As he hit the bottom of the slope and started across the valley, running and angling right toward the wagon fifty yards away, rifles whip-cracked fiercely from along the creek. The slugs chewed into the grass on either side of Cuno's stomping boots.

He squeezed off two shots from his right hip, then, approaching the wagon with its prisoners snarling like circus lions and the marshal sitting with his back to the rear wheel, dove behind the front wheel as another slug barked into a log on the wagon's other side.

Another sparked off the outside wheel with a sharp, ear-ringing clang.

"Hey, Junior!" one of the prisoners growled. "What the hell you think you're doin'? This ain't *none* of *your* affair!"

PRAISE FOR PETER BRANDVOLD AND HIS NOVELS:

"Action-packed . . . for fans of traditional Westerns."
—*Booklist*

"Make room on your shelf of favorites; Peter Brandvold will be staking out a claim there." —Frank Roderus

"Recommended to anyone who loves the West as I do."
—Jack Ballas

"Takes off like a shot." —Douglas Hirt

"A writer to watch."
—Jory Sherman, author of *The Savage Curse*

Berkley titles by Peter Brandvold

The .45-Caliber Series
.45-CALIBER WIDOW MAKER
.45-CALIBER DEATHTRAP
.45-CALIBER MANHUNT
.45-CALIBER FURY
.45-CALIBER REVENGE

The Sheriff Ben Stillman Series
HELL ON WHEELS
ONCE LATE WITH A .38
ONCE UPON A DEAD MAN
ONCE A RENEGADE
ONCE HELL FREEZES OVER
ONCE A LAWMAN
ONCE MORE WITH A .44
ONCE A MARSHAL

The Rogue Lawman Series
BULLETS OVER BEDLAM
COLD CORPSE, HOT TRAIL
DEADLY PREY
ROGUE LAWMAN

The Bounty Hunter Lou Prophet Series
THE GRAVES AT SEVEN DEVILS
THE DEVIL'S LAIR
STARING DOWN THE DEVIL
THE DEVIL GETS HIS DUE
RIDING WITH THE DEVIL'S MISTRESS
DEALT THE DEVIL'S HAND
THE DEVIL AND LOU PROPHET

Other titles
BLOOD MOUNTAIN

.45-CALIBER WIDOW MAKER

PETER BRANDVOLD

BERKLEY BOOKS, NEW YORK

THE BERKLEY PUBLISHING GROUP
Published by the Penguin Group
Penguin Group (USA) Inc.
375 Hudson Street, New York, New York 10014, USA

Penguin Group (Canada), 90 Eglinton Avenue East, Suite 700, Toronto, Ontario M4P 2Y3, Canada
(a division of Pearson Penguin Canada Inc.)
Penguin Books Ltd., 80 Strand, London WC2R 0RL, England
Penguin Group Ireland, 25 St. Stephen's Green, Dublin 2, Ireland (a division of Penguin Books Ltd.)
Penguin Group (Australia), 250 Camberwell Road, Camberwell, Victoria 3124, Australia
(a division of Pearson Australia Group Pty. Ltd.)
Penguin Books India Pvt. Ltd., 11 Community Centre, Panchsheel Park, New Delhi—110 017, India
Penguin Group (NZ), 67 Apollo Drive, Rosedale, North Shore 0632, New Zealand
(a division of Pearson New Zealand Ltd.)
Penguin Books (South Africa) (Pty.) Ltd., 24 Sturdee Avenue, Rosebank, Johannesburg 2196,
South Africa

Penguin Books Ltd., Registered Offices: 80 Strand, London WC2R 0RL, England

This is a work of fiction. Names, characters, places, and incidents either are the product of the author's imagination or are used fictitiously, and any resemblance to actual persons, living or dead, business establishments, events, or locales is entirely coincidental.

.45-CALIBER WIDOW MAKER

A Berkley Book / published by arrangement with the author

PRINTING HISTORY
Berkley edition / May 2009

Copyright © 2009 by Peter Brandvold.
Cover illustration by Bruce Emmett.

ISBN: 978-0-425-22800-5

BERKLEY®
Berkley Books are published by The Berkley Publishing Group,
a division of Penguin Group (USA) Inc.,
375 Hudson Street, New York, New York 10014.
BERKLEY® is a registered trademark of Penguin Group (USA) Inc.
The "B" design is a trademark of Penguin Group (USA) Inc.

PRINTED IN THE UNITED STATES OF AMERICA

10   9   8   7   6   5   4   3   2   1

For Grandma:
Alta Brandvold
of Bottineau, North Dakota.
She will turn ninety-nine this July,
and she's still got the bark on.

1

"WHAT'S THE MATTER, young fella? Ain't ya never seen the devil's hounds up close before?"

Sitting on his skewbald paint, Renegade, Cuno Massey poked his flat-brimmed plainsman back off his forehead and gazed through the bars of the jail wagon parked along the wide dusty street of Buffalo Flats, Wyoming Territory. Four men reclined inside—as owly, soulless, and deadly a quartet of unshaven, low-at-heel privy scum as the husky young man had ever seen.

As he'd ridden into town a minute ago, one of the prisoners had caught his eye—a big half-breed with a knotted scar where his left ear had been and an even bigger scar where his hair had been. A silver hoop dangled from his sole remaining ear, and a sheer, granite wall conveyed more expression than this man's blue-green eyes.

"This hound here," Cuno said, nodding toward the half-breed. "I saw him hauled off to jail up in Dakota. Cut a whore's throat."

In fact, Cuno, having heard the girl scream in the Missouri Saloon down near the Bismarck river docks, had rushed upstairs to see the half-breed stumbling around the room holding a bloody Green River blade in one hand, a bottle in the other, while the girl flopped around, bleeding her life out on the floor beside the rumpled bed.

One kick from Cuno's boot had dislodged the knife. Stomping the drunk, raging half-breed down on the floor in the whore's own thickening blood pool and holding him down with one boot and a spur rowel, he'd waited until a deputy town marshal had come with a sawed-off shotgun and manacles and hazed the pie-eyed half-breed off to jail.

"Wouldn't have been in Bismarck, would it?" asked one of the two deputy U.S. marshals tending the wagon—a tall, rangy, sandy-haired gent with one wandering eye. He was mashing wheel dope into a hub of the wagon's left rear wheel.

"It would."

The lawman chuckled and stirred his dope stick around in the bucket on the ground near his scuffed, grease-smeared boots. "That jail didn't hold ole Fuego here for long. That night, the town marshal's woman found the marshal and two deputies hacked up in the jailhouse like wolf-killed antelope, and the half-breed long gone."

The deputy federal lawman rammed the dope stick in and out of the wheel hub, sweating and panting with the effort in the hot, high-country sun. "A sheriff ran him to ground up in Standing Rock, few days back. We're takin' him over the mountains"—he glanced at the cool, blue, fir-clad peaks of the Mexican Mountains humping up in a near-straight line across the southwestern horizon—"to the federal pen."

"Got a hang rope waitin' on him and his kith in Crow Feather," spat the second marshal—a gray-bearded, rotund gent, a hard fifty years old—adjusting the hams and collars of the two mules standing hang-headed in the wagon's hitch.

The older lawman was smoking a short, black stogie while his high-crowned, tan sombrero shaded his craggy, gray-bearded face and sweat basted his red calico shirt to his chest and flabby belly. Wisps of salt-and-pepper hair curled down around his leathery cheeks.

He grinned and winked at Cuno. "After a proper jury trial, of course."

"Don't doubt it a bit."

Cuno turned back to the half-breed, who stared through the bars at him, his eyes as expressionless as before but now with his thick, mustached upper lip lifted above his large, rot-encrusted teeth, as though he'd been half listening to the conversation and enjoying it.

Cuno pitched his hat brim to the two marshals, then nudged Renegade forward. "Good trip to you, then."

"Oh, I s'pect we will," the older gent chuckled mirthlessly, grunting as he adjusted a heavy harness on the off mule's neck.

Cuno turned Renegade around the front of the mules, in the shading arbor of the Buffalo Flats Saloon next door to the general store before which the jail wagon was parked.

He intended to head into the saloon for a dust-cutting beer before laying in trail supplies and continuing his journey to Crow Feather, where he hoped to secure a freight-hauling contract for him and his freighting partner, Serenity Parker, who was waiting for him there. Cuno had convinced a banker in Sweetwater—a man who'd fought in the War Between the States with Cuno's late father—to grant him a loan with practically no collateral.

"Say there," said the younger deputy from over the backs of the mules. "You wear that forty-five like you know how to use it."

Cuno put Renegade up to the hitchrack flanked by a seed-flecked water trough.

The deputy cocked his head and narrowed a speculative eye. "Care to throw in? It's a long ride, and we could use another hand. There was supposed to be three of us, but ole Milburn Hardy's down with the pony drip."

"Obliged for the offer," Cuno said, swinging down from his saddle. "I'm heading in that direction, but I'm splittin' wind and powderin' sage. A business partner's waiting for me."

"A dollar a day an' found," the younger deputy said,

canting his head to the other side and raising his eyebrows enticingly. He let his blue-eyed gaze flick to the Colt .45 thonged low on Cuno's right thigh clad in smoke-stained deerskin as he added, "Good as pistolero pay in these parts."

"'Preciate it," Cuno said with a cordial nod. "Like I said, as soon as my horse is rested, I have to raise some dust."

After loosening Renegade's saddle cinch and slipping the bit so the horse could draw water, Cuno hoofed it up the saloon's three creaky steps, swiping dust from his gun belt and deerskin breeches with his hat. The whang strings of the tan buckskin tunic drawn taut across his broad, muscular chest swung to and fro as he moved, spurs ringing on the cracked boards.

Annoyance at the "pistolero" remark nipped him. It was true that he knew how to use the ivory-gripped Colt .45 he'd inherited from an old gunfighter friend, but he'd been forced to learn to use it—and to use it well—by the men who'd killed his father and stepmother . . . by the necessity of hunting those men across three territories and killing them and others who'd gotten in his way.

He'd been forced to keep in trim with the Colt by the further sundry men and unfortunate events—bounty hunters like Ruben Pacheca, and the gang that had killed his young, pregnant wife—that had dogged his heels like tin cans tied to a horse's tail.

He wasn't proud of his violent past. He didn't want to be identified with it, nor for his future to be tainted by it. He was not his gun.

"I don't blame you, son," the older lawman said, lifting a feed sack from the long ears of the right mule. "Can't say as I blame you one bit for refusing a job haulin' these vipers to their grisly rewards across that blister on the devil's ass known as the Mexicans. If Svenson an' me weren't married to the meanest, ugliest hags in the territory, who believe the best husbands are those with good-payin' jobs that keep 'em out of the house for weeks at a time, we wouldn't be doin' it, neither!"

The oldster threw his head back, guffawing so loudly that a couple of dogs sniffing around the trash-strewn boardwalk on the other side of the street wheeled and barked with their hackles raised.

Movement drew Cuno's attention back to the jail wagon.

One of the prisoners—a burly, hard-bodied gent with a broad face, wedge-shaped nose, and greasy, dark red hair tied in a queue with a strip of moose hide—knelt at the wagon's rear end, pressing his groin up against the bars. Hands on his hips, he sort of twisted from side to side, sending a thick yellow piss stream into the street behind the wagon, drawing an arcing, wet line back and forth in the dust.

Chuckling, he turned his face toward the boardwalk to Cuno's left, and a lusty smile dimpled his sun-browned cheeks. "Hello, ladies. How're you two fine-lookin' little fillies doin' this afternoon?"

Cuno turned as two young women in summer-weight frocks and bonnets, both wearing white cotton gloves and with wicker shopping baskets looped over their forearms, mounted the boardwalk from the cross street, high-stepping toward Cuno and the marshals.

The pretty blonde in the red frock stopped abruptly, lower jaw hanging as she stared with disbelief at the jail wagon. Her friend, a chubby, round-faced brunette in a formfitting green number with white lace, cut her girlish chatter off to follow her friend's horrified stare.

When her eyes found the prisoner, her pudgy cheeks and pug nose turned crimson.

The gent at the back of the wagon continued evacuating his bladder, grinning, winking, and gyrating his hips. He added a few grunts and sighs for effect, scrunching up his cheeks with devilish mocks and jeers.

The brunette gasped more quietly than her blonde friend. Clapping her free hand to her bosom, she stood frozen, staring with incredulous awe. The blonde inched forward. Glaring at the discourteous prisoner, then raking her gaze from Cuno and the marshals, as though including them all in her scathing condemnation, she jerked her friend around by the arm.

Together, casting horrified and castigating looks behind them—though the brunette looked more than a little fascinated, as well—they retraced their haughty steps back down the boardwalk and across the intersecting side street, until they'd disappeared amongst a handful of drummers and stockmen patronizing the next block.

"Goddamnit, Simms!" The younger marshal slammed his dope stick against the bars before the face of the red-headed prisoner, showering all four men with grease and evoking indignant grunts and curses. "How many times I gotta tell you to behave amongst civilized folk? You try that again, I'm gonna blow your noodle off with my Remy!"

Simms directed his dwindling piss stream toward the older marshal, who jumped back, red-faced with rage. All four of the prisoners laughed and hollered and rattled the chains of their handcuffs and leg irons. Even the half-breed suddenly sprang to life, whooping and clapping his hands madly, silver hoop ring glinting in the midday sun.

The dogs across the street were barking at the wagon again while warily backing off toward a trash-strewn alley between a harness shop and a feed store.

"Like I said, have a good one," Cuno muttered with a dry chuckle as the older lawman joined the fray, ramming the butt of a double-barreled shotgun against the bars, futilely ordering his charges to stifle themselves.

Cuno wheeled and, letting the din drift off behind him, passed through the batwings and into the saloon. Cool shadows and the smell of beer, hard liquor, tobacco smoke, and sawdust washed over him—a refreshing reprieve from two days of blistering sun, trail dust, the ceaseless smell of scorched juniper and alkali, and the constant threat of blood-hungry Crows sporadically raiding up north.

As was part of the price you paid for being gun handy and having paved your back trail with dead men and enemies, Cuno paused just inside the batwings and took a quick but cautious gander.

The big mahogany bar and mirrored back bar ran along the right wall. A woman stood still as a statue behind it—a wizened scarecrow of indeterminate age but with a face cobwebbed with deep lines and pocked with moles and coffee-colored blemishes. Her brown hair, piled impeccably atop her head, owned not a strand of gray. Under a conservative purple dress buttoned to her wattled throat, she was skinny enough, as Cuno's father used to say, that you could have stuffed her down a gun barrel and still been able to shoot.

Along the left wall stretching back into near darkness lay a good dozen or so tables, only two of which were occupied—the one nearest the front window to Cuno's sharp left, almost flanking him, and one in the semishadows near the middle of the room, near a cold, black woodstove and the head of a grizzly snarling down from a square-hewn ceiling joist.

The two men near the window sat side by side on a plankboard bench, their backs to the wall. They were shabbily dressed hombres, with pistols on their hips beneath the table, a Winchester carbine leaning against the wall, within easy reach of the man on the right.

The one nearest the window was gazing out the flyspotted glass while the man beside him, arms crossed on his chest, boots propped on a chair, regarded Cuno dully beneath a flat-brimmed, cream hat bearing a crow feather, a faint sneer curling his thin-mustached upper lip.

The one nearest the window turned to Cuno. They locked gazes for a stretched second.

Cuno slid his eyes toward the other gent, who sat so close to his friend that their shoulders nearly touched. The gent near the window looked at the gent beside him, gave an annoyed grunt, and nudged the other man with his shoulder. Flushing slightly, the man with the feathered hat slid a few inches down the bench from his friend, then resumed sneering through the shadows at Cuno.

Cuno sauntered toward the bar, quickly sizing up the three men at the other table—two playing cards while the third, with long, tawny hair curling over his shoulders, slumped down in his chair, arms around one drawn-up knee, his felt hat with a braided leather band tipped low over his eyes, as though he were dozing.

The cardplayers glanced at Cuno as he passed their table—both wearing dusters and dust-caked sombreros, one bearded, the other with a shaggy, gray-flecked mustache, bandoliers crisscrossed on his chest—then returned to their card game, speaking in hushed, desultory tones as they flopped down their cards and clinked coins together.

Several yards down the bar from the table, Cuno turned toward the mahogany and rested a boot on the brass foot rail. The old woman had been slowly swiveling her head toward him as he'd moved along the bar, her eyes expressionless.

Now, taking a deep drag from a long, black cigarillo, she said in a man-husky voice almost too low to be heard above the thud of hooves and creak of wagons outside, "If you're here for cooch, my girls're upstairs. But all mattress dances are paid for in advance, and go easy on the furniture. If you're here for hooch, it'll be twenty-five cents a shot, and I take no responsibility for sterility, insanity, or blindness."

The woman's eyes brightened slightly as she glowered at Cuno through a harsh black cloud of Mexican tobacco smoke. Her shoulders jerked as though from a slight ague. What sounded like the last faltering croaks of a near-dead chicken bubbled up from her scrawny chest.

After a few puzzled seconds, Cuno realized she was laughing.

2

"I'LL FORGO THE mattress dance this time through."

Cuno eyed a plate of sliced beef, ham, and cheese, and another of crumbly wheat bread. Flies were making a meal of the moldy cheese, and the bread looked dry as hardpan. Still, after two days of beans and jerky, the complimentary bar fare made his stomach mewl with hunger.

"Just the suds and the fixin's there, if they go with the suds."

The old woman planted her cigarillo in a wooden ashtray carved in the shape of a bobcat paw. She grabbed a glass schooner off the back bar and pulled a frothy beer.

Scraping the foam head with a flat stick, she glanced at the two three-gallon jars flanking the meat and bread. Both were filled with murky brine rife with the smell of vinegar and spices. One contained eggs. The other held hog knuckles. The eggs were clustered atop what appeared a coiled sand rattler complete with head and tail. Razor-edged fangs showed between the half-open jaws.

"Don't run from my pickles, neither." She set the beer in front of Cuno, knocked ashes off her cigarillo, and stuck the long, black cylinder between her froggy lips. "Best in the territories."

"What's the snake add?"

"Secret I learned from my late Mexican husband. Claimed he cooked for General Santa Anna." The spidery old barmaid drew another deep puff, batting her long eyelashes against the smoke curling up in front of her face. "That old rattler not only lends a certain sagey flavor, ole Paco claimed it enhanced a man's virility."

She winked as that croaking laugh rumbled up from her sparrow's chest again and she tapped more ashes off her cigarillo. "I don't guarantee any such thing, but I'll tell you this. Ole Paco was a virile son of a bitch till the day he died with a cancer the size of a coffee mug hanging off his neck."

Cuno sipped the frothy beer, warm but somehow still refreshing and instantly tempering the windburn and sunburn that gnawed not only his face but every inch of hide on his hard, muscular frame.

"No offense to Paco, and I ain't braggin', neither, but I believe I'll pass on the eggs," he said, setting the glass atop the bar and moving down toward the meat and cheese. "But I'd build a sandwich."

"Build you a big one."

The old woman ran an admiring gaze over Cuno's taut, brawny frame. Fully half of his twenty-two years had been devoted to back-and-bellying freight in and out of cabin-sized, iron-shod Murphy wagons and maneuvering four-mule and six-mule hitches across cold, steep mountains and windy plains.

Those years had ridged, sculpted, and swelled his chest and arms, broadened his shoulders, hammered his flat belly to the texture of sun-cured rawhide. They'd bulged out the thighs and calves of his scarred deerhide breeches, drew his fair skin taut across high-boned, tapering cheeks, a dimpled chin, and anvil jaws, and spoked the deep-tanned flesh around clear, lake-blue eyes.

His rope-burned hands were large and red as fresh-carved roasts. During long freight runs manipulating the

long rein ribbons trailing out to belligerent teams, his forearms, as round and corded as cedar fence posts, often
pitched and flexed until they tore out the sleeves of his
buckskin tunics and work shirts.

His yellow-blond hair, perpetually sun-bleached, hung
down from his tan, flat-brimmed, low-crowned plainsman,
brushing his shoulders.

"Looks like you could hold all that food and more," the
old woman observed through swirling, webbing tobacco
smoke. "I got plenty. Don't get many through these days,
since the gold pinched out. Bet you could use your ashes
hauled. Want me to call Carlotta? She's the only girl I got
that could handle a young man of your size and obvious
vigor." That cryptic laugh again. "Mamie's prettier, but I
fear you'd snap her back!"

"This'll do me," Cuno said, patting a thick sandwich together, then taking a long sip of the beer.

The old woman grumbled her cryptic disapproval and
drifted down the bar in a cloud of wafting, nose-wrinkling
smoke to a dime novel open at the other end of the mahogany.

Cuno leaned forward, elbows on the bar, and went to serious work on the sandwich and beer, thoroughly enjoying
both in spite of the beer's warmth and the dry bread and
moldy cheese. He'd nearly devoured half the sandwich when
one of the cardplayers flanking him growled, "Girl, get on up
there and get me a sandwich before that big rannie devours
the whole damn mess. A couple more whiskeys, too."

Chewing, Cuno peered into the back bar mirror. The
long-haired man sitting with the cardplayers, hugging a
knee to his chest, lifted his head suddenly. The flat hat brim
fell back to reveal the pretty, oval face of a scowling girl.

"Get your own goddamn food," the girl said.

The two cardplayers stared across the table at each
other. Suddenly, the man who'd given the order threw his
left arm out from his side.

There was a sharp crack as the back of his hand
smacked the girl's right cheek. Head whipping sideways,

tawny hair flying, and hat tumbling off her head, she and her chair went over backward and hit the floor with a raucous thud and a slap of bare hands against floor puncheons.

The girl scrambled to her feet in a rage, throwing her chair aside. "Goddamn you, Pepper!"

Teeth gritted and eyes slitted, she lunged at the man, right fist extended, a steel blade flashing in the wan light from the window. Pepper loosed a high-pitched laugh as, twisting around in his chair, he grabbed both the girl's wrists and jerked her down to her knees.

The knife clattered onto the floor.

The girl cursed as she fought against the man's grip holding her down in front of him. Her crimson cheeks bunched with pain as Pepper crouched over her and drove her toward the floor. The man on the other side of the table held his cards, waiting to resume play, and laughed.

"Now, Miss Johnnie," Pepper said, "you gonna do what I tell you, or do I have to snap these pretty little wrists for you? I could. I could snap these wrists like a sparrow's *neck*!"

Cuno's right hand hovered over the Colt .45 thonged low on his right thigh. His instincts, honed over the years and from dealings with such men as those before him now, were to help the girl by slapping leather and drawing iron. Opting for a less aggressive stance, he grabbed the two plates off the mahogany and moved toward the table.

The head of the other cardplayer snapped toward him. "Hold up there, big boy."

Cuno stopped halfway between the bar and the table. Two large, round maws of a double-barreled shotgun stared at him from atop the second man's pin-striped left thigh, in the shadows beneath the table. The square-faced, dull-eyed man held his cards atop the table in his left hand while his right was obviously wrapped around the barn blaster below.

"I don't recollect Pepper askin' fer any help," he snarled. "So why don't you turn around and set them plates back on the counter where they was?"

Pepper had turned toward Cuno now, too, grinning with

drunken delight as he continued to hold the girl low in front of him. He had long, dark brown hair, a soup-strainer black mustache, and a goatee. The girl grunted painfully, chin dipped toward her chest.

"Stan's right. I didn't request no assistance." Pepper winked and stretched a mirthless grin. "Now, put the fuckin' plates back where they was so my pretty little gal here can fetch me a snack like I just told her." He shot a glance at the old woman standing statue-still behind the bar, cloaked in wafting tobacco smoke. "Two more drinks, Agnes. Johnnie'll fetch 'em."

Cuno held the plates out in front of him, his mild expression belying the angry burn in his belly. "But if I bring 'em, she won't need to." He hiked a shoulder and added in spite of himself, "Then neither one of you will have cause for a tizzy fit."

"I know," the old woman crowed, her high, raspy voice echoing around the room. "Why don't *I* haul it out there, and save you *all*—!"

"Shut up, Agnes!" Pepper snapped, cutting the woman off but keeping his eyes on Cuno. "What's it gonna be, big boy? You gonna set down them plates or is Stan gonna have to clean out your belly button?"

Cuno looked at the twin shotgun maws yawning at him, then at the sneer on Stan's hard face. His heart thudded. Fury burned through him. The girl stared at him from the other side of the table. Her head, with strands of mussed, tawny hair in her eyes, was level with Pepper's belly. Her gaze was skeptical, vaguely befuddled, her lips bunched with pain and with contempt for the man clutching her wrists.

Cuno slid the plates back onto the bar. He should have followed his first instinct and hauled his .45 from its holster. A quiet life had to start somewhere, but he should have known that place wasn't here.

"Well, then," Pepper drawled, turning back to the girl kneeling before him. "Let's try that again—shall we, Johnnie girl?"

As he loosened his grip, the girl jerked her hands back, glaring up at Pepper as she slowly scuttled away on her knees, massaging her wrists and flexing her fingers. Her hard, cunning eyes told Cuno she was thinking about the knife on the floor to her right.

Holding Pepper's gaze, the girl rose slowly, defiantly, and stooped to retrieve her hat. She pressed a dent from the crown, set it on her head, gave Pepper another cool, lingering stare, then moved out from behind the table and strode up to the bar, her stockmen's boots skidding across the puncheons.

She was tall and slender, with a womanish curve to her hips, and she moved with a headstrong, confident grace. But her smooth, peach-colored skin, slightly tanned, told Cuno she wasn't yet twenty. Gray-blue eyes, innocent despite her girlish attempts to give them a jaded cast, glistened in the light from the front windows, framed by buffeting wings of straight, tawny hair.

She wore a man's gray wool shirt decorated with black zigzagging stripes across the front. Her breasts were small and round, and a couple of inches of alluring cleavage shone through the gap offered by the first three open bone buttons. A turquoise ring hung from a sweat-darkened leather thong around her neck, nestling in the V of the open shirt, above the lace trim of a white camisole.

She stole a glance at Cuno as she grabbed the plates off the bar. Turning around, she favored Cuno with another lingering look, a faintly incredulous, almost disdainful cast now in her eyes. Blinking slowly, dismissively, she sauntered back to the table, plunking both plates down before turning back to retrieve the two shot glasses Agnes had filled.

"Why, thank you, sweetheart!" Pepper exclaimed, grinning mockingly up at the young, tawny-haired girl when she'd set both whiskeys on the table before him and Stan. "You didn't have to go to all that trouble!"

He and Stan laughed as they built sandwiches over their facedown pasteboards. The two other men by the window chuffed bemusedly, wearily, as they slouched in their chairs, the one in the window keeping his eyes skinned on the dusty street outside the saloon, as though waiting for someone.

Outside, the din from the prison wagon had faded. Cuno remembered half hearing, in the midst of the trouble with the girl, the marshals yelling at their mules while cracking a blacksnake over their backs and the rattle of wagon boards and welded strap-iron bars as the wagon had rolled into the street and, presumably, out of town.

The girl stole another sidelong glance at Cuno leaning with one arm on the bar behind her, near Agnes standing statue-still again in her fetid smoke cloud. She sauntered back around the table, nonchalantly dragging her heels. She picked up her chair and plopped down into it, poking her hat brim back off her forehead, and lifted one boot onto the chair seat, throwing an arm around her knee.

She cast her bored, tired gaze toward the window. "When we gonna fog it outta this dump?"

"When I say so," Pepper muttered, leaning forward to bite into his sandwich. Talking with his mouth full, he picked up his pasteboards. "Now then, where the hell were we, Stan, before we was so rudely interrupted by Miss High-and-Mighty?"

As the men ate, drank, and continued their game, and the girl stared out the window with the same air as before, Cuno saw that the shotgun had disappeared from Stan's lap.

Cuno turned back to his beer and picked up his half-eaten sandwich. Who these people were and what they were after was none of his business. He had his own business to worry about. Namely, his own urgent desire to secure a freight contract with the sutler at Fort Dixon, near Crow Feather in the southern territory.

The bank loan he'd acquired in Sweetwater was for two six-mule hitches and for two new Murphy high-sided rollers cut under and heavy-braked for rugged mountain terrain. All he needed now was one more freighter, an outrider, and the contract with Fort Dixon, and he'd be set for another year or two.

After a couple of runs, and it looked as though his contract would be renewed, he'd buy a small warehouse and corral in Crow Feather or Cheyenne and maybe put cash down on his own shack so he didn't have to hole up in boardinghouses and flea-bit hotels between runs.

Maybe he'd even think about starting a family again, with the right woman.

He finished the sandwich and beer faster than he'd intended—before he'd given Renegade enough time to rest—so he ordered one more beer and considered one of the hog knuckles.

A soft whistle sounded in the front of the room. Cuno turned to see the two men at the table by the window lazily gaining their feet, the one closest the window staring toward the two cardplayers and the girl while the other man stretched and hitched his double-rigged cartridge belts higher on his narrow hips.

"Come on, now, Gene," Stan complained. "I'm finally winnin' back some of the money this cheatin' privy skunk fleeced me for in Cody!"

"The other fellas are movin'—let's go," Gene ordered mildly, lifting his hat and running a hand through his thin, blond hair as he headed toward the door.

The other man nearest the front chuckled mockingly at Stan, who scowled down at his cards and winnings pile. Pepper whooped as, sliding his chair back, he scooped a small pile of coins into his hat. His long, dark brown hair danced around his shoulders.

Cuno saw, as the man dumped the coins from the hat into his other hand, then deposited the coins in a pocket of his black denims, that Pepper wore a pistol on both thighs, butts forward. Another shoulder holster peeked out from under his open duster. One of his mule-eared boots bulged with a hideout gun.

As Pepper and the girl headed for the door, the girl walking briskly, stiffly ahead of the long-haired gent, Stan scooped his own coins off the table. "Hold up a minute, damnit! Christ, what's the big, damn hurry all of a sudden?"

When he'd shoved his winnings into his pockets, Stan turned toward the door. His cream duster flapped open to reveal that he, too, carried a brace of pistols in the cross-draw position. His sawed-off ten-gauge hung from a lan-yard down his neck, swinging low across his cartridge belts.

Striding toward the still-shuddering batwings, he glanced over his shoulder at Cuno and stopped suddenly.

"I'll be along!" he shouted toward the doors from which the sound of creaking saddle leather emanated.

He turned and angled back toward Cuno. Cuno's left hand held the handle of his beer glass, his right boot propped on the brass foot rail.

"Gonna grab me one more bite of cheese," Stan yelled.

Stan stopped in front of Cuno. Cuno held the man's faintly sneering gaze as Stan snaked his right arm out across the bar to snatch a thick wedge of moldy cheese from one of the free lunch plates.

Taking a bite of the cheese, he winked at Cuno, nodded, and turned toward the door. He hadn't taken half a step before he stopped suddenly and swung back toward Cuno sharply, raising the shotgun hanging from the lanyard around his neck and, holding the barn blaster like a war club, rammed the butt toward Cuno's head.

Having read the man's intentions in his red-mottled face and cow eyes, Cuno dropped his head toward the bar. Stan grunted as the shotgun whooshed through the air. The man's eyes snapped wide with shock as, propelled by his own momentum, he turned nearly a full circle before reset-ting his feet.

When he did, Cuno lunged forward and slammed his right fist wrist-deep in Stan's belly. The air left Stan's lungs in a loud surge, spittle flying out from the man's furred lips.

As he buckled at the waist, his head tipped sideways to-ward Cuno's chest. Cuno smashed his fist, knuckles out, against the side of Stan's head.

"Uhnnn!" The hard case's head jerked as he dropped to a knee, his eyelids fluttering as though to shake away the stars dancing behind his retinas.

Cuno grabbed Stan's collar and hammered another right jab against Stan's left cheek, high on the bone and feeling the flesh tear beneath his knuckles. Holding the man firmly upright, Cuno slammed three more quick, piston-like blows against the same cheek, the solid smacks echoing around the room like distant pistol fire.

Stan yelled like an enraged, trapped coyote with each blood-drawing smack.

After the last blow, Cuno released the man's collar and jerked the shotgun up over Stan's head. Stan dropped to his hands and knees, blood dribbling in several streams from his laid-open cheek to the spur-scarred floor.

He breathed heavily, groaning, as though he'd run barefoot a long way over harsh terrain.

Cursing, he cupped his hand over his cheek and glanced up and sideways at Cuno, fear showing in his close-set eyes. Cuno stepped back away from the man and hefted the shotgun in both his hands, glancing down at the gut shredder bemusedly, as though pondering a fitting use for the savage weapon.

"No," Stan croaked, "please . . . don't . . ."

Cuno flipped the shotgun's latch, and the gun opened. Plucking the wads from each barrel, Cuno flipped them back over his shoulder. They clattered across the puncheons.

Cuno snapped the gun closed, then threw it down to the cutthroat staring up at him skeptically, blood dribbling over his jaw and neck and onto the floorboards below. The gut shredder glanced off Stan's shoulder and hit the floor with a thud.

Cuno set his hand on the butt of his holstered .45 and glared down at him. "Let's be strangers, Stan."

Relief washed through Stan's anguished eyes as he grabbed the empty shotgun and gained his feet. He pulled a dark blue handkerchief from his back pocket and pressed it to his cheek. Keeping his eyes on Cuno and holding the shotgun down low in his left hand, he stepped backward toward the front of the room.

He backed through the doors, looped the shotgun over his shoulder, and jogged down the steps to the hitchrack where the other horses had been tied. Only a single chestnut remained.

Stan swung into the saddle and spurred the mount west, crouching low in the leather and holding his handkerchief to his cheek. The drumming of his hooves dwindled quickly, replaced by what sounded like a dry, ululating wheeze rising slowly above the distant bark of an angry dog.

Cuno turned to the barmaid, Agnes, standing behind the bar in her perpetual, smelly smoke cloud. The skinny woman held a fresh cigarillo to her lips as she peered out the window in the direction Stan had fled.

Her thin lips spread a wide, false-toothed smile, and she shook her head slowly from side to side, shoulders jerking as that queer cackle fought its way up from her shriveled lungs.

3

"I CAUGHT SUCH a bad case of the clap from the girls over to Miss Carlotta's Purple Garter Sportin' Palace that I thought the pony drip was gonna burn a hole right through my longhandles!"

Riding ahead of the jail wagon rattling over a rutted, two-track trail, the town constable of Buffalo Flats, Neil Ardai, slapped his denim-clad thigh and directed a laugh over his shoulder at the two deputy U.S. marshals slouched in the wagon's driver's box. "And you wanna know the kicker?"

"What's the kicker, Neil?" asked the younger of the two federal lawmen, Chuck Svenson, with a faintly distracted air as he skidded his wary gaze back and forth across the rising and falling trail winding between low, pine-clad slopes.

"My wife never had a clue!" Ardai slapped his thigh once more, turning nearly full around in his saddle. His thick black mustache rolled up under his nose as he laughed, tears of mirth trickling down from his deep-set, cobalt eyes.

The older marshal, sitting on the left side of the seat,

holding the leather ribbons loose in his gloved hands, snorted and shook his head. "You an' the missus must have a real close relationship, Neil. That's heartwarmin' as all hell."

Ardai turned forward in the saddle of his cream-maned vinegar dun and raised an arm to sleeve tears from his cheeks. "You know Lucyanne, Bill. Girl didn't weigh a hundred pounds when I married her, and she was as sweet as a dish full of chocolate fudge. Now, only two years after our big church weddin', she's put on more tallow than a she-buff in January, and grew herself a nice, long, forked tail to go with her acid tongue. I swear that girl so much as turns a glance on a rose, it turns black and tumbles off the vine. Goes up in a smoke puff!"

"Jesus Christ!" Landers exclaimed. "You don't s'pose her and my wife are *kin*, do ya, Neil?"

"Hey, Neil," Svenson broke in with an annoyed furrow of his sandy brows, his wandering eye turning darker as he stared toward the narrow stream rushing through a boulder-strewn bed off the right side of the trail. "You sure this is the way to the cutoff you were talkin' about? I don't see no way through the ridge over yonder, let alone across that stream."

"Not to worry, Chuck," Ardai said. "I use the cutoff all the time when I go out lookin' for deer or griz. You won't see it till you're right up on it, and that's the beauty of the thing. If you two can make it through that first gap in this here ole wagon . . ." The constable threw a hand up and looked again over his shoulder, his eyes wide and earnest. ". . . And I ain't sayin' you can, as I never tried to take a wagon through there, just a saddle horse. But if you *can* make it, no one shadin' your trail will ever follow you through that cutoff. If they're not from around *here*, they won't know about it. The only reason *I* know about—"

"Don't mean to sound impatient," Landers said, cutting the constable off again, "but shouldn't we have come *upon it* by now?"

Landers snorted and shook his head. "Don't mind him,

Neil. Chuck here's convinced someone's shadin' us, though I ain't seen nothin' but dust devils foggin' our trail since we left Cody, and while my eyes might be eleven years older than his, I can see twice as far and smell cut-throats from two miles away *downwind*!"

"You yourself are smelly enough to choke a cur off a gut wagon," the younger marshal barked back at him. "You didn't see the group in the Buffalo Flats Saloon like I did when I went in for the whiskey and sandwiches. There were five of the sons o' bitches . . . and they all looked like *cold-steel* artists." Sevenson jerked a thick, brown thumb over his shoulder. "Friends of one or more of these bastards behind us, I say . . ."

One of the men lounging in the jail wagon—"Colorado" Bob King—gave a coyote-like howl and laughed. "Friends of one or more of us—you got that right, Chuck!"

Gritting his teeth, Svenson turned and rammed the back of a clenched fist against the front wall of the welded strap-iron cage. He glared at the lanky, Texas-born regulator and bank robber—a bizarre-looking cuss with sinister, Nordic features complete with high, tapering cheekbones and slanted, snakelike eyes. Four gold front teeth glistened on his upper jaw. Long, silver hair hung straight down from his black bowler hat to the shoulders of his dusty frock.

Though born in Texas, the thirty-eight-year-old outlaw had acquired the "Colorado" handle because, according to legend, he'd robbed more banks and killed more men in that territory than any other white man in frontier history.

On the back of one hand King had tattooed a running rabbit with a horrifed look in its eye. On the back of his other hand was a plunging hawk, wings and talons out, beak open, ready to rip and tear.

"I done told you to address me as Marshal Svenson, *Bob*. And keep your goddamn voice down, or I'll come back there and smash your head like a ripe melon."

"You keep threatenin'," said Colorado Bob, resting an arm on one upraised knee while he smoked and swayed easily with the wagon's pitch and lurch, his gold teeth flashing in the afternoon sunshine angling through the pine tops. "And me . . . I just keep right on quivering . . . shakin' right down to my boot toes . . ."

He flicked ashes from his tightly rolled quirley and took a deep drag, narrowing his slanted eyes at Svenson with an even more sinister air than usual.

The others sitting or lying on the bed of the wagon around him—Frank Blackburn and the man who'd pissed out of the wagon in town, Brush Simms—laughed or chuckled as they stared at Svenson.

Fuego seemed customarily ensconced in his own crazy head. The scalped, one-eared half-breed merely lay, bare-chested, on his wadded-up shirt and jacket, grinning at the sky as if thoroughly enjoying the story he read in the clouds.

"Goddamnit!" Face pinched with fury, Svenson reached under the driver's seat for his twelve-gauge shotgun. "That seals it! Bill, stop the wagon!"

"Pull your horns in there, Deputy!" the older marshal roared, scowling at his partner as the wagon continued rocking and bouncing over the deep-rutted trail. "You ain't gonna do no such thing. You keep lettin' those crazy bastards bait you into their wolf trap, you'll get your head chopped off. Now, put that Greener back under the seat and wipe the spit off your chin. You're a professional, goddamnit. Act like one!"

"That's what I've always said," said Frank Blackburn, leaning against the back of the wagon. "A professional man like yourself there, Chuck, should at least *act* like one."

Blackburn grinned. He was a muscular, almost midget-sized hard case in his mid-twenties, with short blond hair under the funnel-brimmed hat secured beneath his chin with a horsehair thong. His stout arms, sleeves rolled up above his bulging biceps, were crossed on his broad chest, and his short, muscular legs jutted in front of him, his hand-tooled, calfskin boots crossed at the ankles.

"I'll act however I feel like acting." Svenson gave the man a hard, sidelong look through the bars behind him.

"And if you got men comin' to try to spring you, Blackburn, you'll see how I act when the chips are down. *Comprende*, amigo?"

"Save the Mex talk for Fuego," Blackburn growled, glancing at the Mexican lying beside him, still staring dreamily at the puffy summer clouds, as though he were a kid lounging in a tree house.

Svenson gritted his teeth, heart pumping boiling oil through his veins, but before he could continue the heated banter, Neil Ardai said, "This is the place, fellers."

"Where?" Landers said, staring through the scattered poplars lining the stream, which curled along the base of a rocky, sandstone ridge.

Riding his vinegar dun about twenty yards ahead of the two wagon mules, Ardai chuckled. "That's the beauty of it. Still can't see it, can you?" He glanced over his shoulder. "Bill, the bank drops around that next bend. Follow me down to the river. You'll see a rocky ford through the trees. That's where we cross the stream."

Ardai gigged his horse into a jog ahead. When Landers and Svenson rounded the bend, they dropped down the shallow bank and rolled out across the riverbed, through a gap in the poplars lining the stream. The water flattened and widened as it slid over a rocky ford—a foot deep at the deepest, Bill Landers thought as he surveyed the crossing.

Riding ahead, Ardai directed the marshals around trouble spots. The wagon leapt, bounced, pitched, and shook as the wide, iron-shod wheels rumbled over the rocks, splashing water up around the bed and evoking indignant yowls and curses from the prisoners.

Ahead, the marshals saw no passage through the sheer, stone ridge on the other side of the stream until they pulled the wagon up the opposite bank and followed Ardai ahead and left. They swerved around junipers, cedars, and huge, cracked boulders fallen from the ridges. When they were a hundred feet from the base of the southwestern cliff, a long vertical shadow appeared in the high, pocked, and crenellated stone wall.

Landers chuckled as, yelling at the braying mules, he watched the shadow darken and widen before him. Suddenly, the wall seemed to split and, as though a door opened and pulled back to the left, the opening in the canyon wall yawned—only about fifty feet wide and littered with brush and rocks, but an opening just the same.

Large enough for the wagon.

Yelling and pointing out obstacles, Ardai led them farther through the gap and down a twisting canyon that narrowed to little wider than the wagon's rear wheels in places. They had to stop at one point and, using a wagon jack and two crowbars, lever a boulder out of the path. Five minutes later, the canyon opened until it was nearly as wide as the one they'd just left, and threaded with a trickling feeder stream.

"Should be smooth sailing from here on," Ardai said, rising proudly in his stirrups and surveying the terrain ahead, which was slowly filling with early evening shadows. "At least, for as far as I've taken this canyon right down the middle of the Mexicans!"

"This meets up with the Cheyenne River?" asked Svenson, standing in the stopped wagon's box, resting his shotgun over a shoulder to look over the cut.

"It forks and doglegs. Stay to the west. When you see Sleeping Bear Butte—you'll recognize it on the right side of the canyon—hang a left. You should meet up with the Cheyenne in about two days. Only take you about two more after that to reach Crow Feather."

Ardai neck-reined the dun around to head back toward the wagon. "I best get back to Buff Flat, keep an eye on the drunks I have in lockup. Happy sailin', fellas. If I see any hombres look like they're shadin' ya"—he affected a hard, earnest grin and a dry chuckle—"they won't be shadin' ya fer long."

"Much obliged, Neil," Landers called, reaching under his seat for a canteen while Svenson continued standing and running his eyes along the rocky, fir-and-pine-stippled ridges humping around him.

A skeptical look darkening his wandering right eye, the junior deputy muttered, "I'll thank ya, too, Neil, if we don't get so lost even the devil can't find us."

"Oh, you'll be wishin' the devil finds ya." At the back of the wagon, Frank Blackburn chuckled. "When the fellas that do find ya, *find ya!*"

Simms and King joined the short, muscular hard case in a chorus of coyote-like laughter while Fuego just stared at a nearby pine top, absently fingering the horrific-looking place where his ear had been.

Constable Neil Ardai splashed back across Buffalo Creek and gained the main trail, swinging the vinegar dun back toward town. His black eyebrows furrowed suddenly over his cobalt eyes, and he drew back on the dun's reins, stopping the horse in the middle of the trail.

"I work too damn hard," the constable said, leaning back over his cantle and reaching into the right saddle pouch.

He fished around under the flap for a few seconds, grunting as he dropped his hand down lower in the near-empty bag. A celestial smile spread across his mustached mouth. Straightening, he lifted a corked bottle up over his horse's hip and swung it forward, raising the bottle in front of his head to gauge the level of remaining amber liquid.

A good two inches.

That oughta hold him till he got back to town.

He wrenched the cork from the lip with his teeth, spat it into the brush along the trail, then set the bottle against his mouth and hefted it high. Two gurgling jugs, and the bottle was empty.

Ardai lowered the empty vessel with a rasping, satisfied sigh and flipped the bottle back over his shoulder. It shattered against a rock, the crash muffled by the rush of the river through the trees to his left.

Singing quietly about an unladylike lady named Maureen, Ardai gigged the dun back along the river, heading upstream toward Buffalo Flats. He was halfway back, rounding a long bend between high banks, the air sharply tanged with pine, when he reined up suddenly.

The constable stared straight ahead, down a long, curving slope through columnar pines.

The drumming of many hooves grew louder and louder.

A half dozen riders . . . riding fast . . . straight toward him.

4

ARDAI'S THROAT DRIED as he stared down the shaded slope. His gut tightened, and he laid his right hand over the polished walnut grips of his holstered .44.

The riders appeared, silhouetted figures rounding the bend through the pines, bobbing and pitching with the strides of their loping mounts. As they moved around the bend and headed for the hill upon which Ardai sat, statue-still though his heart thudded heavily, the lead rider, lifting his gaze and widening his eyes, reined back sharply, raising his right hand for the others to do likewise.

When all five well-armed, hard-faced riders sat their snorting, fidgeting mounts at the base of the low hill, staring up bemusedly at Ardai, the constable knew without a doubt who they were and what they were after.

He didn't recognize one of them.

But he knew . . .

A silence stretched, relieved only by the squawk of saddle leather, the faint rattle of trace chains, and the horses' scuffs and stomps. The breeze sifted through the pine tops, making a nearby trunk creak. All the men stared up the hill at Ardai staring down at them.

One, he saw, was a pretty, tawny-haired girl in men's rough trail gear. She, too, wore a holstered pistol, in the cross-draw position up high on her left hip. A saddle-ring carbine jutted from the sheath under her right leg. Resting her gloved hand on her pistol grips, she cast a cautious glance up the hill at the constable, then around the men gathered about her.

The lead rider—lanky, with long, dark brown hair, mustache, and goatee, and with a broad, scarred nose—spit a fleck of trail dust from his lips and narrowed a dark eye. "Afternoon, Constable."

Ardai felt as though the copper eagle on his cracked leather vest were burning a hole through his skin. He only nodded. His gloved hand resting atop the .44 was sweating profusely.

The lead rider straightened his head and frowned, a sneering, defiant note in his voice while his eyes acquired a mock-serious cast. "Say, you haven't seen a jail wagon around here somewheres, have you? A jail wagon driven by two deputy U.S. marshals and carrying the meanest, ugliest-lookin' quartet of bastards you've ever seen in your ill-fated, too-short life?"

The other men chuckled and slid their sneering gazes from Ardai to the lead rider and back again. One of them had a long, nasty gash across the nub of his left cheek. A horse nickered. The stream curving off to the left made a soft rushing noise on the other side of the poplars.

"Well, now," Ardai said, cocking his head to one side and trying to put some authority into his voice, "why would you fellas be trailin' a jail wagon loaded with federal prisoners?"

The group looked around at each other as though at a secret joke.

Then the leader turned back toward Ardai. As though in response to the dumbest question he'd ever heard, he said, "Why, to run 'em down, kill the marshals, and spring our three amigos. Whadoya think we're trackin' 'em for—to offer 'em a drink and fresh-cut roses?"

More snickers and chuckles from the men around the

leader. Nervously, the girl flicked her eyes back and forth between the constable and the lead desperado, her features tense and apprehensive.

Ardai held the leader's sneering, level, faintly challenging gaze. The man had slid the wings of his duster back behind a brace of big .45s. He leaned smugly forward on his saddle horn.

The constable's heart thudded so hard he thought it would crack a rib. The dreamy effect of his pull on the whiskey bottle had worn off entirely, leaving him washed out, sluggish, and scared as hell. He'd never faced a pack of trail dogs as obviously feral as the ones he faced now. Buffalo Flats was a relatively quiet little town. And Ardai had no real training as a lawman. Before, he'd sold whiskey to remote northern Colorado roadhouses and trading posts and pimped his own whores on the side.

He considered lifting his hand from his weapon, turning his horse around, and riding back the way he'd come. Screw pride. He was getting paid only twenty dollars a month, and he spent that much on girls, cards, and whiskey. But, if he gave these men his back, they'd beef him from behind.

He was stuck between a rock and sheer mountain wall.

Flicking his gaze around the sneering riders down the hill before him, he tightened his hand around his .44. Maybe he could kill one or two and set the group's horses leaping and befouling the aims of the other shooters. Deep down, he didn't think it would work, but his anxious mind was reeling too fast for rational thought.

As if from far away, Ardai heard himself give a savage, unpremeditated yell as he slipped the revolver from its holster and thumbed back the hammer.

But he had the gun only half raised before the lead rider, in a blur of lightning-quick motion, drew his matched Colts from their cross-draw holsters, raised them above his horse's head, and angled them up the hill.

Both Colts roared, belching smoke and fire, at the same time.

* * *

A red-tailed hawk perched on the toe of the dead man's right boot, staring at Cuno Massey with proprietary anger in its gold-speckled, copper eyes.

Cuno swung down from Renegade's back, dropped the reins, and looking around warily with one hand on his .45's grip, sidled over to the dead man.

The body lay belly up across a boulder. Blood bibbed the man's vest and pin-striped, collarless shirt, even staining the gold pocket watch dangling just above the ground from the dead man's vest pocket. It completely covered the copper badge attached to the vest, so that Cuno, keeping an eye skinned on the terrain around him, in case the shooter was still around, had to lean down to make out the words TOWN CONSTABLE etched across spread eagle wings, with BUFFALO FLATS written across the furled flag upon which the eagle was perched.

He also had to look close to see the two, quarter-sized holes in the man's upper chest, spaced about six inches apart in a straight line. Dead, no doubt, before he'd hit the ground.

Cuno straightened and looked around carefully. A vinegar dun cropped bluestem a ways down the hill and off the trail's right side, near the cottonwoods lining the stream. Aside from the horse, there was no other movement.

The man had only been dead a half hour or so, but it appeared the killer or killers were gone. Inspecting the two-track trail, he saw that a half dozen or so riders had passed recently, as had an iron-shod, wide-wheeled wagon.

Probably the jail wagon.

He looked around again, then let his gaze fall back upon the dead lawman. Perplexity needled him, and his inner voice began to whisper. Stop thinking, it told him. Your business—your *only* business—is in Crow Feather.

Cuno turned away from the dead man and stepped into his saddle. He had no time to waste. He had to get that contract secured before someone else beat him to it. Western military outposts offered only a couple of contracts each year, and if the bid was right, they were usually awarded on a first-come, first-served basis.

But he couldn't leave the man draped over the boulder for the scavengers.

He rode too quickly out to where the vinegar dun grazed. The horse spooked, jogged off downstream a good hundred yards, nickering and fiddle-footing and stepping on its reins, before Cuno finally got it cornered in a thick stand of willows and poplars.

Grabbing the dun's reins, he led the still-nickering horse back to its dead rider. Neither Renegade nor the dun cottoned to the smell of fresh blood, so Cuno had to tie both horses to separate pines along the trail.

Wrapping the constable's blanket roll around the body, Cuno back-and-bellied him over his saddle, and tied his wrists to his ankles beneath the horse's belly. When he'd draped the man's hat, which he found along the trail, over the saddle horn, he aimed the horse back toward town, then slapped his hip with the flat of his hand.

The horse whinnied and, shaking its head at the blood smell, galloped buck-kicking down the trail and around the bend behind the darkening pines. The hooves' drumming dwindled quickly beneath the stream's incessant murmur.

Cuno sleeved sweat off his forehead and looked around the slopes and the streambed once more. He walked over to where Renegade stood tied to the pine, swishing its tail. A late breeze had lifted, blowing the silky clay-colored mane. The skewbald paint regarded Cuno expectantly over its shoulder.

"What do you say we try this again, fella?" Cuno said, grabbing the reins and swinging up into the saddle.

He backed the horse onto the trail and urged it downstream. Renegade nickered as he lengthened his stride down the long, gradual hill cloaked in shadows angling out from the ridge and turned at the bottom around a cedar-clad scarp. As horse and rider progressed down the long, narrow valley, following the twisting course of Buffalo Creek, the light faded and the breeze gained a chill, late-summer edge.

Wanting to keep pushing—he'd stop only when he

could no longer see the trail, in another hour or so—Cuno reached behind his saddle and fished his red-and-black mackinaw out from under his bedroll. Wrapping his reins around the horn, he shrugged into the coat and, raising the collar, put Renegade into a ground-eating lope across a broad, grassy flat bordered by aspens.

A couple of miles downstream from Buffalo Flats, he followed the wagon trail across the stream at a rocky ford, cleaved a broad canyon, and rose slowly toward a distant saddleback ridge. Glowing stars capped the ridge, kindling brightly in a lilac sky.

Wolves howled along that ridge, and an owl hooted from a nearby branch or knob.

As he rode, keeping his eyes skinned for general trail hazards, which included predatory men as well as animals, Cuno realized his thoughts were edged with a generalized unease.

The dead lawman.

After all the death he'd witnessed in recent years—from the deaths of his mother, father, and then his stepmother to the untimely going-under of the beautiful young half-breed girl he'd taken as a wife and who'd owned the unlikely name of July Summer—death still managed to wriggle around in his gut like bad meat or spoiled milk.

It was a good thing. It meant, that in spite of all the hard knocks and all the lives he himself had been forced to take, he'd managed to retain some semblance of a soul.

Still, he needed no distractions now. After struggling to find a life for himself, one that would honor his dead parents and his dead wife and the child he never knew, he was finally on the trail of a crackling future—one that didn't teeter at the end of a gun barrel. He needed to hit Crow Feather in two days or less. No more.

Not just for himself, but for his old friend Serenity, as well. He and the old mountain man and former saloon owner had been through hell paved with goatheads since Cuno's partner, Wade Scanlon, had been killed by renegade white men in Colorado. Together, they'd hunted

Wade's killers and rescued a Chinese girl who'd been kidnapped by the same group.

Afterward, out a load of supplies and an expensive Murphy freighter, Cuno had found his accounts wallowing in red and no contracts on the horizon. He and Serenity had spent the winter swamping saloons in Denver.

Cuno put the skewbald up a steep hill between fast-darkening walls of aspen-sheathed granite.

The lawman . . .

Had the group he'd encountered in the saloon killed him? Why?

Were they after the jail wagon?

Cuno had thought he'd have overtaken the wagon by now. The fact that he hadn't made the worm inside his gut wriggle. But he'd heard no gunfire. The marshals might have taken another route through the Mexicans to Crow Feather, foiling any plans the gang might have had of springing the prisoners.

The thought was still shuffling around in his head when a dull rumbling rose from the thickening night shadows. At first, it sounded like a distant rock slide.

But as the thumps grew louder and were joined by the squawks of tack and the rattle of bridle bits and chains, the occasional chuff of a horse or the throat-clearing of a man, Cuno reined Renegade off the left side of the trail. He put the horse up a steep grade and drew rein behind a vertical knob of eroded rock spiked with cedars. Leaning forward, he cupped a hand over the stallion's nostrils, and peered around the knob's left side.

The hoof thumps rose like the beat of several Indian war drums. Occasionally there was the ring of a shod hoof clipping a stone.

Shadows moved, rising and falling behind the rocks and shrubs and sliding from left to right along the trail below. As the riders passed, Cuno swung his head to peer around the knob's right side. The silhouettes of men and horses flicked behind shrubs and rocks and disappeared behind another squat knob rising from the slope to Cuno's right.

One of the riders said something in a tight, frustrated voice, too far away and too drowned by the clatter of the hooves for Cuno to make out. As quickly as they'd risen, the drumming of the hooves faded off down canyon, echoing faintly. As if to punctuate their passing, a horse whinnied, and then the rasping breeze and distant coyote yips filled the night once more.

The chill breeze slipped down Cuno's wool collar to rake the hair over his sweat-damp back, lifting gooseflesh. He quelled the urge to shiver. That worm in his gut lifted its head and flicked its tail.

They were after the wagon.

Cuno expelled a deep breath and put Renegade down the slope, letting the horse pick its own path in the darkness, hearing rocks rattle behind. As he turned the horse down trail and nudged him with his spurs, he was off again, angling southeast through the Mexicans, darkness like a thick black glove descending quickly while stars kindled brightly and merged—sequins in bunched, black cloth.

Since the trail was merely a faint line rising and falling and curving along the ground before him, Cuno held Renegade to a walk. He didn't want the horse slamming a cannon against an unseen rock or tripping over deadfall. As he rode, he found himself wondering if the dead lawman's horse had found its way back to town.

If so, had the man's family found him?

Absently, he imagined the scene. The wife, having heard the horse's snort or whinny, wanders outside to see the vinegar dun standing in the yard, by a stack of split cordwood. She holds up a lamp and walks around the horse. Maybe a child, or two children, having been waiting for their father since suppertime, run out of the cabin behind her.

The dull, yellow light finds the body humping up beneath the blanket, hanging belly down across the saddle, the man's dark brown hair peeking out from the blanket's open fold . . .

A sudden, bereaved scream shatters the quiet night.

Cuno removed his hat and ran his hand through his long, sweat-damp hair. No matter who cared about him, or if no one cared, the man was dead.

Murdered.

Cuno rode for another hour, until it was so black he could barely see his hand in front of his face. Then he camped in a box canyon, near a small feeder creek, building a small fire for coffee and to warm some beans.

He dug a shallow trough for his hip and slept hard, his two blankets pulled up to his chin against the high-country chill and the breeze that settled after midnight. In his sleep he heard an owl hoot, a distant bobcat scream, and the sporadic scratchings of burrowing creatures. Pinecones thudded dully around him.

He started the next day consciously putting the dead lawman and the jail wagon out of his mind . . . until, around ten a.m., as he took a detour around a section of trail obliterated by a rockslide, a distant rifle shot ripped out across pine-covered slopes, sucking at its own echo.

It was followed by the muffled, almost inaudible bray of a mule.

5

CUNO SAT HIS skewbald paint straight-backed and tense, jaws hard as he stared up the razorback ridge on his right.

Pines covered the slope slashed with charred, crumbling logs from a long-ago fire, and recent deadfall—pines as well as firs, a few aspens. At the lip of the ridge, the forest receded beneath a camel hump of pocked, fluted sandstone.

As his gaze bored a hole through the sky capping the ridge, another rifle shot cracked in the canyon on the other side. The report flatted out shrilly as it echoed across the valley—muffled with distance but crisp and clear on the high, dry western air. Renegade shook his head and stomped his right foot, then shook his head again.

Brows ridging his clear blue eyes, Cuno continued staring at the ridge, his heart thudding dully. Finally, when no more gunshots sounded, he snapped his head forward, clucked to the horse, and continued on his way, up through a broad valley cleaved by a winding, slender stream around which tall, tawny grass grew thick and breeze-ruffled. Flood-killed trees—short-branched and barkless—stood in spare groves on both sides of the slow-moving water.

Keeping his gaze on the trees and the stream, Cuno was practically holding his breath, hoping he wouldn't hear another report, hoping the shots he'd heard had been fired by hunters and not by the renegades trailing the jail wagon.

He'd ridden only fifty yards when another whip-crack broke beyond the ridge, the echo drawing Cuno's gut taut as braided rawhide. Another report sounded, and then another, until a veritable fusillade rose from the far canyon.

When you knew how to use a .45, there were times when you couldn't very well *not* use it.

Cursing the past that had led to his abilities, he neck-reined Renegade back down the faint wagon trail he'd been following, then put the horse up the gradual western slope. Lunging off his rear hooves, digging with the front, Renegade climbed into the tall grass along the base of the hill and lunged up through the grass and chokecherry shrubs until the scrub thinned and the forest began.

The horse picked his own way through the thick timber, leaping deadfalls and turning sharply around occasional boulders and the giant root balls of trees uprooted by previous wind storms. Cuno ducked under branches, occasionally breaking one off. Renegade's hooves thumped softly in the spongy turf, crunching pinecones and needles.

Gaining the sandstone caprock, Cuno trotted the skewbald along the dike's sandy base until he found a ragged defile. He couldn't tell if the cleft offered passage to the other side of the ridge and into the valley on the other side, but it was the only one he'd seen.

Swinging down from the saddle, he quickly tied the horse to a pine branch and shucked his Winchester from the saddle boot.

The shooting continued—the revolver and rifle reports sounding like snapping branches, with the occasional whistling screech of a ricochet. Occasionally, a man gave a clipped, angry shout.

"Stay, boy," Cuno told the horse as, levering a shell into the Winchester's breech, he strode back up the slope to peer into the cavern.

He couldn't see much but rock thumbs jutting from both stone walls and narrowing the passage to a few feet in places. But the gunfire sounded louder in here. He moved forward, crawling over a couple of stacked boulders and sidestepping around a three-foot gap before angling through a dogleg.

Seconds later, he crouched behind a stone upthrust at the other end, peering over the rock and into a broad, sun-splashed valley like the one he'd left. Few trees stippled the slope below him, however. Mostly tall, tawny grass, chokecherry shrubs, occasional aspens, and moss-furred rocks and boulders.

At the far side of the valley, a narrow creek angled along the base of a steep, pine-carpeted spur ridge. Rocks and scattered aspens stood along the creek, and now as Cuno raked his gaze across the canyon, he saw several sets of smoke puffs and orange flashes of gunfire from the rocks and trees.

The shots were directed up toward the middle of the valley, where the jail wagon was parked along an almost-grassed-over wagon trail. The wagon tongue drooped into the trail, the mules gone.

The four prisoners cowered inside the wagon, yelling encouragement toward the four or five men shooting toward Cuno's side of the canyon from the creek.

Another man crouched behind the wagon's left front wheel, firing a Winchester toward the creek. A body humped in the grass just ahead and left of the wagon. The sun reflected off something silver on the man's chest. Likely a deputy U.S. marshal's badge, Cuno thought with a nettling hitch in his gut.

He returned his gaze to the man shooting from the wagon. The gray hair on the man's hatless head, and the rounded shoulders, bespoke the older marshal. The younger one was dead or at least badly wounded. A large patch of glistening red blood shone on the older gent's shirt, across his left shoulder blade. By the way he was hefting his rifle, as though it weighed ten extra pounds, he was losing blood and strength fast.

Cuno moved out from behind the rock, crouching, holding his Winchester low so that sunlight was less likely to flash off the copper receiver chasing. He strode down the slope, hoping he wouldn't be seen from the creek, and crouched behind a spindly cedar and a low boulder sheathed in tawny grass.

He hunkered on one knee, listening to the fiercely sporadic cracks of the gunfire and the whining ricochets off rocks and the wagon's iron-shod front wheels, while he considered the best way to offer a hand. Should he try to move around and flank the attackers, or just drop a little closer to the wagon and return fire at the creek from higher ground?

With a solid two hundred yards currently stretching between him and the creek, he had little chance of hitting any of the well-covered shooters from here.

He'd just decided to try to flank the attackers when movement on his left caught his eye.

A mustached man in a long, cream duster, felt sombrero, and mule-eared, stovepipe boots stole out from behind a rocky escarpment humping up out of the slope about fifty yards below Cuno. Crouching, holding his rifle in one hand, the man directed his gaze toward the jail wagon as he stole down the slope and pulled up behind a triangular boulder sheathed in spindly shrubs.

He was doing to the old marshal what Cuno had planned to do to the gunman's compadres. Less than sixty yards away from the lawman, he had a clear shot.

On the other side of the valley, amidst the angry, sporadic rifle cracks, a man cursed sharply. Cuno looked beyond the wagon to see one of the attackers down on a knee beside a boulder, clutching his thigh. The old marshal, who had scrambled around to the other end of the wagon containing the four snarling, cursing prisoners, snapped off another shot.

The man clutching his knee by the tree jerked straight back and flopped down in the grass beside the stream, throwing his rifle high in the air. It landed in the water with a silent splash.

Behind the wagon, the old marshal chuckled as he ejected the spent brass and levered a fresh shell into the chamber. At the same time, the man downslope and left of Cuno snaked his own rifle around the right side of his covering boulder to draw a bead on the marshal's back.

Cuno snapped his Winchester to his shoulder, squinted down the barrel, centered his sights on the side of the rifleman's head, just above and behind the man's ear, and squeezed the trigger.

The rifle roared as the brass butt plate slammed against Cuno's shoulder.

The boulder in front of the gunman turned red, as though someone had slung an open can of paint at it. The man's head jerked sharply sideways, then straightened, and he seemed to continue to peer downslope for a good three seconds before the rifle sagged in his arms.

His hands opened, the rifle fell, and the man sagged forward on his face. He rolled awkwardly about ten yards down the hill before coming to rest on his back, arms and legs spread wide.

The old marshal had just snapped off a shot toward the creek. Before he could eject his spent brass, he snapped his entire body around toward Cuno, his craggy, bearded face etched with fear.

Crouching behind his covering shrub and racking a fresh shell into his Winchester's breech, Cuno threw up an arm. He thought he saw befuddlement brush across the old marshal's haggard, sweating features. The man's chin dropped slightly as he looked at the dead rifleman sprawled on the slope below the triangular-shaped boulder.

More shouts rose from the creek. Cuno took advantage of the attackers' confusion—they'd no doubt seen the flanking shooter tumble down the hill—by bounding to his feet and scrambling down the slope past the blood-splattered boulder. He hurdled the rifleman's corpse with its ruined head and bulging eyes.

As he hit the bottom of the slope and started across the valley, running and angling right toward the wagon fifty yards away, rifles whip-cracked fiercely from along the creek. The slugs chewed into the grass on either side of Cuno's stomping boots.

He squeezed off two shots from his right hip, then, approaching the wagon with its prisoners snarling like circus lions and the marshal sitting with his back to the rear wheel, dove behind the front wheel as another slug barked into a log on the wagon's other side.

Another sparked off the outside wheel with a sharp, ear-ringing clang.

"Hey, Junior!" one of the prisoners growled. "What the hell you think you're doin'? This ain't *none* of *your* affair!"

Cuno, breathing hard as he pressed his back to the wagon's spoked wheel, beside the bulging hub, glanced over his left shoulder. A small but strongly built, broad-faced gent glared at him from between the wagon's bars.

"Now, the marshal over here is on his last legs, and in about two minutes, you ain't gonna have no one to be fighting for. Understand? So you best beat it back to where you came from. *Got it*, big boy?"

Cuno looked at the marshal at the other end of the wagon. The man's left front chest was bloody, his large belly rising and falling sharply beneath the flaps of his beaded deerskin vest. The gray-bearded man cast Cuno a sidelong glance, a smile of ironic humor as well as searing pain tugged at his lips and long, dust-rimmed, gray-brown mustache. His hat was gone, and thin, sweat-soaked hair curled about his balding head.

"Frank's got a point, kid." The old marshal coughed. "Bastards jumped us when we were watering the mules at the creek. Didn't figure it. Didn't see it comin.'" He coughed again, sucked a rattling breath. "Ardai was so damn sure they'd never track us through this canyon."

"Ardai's a fool," barked the red-haired prisoner, who'd pissed through the wagon's bars in Buffalo Flats, poking his wedge-shaped, sunburned nose through the bars as he glared down at the marshal. "Joe Pepper's got Dud Manover ridin' with him. Manover can track a snake across a boulder field in the drivin' rain!"

A couple more slugs tore into the sod around the wagon, another clanging off one of the wagon bars. As the cracks resounded around the valley, one of the prisoners—the tall, Nordic-looking hombre with long, silver hair and gold front teeth crawled over to the wagon's far side. "Goddamn you sons o' bitches! Watch where you shootin'!"

The red-haired gent followed suit with, "Ain't much good springin' us if we're *dead*, now, *is it*?" He turned to the rangy, silver-haired man. "Which one fired that shot—did you see, Bob? Faraday, wasn't it?"

The short, stocky gent called Frank shook his head. "The old mossy-horned badge toter done shot Faraday. He's the one on his back by the creek. I think there's only three left—Shepherd, Pepper, and Stan McDonald."

Cuno had crawled beneath the wagon on his belly, holding his rifle up in front of him, cocked and ready. As the prisoners scuffed around in the wagon above his head, making the springs and wooden undercarriage squawk and creak, he cast his gaze across the grassy, cedar-stippled valley toward the creek.

There was a low hump of ground halfway between the wagon and the water, and he thought he'd seen a hat crown sway above the bending weed tips capping the hump.

"Pepper and McDonald's all we need," he heard one of the prisoners sneer above his head. "Them're the cold-steel boys, sure 'nough. Boys, we'll soon be free as the damn jackrabbits and on our way to that payroll box."

"If Pepper and McDonald don't kill us instead of that fool kid and the mossy horn." Bob shouted loudly through the cracks between the wagon's stout floorboards. "Hey, kid, where'd you go, anyways? Just what in the hell do you think you're *doin'* under there?"

Ka-blam!

Cuno's rifle rammed his shoulder and leapt in his hands. He stared down the smoking barrel. The man who had just poked his head up above the low, grassy mound suddenly disappeared.

"On the right, kid!" the old marshal rasped. "I'm outta shells!"

Cuno opened his Winchester's breech, and the smoking spent cartridge flew back behind him. Seating a fresh shell, Cuno slid the rifle right. Another man—one with blood gleaming on his left cheek—bolted out from behind a boulder about forty yards from the wagon.

"Look out, Stan!" One of the prisoners shouted. "The kid's under the wagon!"

Stan stopped, snapped his rifle to his shoulder. The maw spat smoke and flames. At the same time the slug ground into the dirt three inches from Cuno's right elbow, the report reached Cuno's ears. A quarter-second later, Cuno triggered his Winchester three times quickly.

Stan grunted as all three slugs took him through the center of his chest, lifting him a foot in the air and punching him straight back.

"*Ohhhhhhhh!*" one of the prisoners lamented as Stan hit the ground shoulder first on his back, boots and spurs soon following. His rifle clattered into the brush beside him.

Silence. No movement in the wagon over Cuno's head.

There was only the sighing of the wind ruffling the grass and the occasional peeps of birds in the trees along the creek.

The old marshal wheezed a taut laugh. "I'll be damned, kid. You got the son of a bitch."

Raking his gaze back and forth across the canyon, Cuno thumbed more rounds from his cartridge belt into his rifle's loading gate. "Should have finished him off in Buffalo Flats." He drew a deep breath. "If I counted right, there's one more."

6

CUNO'S LAST WORDS hadn't died on his lips before a girl's scream rose from the creek.

A man in chaps, a funnel-brimmed hat, and a dark brown shirt ran out from a tight clump of aspens, water splashing up around his knees as he jogged across the stream, a rifle in his hand. He angled toward a trough in the steep, opposite bank.

Another figure—slender and with long, tawny hair—ran along behind him.

It was the girl from the Buffalo Flats Saloon whom Pepper had backhanded. She yelled sharply, closing on the brown-shirted man. The man wheeled, swinging his rifle around and smashing the butt across the girl's forehead.

Her scream reached Cuno's ears after she'd wheeled and fallen in the shallow water and the man had continued slogging through the water toward the trough.

Cuno scrambled out from beneath the wagon, ran into the meadow, and dropped to a knee. Backshooting disgusted him, but better to backshoot a man than let him ride off to return later to finish the bloody job he'd started.

"Look out, Shepherd!" the red-haired prisoner called from behind Cuno. "The kid's drawin' a bead on ya!"

Cuno fired. Dust puffed from the bank in front of the brown-shirted man. He flinched and jerked a quick look over his shoulder as he splashed onto the opposite shore and scrambled toward the trough angling down the cutbank.

Cuno fired two more quick rounds, both slugs pounding the bank on either side of the man now scrambling up the steep, eroded trough, using his rifle like a cane and frantically pulling himself up by protruding roots with his other hand.

Cursing, Cuno ran forward and racked a fresh shell.

Behind him, the prisoners whooped and hollered encouragement to their friend Shepherd. Cuno stopped, drew aim again as his target tossed his rifle over the bank and hoisted himself up over the lip with both arms.

Cuno's rifle thundered twice more. Both slugs blew widgets of stone and clay from the side of the cutbank as the brown-shirted man threw himself into the grass atop the lip and, grabbing his rifle, rolled into the thick, shaded timber beyond.

One of the prisoners guffawed and rattled the bars of the jail wagon. "Missed him, big boy! Missed him clean!"

"But don't worry," yowled one of the others. "He'll be back . . . with more!"

There was a fleshy smack. "Shut your fuckin' trap, Simms!"

The man's return was what Cuno was afraid of. He took his Winchester in one hand and bolted forward into an all-out run, boots pounding and spurs trilling, grass crunching beneath his feet. Vaguely, he heard the prisoners behind him cursing and arguing, someone smacking the bars angrily.

He made the trees and cut straight into the stream, glancing at the girl, who'd crawled onto the canyon-side shoreline and now lay on her hip and elbow. She held a hand to her bleeding forehead as her eyes rolled and fluttered, dazed.

Ten long strides and Cuno was at the trough, climbing fast, grabbing exposed roots. His wet boots squawked and slipped in the clay already muddied by his fleeing quarry.

When he'd pulled himself up and over the lip, he remained crouching, rifle ready, as he raked his gaze around the columnar pines and firs looming around him. When no shots exploded from nearby boles, Cuno moved forward.

His heart pounded as he began jogging slowly, sweeping his gaze around the trees, stalking the last surviving bushwhacker—aside from the girl. Ahead, several horses whinnied amongst the angry chittering of squirrels. Cuno lengthened his stride, heading up the pine-clad slope, leaping deadfalls, holding his rifle up high across his chest.

There was the clatter of pounding hooves and more whinnies and knickers. Twigs snapped under running hooves.

Cuno ran harder, his breath whooshing in and out of his broad chest, his knotted red bandanna flopping over his shoulder. When he got to the crest of the hill, he looked down into a narrow, brush-and-willow-choked gorge. Beyond, where the gorge opened out into a series of sage-covered hogbacks, the brown-shirted man galloped into the distance astride a lunging steeldust.

Five other horses fanned out around him, buck-kicking angrily and trailing their reins.

Cuno raised his rifle and snapped off three quick shots, but the bouncing rider was a hundred yards away, rising and falling over the hogbacks. Cuno couldn't even see the dust or grass blown up by his errant rounds.

He bit out a sharp curse. He watched the fleeing rider disappear down the other side of a steep rise. The other horses scattered amongst the rolling, cedar-spotted hills, dwindling quickly until they were gone.

Cuno turned and tramped back the way he'd come, run-sliding down the slippery trough to the stream. The girl sat along the opposite shore, her back against a rock, knees bent.

Her shirt and jeans were soaked, and her tawny hair hung in wet strands to her shoulders. Her forehead was swollen and bloody around a vertical gash on her left temple. She rested her arms on her knees and watched Cuno without expression.

She'd found her wet hat and snugged it down on her

head, the brim shading her eyes. She moved her head to watch Cuno cross the stream. As he started up the bank about ten feet away from her, he turned to her and tossed his chin back toward the steep cutbank.

"Where's he headed?"

She said in a voice so soft and without inflection that the stream nearly drowned it, "How should I know?"

Cuno didn't know what to make of her. She'd been part of the group and yet, back in the saloon, she'd seemed removed from it. He should throw her in the jail wagon, but then there was the complication of throwing a girl to four snarling male coyotes . . .

Screw it. She'd had her horns dulled by Shepherd.

He turned away and tramped through the trees and across the meadow, cutting between the two dead men— Stan and Pepper—lying in bloody heaps amidst the waving bluestem and wheatgrass. When he got back to the wagon, the prisoners were sitting against the barred walls, regarding him skeptically.

The big, one-eared Mexican, Fuego, sat with one forearm draped across a lone upraised knee, head canted as he studied Cuno like an artist might study an image he'd like to paint.

Only, unlike your average artist, Fuego's blue-green eyes were opaque with needling menace—a deep-seated, animal-like threat the likes of which Cuno hadn't confronted since his dealings with the savage bounty hunter Ruben Pacheca. Remembering Cuno's part in the Mexican's incarceration, Fuego was, without a doubt, imagining the south-of-the-border style revenge he intended to exact on the husky blond freighter, first chance he got.

"Hey, kid," said the stocky gent with a wide, clean-shaven face and steel-blue eyes. He was short enough that he could stand in the wagon without stooping, and he stood now, thick fists wrapped around the bars of the cage's rear door. "Grab the marshal's key off his belt and open the damn door. Hurry up. You don't wanna die out here. This ain't your fight!"

Ignoring the man, Cuno walked around the rear of the wagon and crouched down before the marshal. The oldster sat where Cuno had left him, leaning back against the wheel, legs stretched straight out before him, rifle crossed on his lap.

He was just beyond the reach of the jail cage and the four seasoned killers within. He had one cartridge pinched between the thumb and index finger of his left hand, as though he'd started reloaded his rifle but was too fatigued to follow through.

His chest rose and fell heavily. His eyes had been closed but as Cuno's shadow passed over his gray-bearded face, his lids fluttered open.

"You get the other one?" he rasped.

Cuno shook his head. "How bad you hit?"

The man shook his head as if to say he wasn't sure. "Think my shoulder's shattered." He glanced at the blood bibbing his gray duck shirt over which he wore a beaded deerskin vest to which his marshal's badge was pinned. "'Bout half drained, too, I reckon. Stuff my neckerchief in the hole, will you?"

Cuno leaned his rifle over a sage clump, then unknotted the sweat-stained green cloth from around the marshal's leathery neck.

"Bullet go all the way through?"

The marshal nodded. "In through the back, out the front. Bastards backshot me. Drilled Chuck through the kneecap, and when I tried to help him to cover, they shot him through his neck. Got me when I was runnin' toward the wagon."

Cuno stretched the man's neckerchief out before him, started a tear with his teeth, then ripped the cloth in two with his hands. "You have anything to clean it with?"

The old lawman tossed his head toward the front of the wagon. "Bottle under the seat . . . in the grain sack."

Cuno moved up the side of the wagon, ignoring the prisoners' owly stares and snarls and the continued threatening pleas of the short man called Frank to blast the lock off the cage's door. He shoved aside several croaker sacks of camping supplies before he found the bottle stuffed in a bag of parched corn.

When he'd soaked both pieces of cloth with the whiskey, he moved back to the marshal and extended the bottle.

The oldster chuckled dryly. "Obliged, kid."

When the man had taken a couple of hard pulls, Cuno wadded both pieces of cloth tightly in his fists, wringing out the excess whiskey. He pulled the marshal slightly forward and scuttled around beside him to inspect the entrance wound in his back.

"I feared they mighta sent someone from the north to blast the prisoners outta the cage."

"Maybe you should have let them go and saved your own hide." Cuno found the hole just below the man's left shoulder blade and, gritting his teeth, stuffed the neckerchief into it. "Maybe you still should . . ."

"*Gnnahhhh!*" The old marshal drew his mouth wide. Shock and misery glazed his eyes as Cuno tamped the whiskey-soaked cloth into place. The old lawman stopped breathing for about five seconds, and then he let out some air before sucking a deep, slow breath. "No lawman worth his salt'd let them critters out to run wild upon the land. No, sir. Not as long as I still got blood to bleed with."

Cuno shoved the man back against the wheel and leaned his head close to locate the exit hole in the man's chest. It was about six inches down from his shoulder.

"Ready?"

"Wait!"

The marshal lifted his whiskey bottle in a quivering, blue-veined hand. The bottle shook so hard that he missed his mouth twice before finally slipping the brown lip inside. He tipped back another long pull, his Adam's apple bobbing like a duck on a millrace.

"Hey, save some for us, Landers," said the prisoner with the long, silver hair, sitting with his back to Cuno and the old marshal but turning his head to peer over his shoulder. "We're gonna have us a hoedown after you're dead."

The lawman lowered the sloshing bottle with a raspy, whiskey-fetid sigh. He looked up to see Cuno staring at the man. "That's Bob King. Colorado Bob. Don't look into his eyes too long." The marshal chuckled. "They say it'll drive you loco, sort of like sleepin' in the moonlight."

Despite the warning, Cuno held the man's snaky, slant-eyed gaze. "Don't doubt it a bit."

Colorado Bob King stretched a slow, thin-lipped smile teeming with nearly as much menace as the eyes of Fuego. His gold teeth glistened. As he squeezed the bars in his fists, the tattoos on the back of his hands shifted and clarified—the rabbit on one, the hawk on the other.

Cuno spat to one side, then leaned forward again and shoved the wadded cloth into the old marshal's bullet hole.

The man scrunched up his flushed, sweaty face and turned his head to one side, groaning deep in his chest. The cords in his neck stood out like ropes.

"Jay-*zuzzzz* Keee-*rist*, that smarts!"

He swallowed, let the muscles in his face slacken. "But I do appreciate it, kid. Now, if you'll be so kind as to help me retrieve my mules, I'll try to get this heap movin' again . . . before that backshootin' son of a bitch brings more of Oldenberg's boys."

The man had grabbed Cuno's shoulder and began pulling himself to his feet. Cuno shoved him back down. "You're not gonna do any walking with that shredded shoulder. I'll fetch your mules. Then we'll see if you're fit to ride."

"I gotta ride. Gotta get this vermin to the lockup in Crow Feather. They done already been sentenced up in Cody, but the judge wanted 'em to hang in Crow Feather. That's where they robbed the army payroll detail. The widows of the men they killed put in a special request to see these coyotes' necks stretched while they sipped tea and ate pound cake."

Landers laughed, coughed, and spat.

"We'll see about that."

Cuno cursed inwardly again as he moved around the

front of the wagon and tramped off into the meadow. The old marshal's shoulder was shot to hell. He wouldn't be able to drive the wagon. It was doubtful that he could even ride without the jarring bleeding him dry.

And if the Oldenberg whom the man had mentioned was the notorious thieving killer and gang leader Karl Oldenberg, even the long-odds bets were off.

But, like the man said, he had a wagonload of prisoners to haul to Crow Feather. They weren't just stock or hay thieves, either. If all four weren't seasoned killers, then Cuno didn't know shit from Cheyenne.

Someone would have to get the wagon to Crow Feather. If Cuno had to do it, he'd be delayed a good three or four days. Likely, he'd lose the freighting contract not just for himself but for his old pal Serenity Parker, as well.

He crouched over the younger marshal, who lay on his hip and shoulder, legs scissored widely, thick red blood coating his neck and chest. His hat was gone but his sweaty, sandy hair still retained its shape.

Cuno grabbed a shoulder and turned the man over on his back. His sightless eyes stared at the sky over Cuno's shoulder. His parted lips formed a perfect O.

Irrational guilt plucked at Cuno as he stared down at the dead man. Finally, he brushed his open palm across Svenson's face, closing his eyes.

"Sorry, partner."

Cuno straightened the man's legs and crossed his arms on his belly. Leaving the body half concealed in the waving grass, he tramped off toward the northeast side of the canyon where he'd spied the wagon mules foraging in the trees along the creek. As he walked, he kept an eye skinned on the ridges.

The man called Shepherd wouldn't be back yet, but he'd come. And, if he was a member of Karl Oldenberg's gang, who'd been plundering mining camps across Wyoming for the past two years, he'd bring more.

Many more . . .

7

THE MULES WERE a couple of mixed-breed duns. They were docile, rested, and watered enough that they balked little at being led back across the canyon to the wagon.

When Cuno had both hitched to the traces, and he'd checked the snaps, buckles, hames, tongue, and double-tree—he wanted no problems in case they needed to high-tail it—he checked on the marshal.

The oldster sat where Cuno had left him, dozing in the sunlight that was beginning to angle slowly now over the western ridges, drawing shade out from the jail wagon. The man held his bottle in one hand between his thighs.

At least he appeared to be dozing. The marshal's cheek twitched slightly as flies buzzed around the blood jelled on his chest, but he didn't seem to be breathing.

Cuno touched his shoulder, and the man snapped his head up, eyes bright, almost lucid, in fact.

"Got the mules hitched to the wagon," Cuno said. "As soon as I fetch my horse, we'll be ready to roll . . . if you still wanna give it a try."

"Did you check on Chuck?"

Cuno nodded gravely.

"No time to bury him. Maybe we could haul him along, bury him along the trail somewheres . . . ?"

Again, Cuno nodded. "I'll lay him over my horse."

The old man threw an arm forward. "Pull me up, young'un. I'll get rollin' while you fetch your horse and Chuck."

Cuno doubted the man would make it, but it was worth a try. He pulled him up and, throwing one arm around his neck, led the man up toward the wagon box.

"Jesus, you don't look good, Bill," said the short, muscular prisoner, Frank Blackburn, wagging his head gravely as he stared through the bars.

The other prisoners, even the silently menacing Fuego, were staring expectantly at the wounded lawman.

"Ah, go diddle your mother, Blackburn," the marshal rasped.

"I'd do that," Blackburn said, grinning and canting his head toward the wagon's rear door. "Just as soon as you open the door o' this here cage . . ."

The marshal stopped near the left front wheel and looked over the mules. Glancing at Cuno, he said, "You've rigged a team before."

"Time or two." Cuno steadied the wounded marshal as the man put a foot on the wheel hub and climbed heavily, grunting painfully and sucking air through his teeth, into the driver's box.

Standing, he looked over the team once more, raking his gaze back and forth across the collars and hames and the chains securing the rig to the tongue. "Yessir, you'll do."

One-handed, he began unwrapping the reins from the brake handle.

"I'll be along shortly." Cuno turned and began striding back toward the western ridge and the defile in the caprock humping up above the pine forest.

Behind him, the old marshal shook the reins across the mules' broad backs and yelled, "Get along there, now, you useless sacks of mule flesh!"

As the jail wagon began rattling up trail, Blackburn called behind Cuno. "Don't worry, kid! We'll take good care of him!"

Between mule-directed harangues, the marshal told Blackburn to do something physically impossible to himself, and, as all the prisoners except Fuego laughed, the wagon crested a low ridge and began dropping down out of sight.

Cuno found Renegade contentedly foraging where he'd left the horse on the other side of the spur. Locating a slightly wider defile about fifty yards away from the first one, he led the horse through the gap and down the mountain.

When he'd tied the body of the dead marshal to Renegade's rump, he began to fork leather, then, remembering the girl, stopped and turned back to the creek. No sign of her. She'd likely run down one of her gang's horses and hightailed it back to where she came from.

Cuno swung up into the saddle and put Renegade up trail in an easy lope. It was only fifteen minutes or so before he spied the wagon rumbling through another broad canyon rippled with rocky dikes and benches and slashed with small gullies. The wagon was a mere brown speck about a half mile ahead and nearly lost amidst the rabbit brush and clay-colored rocks.

Cuno rode up past the prisoners, who were sitting or lying in the bouncing box, all as scowling, sunburned, and dusty as a passel of trapped wolves. Hearing Renegade's clomping hooves, the old marshal jerked with a start, fumbling his rifle off the seat beside him.

"It's Cuno." The blond freighter walked Renegade beside the right front wheel, keeping pace with the slow-moving wagon. "You still kicking?"

"Ah, shit," the marshal said, shoving his rifle under the seat. "I cut myself worse than this shavin'." He glanced at Cuno, squinting one eye. "Cuno, you say?"

"Cuno Massey."

"I'm Bill Landers. Much obliged for the help, young

Massey. I reckon I got her under control for the time bein'. I know you got business ahead, an' I wouldn't want to hold you up no more than I already have."

"That's all right," Cuno said. "I got all the time in the world."

He pulled Renegade up close to the wagon. He wrapped his reins around his saddle horn, then stepped off the horse and into the wagon in one smooth motion, Renegade keeping pace off the wagon's right front wheel. The body of the dead deputy flopped behind the saddle, the man's hair dangling toward the trail.

Cuno sat down beside the old marshal, who had fashioned a sling out of a leather rifle lanyard, and poked his hat back off his forehead. A quick inspection told him the oldster was in worse shape than he let on.

The man was of an older, hardier breed—he wore his hard, rich past in the deep lines in his face and neck—but he couldn't drive the team and endure the wagon's pitch and sway much more than a few miles. The man's cheeks were sallow, his eyes glazed with pain.

Already, fresh blood had begun pumping through the cloth Cuno had stuffed into the hole in his chest. It glistened brightly as it spread out across the shirt and vest, and it rimmed the edges of the man's badge.

"Thought you said you had business in Crow Feather," Landers said, narrowing a skeptical eye at the husky lad.

"Nah." Cuno hiked a shoulder. "Just didn't think I'd look good in a badge. You want me to take over? I've driven a few teams."

"I got it. You know, during the height of the Injun Wars I was shot seven times—all at *once*?"

"Sioux?"

"Nah." The old lawman winced and shook his head. "The noncom I was playin' poker with at Camp Wichita!"

He threw his head back and guffawed until he turned linen white and winced at a keen pain spasm. Coughing, he spat over the wagon's left wheel and drifted into silence.

"How long you been marshaling?" Cuno asked after they'd ridden a half mile or so, just to keep the oldster alert.

"Ten years. I ranched in the Chugwater Buttes 'fore that . . . till rustlers and Injuns run off all my stock and my wife up and left me for a saloon owner in Wheatland."

Landers shook his head again. "Bitch died of syphilis three years later, and it ain't to my credit that I rejoiced when the devil took her black soul. I was badge totin' by then. The feds in Cheyenne needed someone to work the area around here after three deputies got beefed by vermin like these in the back.

"I done cleaned out a good dozen or so gangs holed up from here clear down to the Laramies, the Mummies, and over west to the Wind Rivers. Been half froze, damn near beat to death, arrowed by Crows and Cheyennes, almost drowned by a whiskey peddler named Vernon Gault, and shot in the ass *and* the head by stagecoach thieves and bank robbers."

Landers chuckled and jerked his head back to indicate the men riding in the cage, just out of arm's reach, behind him. "You think I'm gonna let these sons o' bitches run the chute after all that? Bullshit!"

"All four with Oldenberg?"

Landers shook his head. He was sagging forward over his bony knees. His eyelids seemed to be getting heavy, the skin over his cheekbones growing tighter.

"King, Blackburn, and Simms. Fuego's a loner, far as anyone can tell. He was convicted by the judge in Cody of raping a twelve-year-old girl in an old mine shack not two weeks ago, just outside Crow Feather. The girl's father found the bean eater sacked out, drunker'n a Catholic on All Saints' Day, near his poor daughter's cold, naked corpse. Fuego had slit her throat from ear to ear."

Cuno glanced over his shoulder to peer into the clattering cage in which all four prisoners dozed. Fuego lay flat on his back with an arm crooked over his eyes. "After what I saw in Bismarck . . ."

Cuno had started to turn his head forward when the old marshal sagged sideways against him, the reins slithering out of his gloved hands. Cuno snapped the reins up quickly, then straightened as the old marshal, his head on Cuno's left shoulder, gave a long, shuddering sigh and drifted deep into unconsciousness.

The man's chest was bright with amber blood. Both ends of the wound needed to be cleaned out and wrapped with a poultice, or he'd bleed to death soon.

As the old marshal's slow, shallow breaths rattled up like a vagrant breeze across cattails, Cuno raked his eyes across the jumbled hogbacks and sandstone dikes rising between two sheer, red stone cliffs over which several hawks or eagles circled, hunting the rims.

Unfolding on his right was a deep, narrow crease between hogbacks. It was hard to tell, but the crease appeared to lead to the base of the red stone wall. Maybe a box canyon.

Cuno turned the mules into the crease, and the wagon bounced violently over sharp hummocks, scattered rocks, and wild mahogany shrubs. As Cuno had hoped, the crease dead-ended in a well-sheltered box canyon cut a hundred yards into the cliff face. A thin trickle of water curled over a mossy granite wall, rattling over jumbled boulders on its plunge to the sand-bottomed pool below.

"Just what in the *hell* are we doin'?" the prisoner called Brush Simms barked indignantly. The violent passage through the crease had jolted him and the other prisoners around in the cage like dice in a cup. They squeezed the bars in their red fists.

Cuno stopped the wagon about thirty yards and down a slight slope from the pool, the runoff trickling through a narrow, rocky cut nearby. He set the brake, dropped the reins, and slid to the far right edge of the driver's box, dragging the old marshal along as gently as he could.

Planting one foot on the right front wheel hub, the other on a stout wooden brace, he eased the out-cold marshal off the seat. He turned and, holding the man under his sagging arms, stepped onto the rocky ground with the old man sort of dangling off his left hip.

The lawman puffed out his cheeks and flapped his lips as he blew, cursing in his sleep. "Goddamn . . . sons'bitches . . . the whole friggin' lot . . . !"

"You'll get no arguments from me," Cuno muttered.

"Jesus," Blackburn said, squatting at the edge of the cage and peering gravely through the bars as Cuno led the marshal up the slope toward the rattling falls. "That's a damn cadaver you're messin' with boy. Sure as shit up a cow's ass!"

"If you don't think our boys'll find us in here, you got another think comin', young fella!" Colorado Bob King tipped back one of the two canteens hanging from the barred ceiling of the jail wagon. Scowling, he let the canteen flop from its lanyard against a barred wall. "Hey, bring us some o' that water. We're bone-dry over here!"

Cuno resisted the urge to palm his Colt revolver and silence the prisoners with .45-caliber slugs. He eased the old marshal down against a boulder about twelve feet back from the pool and the rattling falls, which spread a fine mist across the nearby rocks and spindly cedar shrubs.

He looked back to see Renegade nibbling wheatgrass a ways off down the crease, then put two fingers to his mouth and whistled. The horse lifted its head with a start and, rippling its withers, stomped up the slope to the pool.

"Just like a damn dog," one of the prisoners chuckled, barely audible above the falls.

Cuno left the old marshal reclining, out like a blown wick, against the boulder while he got up and cut the body of the younger lawman free of Renegade's rump. He eased the body down in the grass, then retrieved his saddlebags and bedroll, setting each down beside the wounded marshal, and began fishing around in the pouches for a bottle of whiskey and wool scrap cloth he'd wound around a flat stick.

Fashioning a couple of poultices from whiskey, rich black mud he scooped out from beneath a rock, and shredded pine bark sticky with fragrant sap, he packed both the old marshal's entrance and exit wounds. He secured the poultices to the wounds with cloth wrapped under and over his arm, then several times around his chest.

That done, he returned the unconscious man's arm to the leather sling, then spread out one of the bedrolls he found in the wagon, and eased the man onto it, resting his head against the grain sack. He drew an extra blanket up to the man's chin, then gathered wood and started a fire to keep him warm.

Soon, when the inevitable fever set in, he'd shake like a leaf in a prairie cyclone.

The next chore in the order of importance was to cover the wagon's tracks leading off from the main trail, and that's what he did, ignoring the prisoners' gripes and threats as he tramped off down the crease. He cut down a cedar sapling and, starting back at the main trail, used the tree to wipe out the wagon and horse tracks as he backed down the crease. He used a deft hand on the tracks, knowing that any good tracker would quickly spot the ruse though maybe not before Cuno detected their presence.

"Hey, junior bub," said Blackburn as Cuno, tossing away the cedar tree, approached the wagon, sweating from his labors in the heat of the mid-afternoon. "It's pretty obvious you're just bound and determined to be a Good Samaritan to that slow-rotting badge toter over yonder."

Cuno paused by the wagon to remove his neckerchief. He looked at Blackburn, King, and Simms staring at him through the wagon's bars, sitting with their backs to the walls. As usual, Fuego sat sort of off by himself, back against the front wall, that dreamy, sinister look in his blue-green eyes as he played with the hair on one arm, beneath the rolled sleeve of his sweat-soaked, buckskin tunic. The silver ring dangled from his lone ear.

"We fellas talked it over," said Colorado Bob King, a grin spreading his thin, pink lips back from his gold teeth and slitting those slanted demon's eyes. "We're prepared to give you five hundred dollars to open that fuckin' door and remove these manacles."

Mopping his forehead with his handkerchief, Cuno grunted and continued toward the falls.

"How 'bout a thousand?"

Cuno turned back to the wagon. The three members of the Karl Oldenberg Gang stood on the near side of the cage, grinning at him through the bars.

Flies buzzed. One of the mules brayed softly, as if sensing Cuno's anger and consternation at not only being held up and probably losing his freighting contract, but at having to listen to the ceaseless caterwauling of these half-human lobos.

Rage boiled up in his head, pushing a red haze over his eyes.

Before he knew what he was doing, his .45 was in his hand, and he was crouching and fanning the hammer.

The Colt leapt and roared.

The prisoners stumbled back, jaws dropping and eyes snapping wide as the .45 rounds clanged, barked, and sparked like lightning off the welded iron bars.

When he'd fired all six rounds, Cuno stared through the wafting powder smoke. All three of the gang members were down and cowering on the wagon's stout wooden bed, snarling and grunting as they shielded their heads with their arms.

Cuno straightened slowly, slowly lowering the Colt, a wry smile pulling at his mouth corners. He thumbed open the loading gate and removed the spent shells as the reports continued to echo around the box canyon.

A foolish move, probably, but it was too soon for the Oldenberg Gang to be anywhere near.

Besides, the .45-caliber tantrum had relieved the tension like an iron piston rammed up his spine.

When he'd thumbed fresh bullets into the Colt, he spun the cylinder and couldn't resist the temptation to spin the gun on his finger before dropping it into its well-oiled holster.

He regarded the men still cowering on the wagon bed. Only Fuego was grinning, showing his stubby, rotten teeth under his mustached lip, peering at Cuno from low in the cabin's front corner.

"Now, how 'bout a little peace and quiet," Cuno grunted as he turned and continued tramping up to the pool where the old marshal was sawing heavy logs.

Behind him, he heard Colorado Bob say softly, "Son of a bitch is packin' a widow maker!"

8

LYLE SHEPHERD CLUTCHED his bloody neck as he put his black gelding up a switchbacking trail in the northwest corner of the Mexican Mountains, cursing under his breath and sucking pinched drafts of air through his clenched teeth.

Another hundred yards up the ridge, the town of Helldorado, jokingly named by the drunken prospectors who'd founded the place not two years ago, swam into view along the broad shoulder of the pine-clad Breasted Butte—also named by the pie-eyed prospectors for the obvious reason that, from a distance, the bluff resembled a woman's bosom.

The stench of overfilled privy pits, goat pens and pigpens, and Chinese cook fires was already so strong that Shepherd wanted to lift his neckerchief over his nose. But that would have required the use of the hand he was using to stem the outpouring of his body's vital fluids.

Blood oozed down his neck and under the collar of his pin-striped, collarless shirt because of the meddling son of a towheaded bitch who'd appeared out of nowhere with a Winchester to foil his party's plans to free their three amigos from the jail wagon.

Damn that younker's exasperating hide. When Karl Oldenberg sent more boys out after that soon-to-be-sorry bushwhacker, they'd bring him back in a half dozen separate bags and throw him to Mrs. Hoavig's hogs. Then they'd pass a jug and bend a couple of whores over rain barrels, in grand celebratory fashion, while the snorting, malodorous pigs thoroughly stuffed themselves.

Shepherd gigged the tired horse up the last switchback. Swerving around several slow-moving prospectors' wagons and a rickety firewood cart, he jogged into the smelly cesspool of a boomtown.

Weathered tents and crude log shanties pushed up on both sides of the rutted, pitted road down the middle of which snaked a narrow trench for carrying away rain and excess waste water. Several dead chickens, a dog, and a goat moldered at the bottom of the deep cut—the same ones that had been there two weeks ago.

Shepherd pushed the black through the rollicking, buckskin-and-denim-clad crowd, and drew rein before the largest building on the main drag. The three-story, unpainted, whipsawed-board affair with a broad porch on two sides and real glass windows on the first story was called, in Helldorado's customary ironic tradition, THE WICK-DIP SALOON AND DANCE HALL with a lesser sign tacked below announcing TITTY SHOWS NIGHTLY!

Snarling and groaning, Shepherd swung down from his saddle, tossed his reins over one of the several hitchracks fronting the place. Still clamping his hand to his oozing neck, he climbed the four steps to the porch.

Halfway to the batwing doors, he heard a low snarl and the patter of padded feet and claws, and he turned to see the spidery, yellow mongrel that lived under the porch bolt toward him from behind a rain barrel, teeth showing, hackles raised.

"Goddamn your mangy hide, dog!" Just before the mutt could clamp its jaws around his right ankle, Shepherd wheeled and kicked. "Don't you bite me, you black-hearted bastard!"

Shepherd's boot only grazed the dog's head, but the cur yowled, wheeled in a blur, and yelping as though it had been peppered with buckshot, galloped down the porch and around the side of the building, its little feet slipping on the heel-polished boards.

"Son of a bitch mongrel never did like me," Shepherd grumbled as, pushing through the batwings, he moved into the saloon's cool, brown shadows tainted with the smell of tobacco, spilled beer, and vomit.

The place was nearly deserted except for three scantily clad girls practicing dance steps atop the stage in the far back, beyond the stairs. Two wizened prospectors arm wrestled at a table to Shepherd's left, under the marble-black eyes of a six-point buck whose head was tacked to a stout ceiling joist.

The two bearded gents in duck coats and suspenders grumbled and cursed and gritted their teeth as their clenched, arthritic fists leaned first one way and then the other only to inch back in the other direction again. Their chairs creaked beneath their shifting weights.

To Shepherd's right, a sleepy-looking blonde stared at him from atop the bar. She wore a thin purple housecoat over a camisole low-cut enough to reveal nearly all of her ripe, creamy breasts. She arched a blonde brow, and the corners of her full mouth rose in her sexy, heart-shaped face.

"How ya doin', Lyle?"

"How'm I doin'? How's it look like I'm doin', Betty?"

"Git stung by a bumblebee, did ya?"

"Yeah, a *lead* bumblebee. Toss me a rag, will ya, so I can try to get some of this bleedin' stopped before I sieve dry and turn pale as those two big titties of yourn."

Betty frowned as she slumped against the bar, letting the edge of the zinc-covered mahogany push her breasts up under her neck, revealing all but the nipples. "I ain't got no spare bar rags you can bloody all up, Lyle. I just did my wash for the week."

"Ah, for chrissakes!" He lunged for a rag lying halfway

down the bar, near the large free-lunch spread upon a blue china serving platter.

"Oh, no, you don't!"

The girl made a dash for the rag, but Shepherd got to it a half second before she did. She slapped her plump little hand down on the damp zinc countertop, where the rag had been resting, as Shepherd shucked it up to his neck and plopped it down on his bloody bullet wound.

"Thanks for the help, you miserable bitch."

"Buster don't even like you."

"Buster's a mangy-assed cur just like you and half the other whores in this dump."

Shepherd dropped his chin to inspect the wound he'd been dabbing the cloth at. He couldn't see the bullet burn, for it was too far up on his neck, but a quick look into the back bar mirror told him it was a long, nasty-looking gash that had missed his carotid artery by about two cat whiskers.

Friggin' dry-gulchin' bastard. And Shepherd had to be the one to inform his boss of the dark turn of events—four men dead and three others still confined to the jail wagon heading for the hangman in Crow Feather.

"Where's Karl?"

"Upstairs," Betty said, wrinkling her nose and standing back to cross her arms on her matronly bosoms, denying Shepherd the continued privilege of her pricey wares. "Said he don't wanna be disturbed for anything but an extreme emergency."

Shepherd gritted his teeth. "Wouldn't you call four men shot deader'n last year's Christmas stew, and me nearly gettin' my head blowed off my shoulders, an emergency?"

Betty turned her head to one side and hiked a shoulder. "Since it's Karl givin' the orders around here, it don't really matter what *I'd* call an emergency, does it?"

"Jesus Christ," Shepherd grumbled as, holding the damp bar rag to his neck, he stomped down the bar toward the stairs on the other side of which the three scantily clad dancers were quietly practicing their kick steps, arm in arm and barefoot. "What the hell am I doin', standin' around talkin' to a damn whore dumber'n that damn cur she throws scraps to under the porch?"

Angrily, he climbed the stairs, boot heels thudding and spurs singing.

Behind him, Betty yelled, "And you can wash that rag when you're through with it, Lyle!"

"You can kiss my ass, you fuckin' bitch!"

"I'm tellin' Karl about the bad language you're in the habit of employin' on the premises!"

"Next time I'll just shoot ya." Shepherd turned his lean, six-foot-three-inch frame at the top of the stairs and jutted his jaw back toward the bar. "How'd that be?"

Smiling woodenly and keeping her left arm crossed on her breasts, Betty raised her right one high above her head, extending her pale middle finger.

Seething, Shepherd swung away from the balcony rail and stomped down the wide hall, the thud of his boots softened by the deep pile carpet runner. On both sides of the hall, paintings of naked women—some frolicking with either naked men, mostly black, or horses—hung on the unpainted board walls, between the unlit bracket lamps boasting either pink or soft blue mantels and bowls.

The building was silent, as it usually was this time of the day, with most of the girls getting their beauty rest in preparation for the night ahead. Shepherd could hear a couple of the girls sawing logs behind the closed, numbered doors. Horse clomps and a dog's desultory barks emanated from outside, beneath the rustle-scuffs of Shepherd's boots on the carpet runner.

He paused by Oldenberg's door, marked with a broad plank on which OFFICE had been painted in green. He took a deep breath and steeled himself for his boss's anticipated wrath. Then he lifted his right hand and knocked.

A strange voice, vaguely similar to Oldenberg's, rose behind the door. "Go 'way."

"Mr. Oldenberg, it's me—Shepherd."

A throat clearing. Someone said something too low for

Shepherd to hear. Then, in the same, only barely recognizable voice: "Awright, come in."

Shepherd turned the knob, pushed the door open, and stepped into the broad, barren office furnished with one massive desk on the far side of the room, fronting two open windows, and a single bookcase on which only two yellow-covered novels and a stack of old newspapers sat under a half-inch of dust.

Against the right wall was a double-sized bed supported by four split pine logs and covered with a ratty quilt of yellow-and-spruce-green squares tied with red yarn. A white porcelain thunder mug peeked out from beneath the bed's heavy frame, its lid on the floor beside it. Nothing adorned the pine-knotted walls—no pictures, paintings, game trophies, or even a gun rack.

"Back so soon? Where's Bob?"

Shepherd turned back to the desk, from which the burly, bearlike growl had risen. Karl Oldenberg sat back in his chair, lower jaw slack. He was a heavy, thick-necked, raw-faced man in his early thirties, with long, stringy hair, muttonchop whiskers, and an untrimmed goatee and mustache.

Like Shepherd and everyone else Oldenberg associated with, he'd been an outlaw practically since birth. But since purchasing the Wick-Dip and becoming a pseudo-respectable businessman, he'd affected a black clawhammer coat over a dark red, linsey tunic with leather ties at the deep V-shaped cut down his broad, fleshy but muscular chest.

In spite of the muttonchops and goatee, he had an oddly boyish face, with a dimple showing through the goatee, and plump, dimpled cheeks. His close-set, light brown eyes were small, and they owned the perpetual belligerence of a schoolyard bully.

Now, however, he had the dreamy look the girls got when they were high on marijuana or opium, which the town's Chinese butcher supplied in return for mattress dances.

"Sorry to say," Shepherd said, sounding as though he

had a cocklebur stuck in his throat, "that Bob ain't with me. Fact, no one's with me."

Oldenberg still spoke in that slow, garbled growl, and his eyes still seemed to own an extra, thicker lens as he said, "What'd you do to your neck, Lyle?"

There was a soft, female grunt from somewhere below Shepherd's boss and, aborting his attempt to answer the man's last question, Lyle dropped his eyes below the desktop.

Between the desk's two encased drawer stacks, half concealed by the room's deep shadows and further obscured by the bright, sunlit windows, a plump, pink, female ass hovered about a foot above the floor, the long, straight fold between smooth, fleshy lobes angled downward.

Squinting his eyes and angling his head, Shepherd could see that the girl was on her hands and knees. Her ass was moving slightly as, up near Oldenberg's chair and between his spread knees, her head bobbed as her mouth issued faint, crackling, sucking sounds, like the sounds a wheel hub makes when it's getting greased.

Startled, Shepherd lifted his eyes quickly and, pretending he hadn't seen the girl beneath the desk, said after several throat clearings and lip smacks, "Took a bullet, Boss. But I reckon I got off lucky. Pepper, McDonald, Faraday, Manover, ole Heck Dawson—they've all gone under."

Shepherd winced as the bullet burn sent a pain spasm down his back and into his loins. He clamped the rag down harder on his neck.

"We had them two badge toters dead to rights. I mean, they was ours, and we was a frog whisker away from springin' Bob and the boys. But some kid right handy with a Winchester slithered down the far side of the valley and took us all by surprise. The damn younker shot Manover and then he took out Pepper and McDonald, too, when the boys tried to storm the damn wagon. I took this here ricochet after Faraday done got his own wick blowed."

Shepherd felt his gut clench as the eyes of his beefy boss regained more of their customary hardness as he stared across the room at his underling. Under the desk, the girl grunted anxiously, and the wet crackling sounds got louder. Her ass rose and fell sharply as she toiled in obvious futility.

Oldenberg lurched back in his swivel chair and, scowling and flushing, dropped his hands to his crotch, his arms jerking as he pushed the girl's head away. "Esther, goddamnit, can't you see I ain't in the mood no more? Get on outta here, now!"

He shoved his chair back toward the window behind him and dropped in his seat a little as he kicked out with both feet. Esther gave a squeal, and Shepherd, still standing and holding the rag to his neck in front of the closed office door, saw the buck-naked whore twist around beneath the desk as she yowled and squealed against Oldenberg's flailing boots.

"Go on, git!" The beefy saloon owner lashed out with his left boot once more, making his belt buckle jingle. But the girl had already scuttled out from under the desk, sobbing, her curly red hair flying about her head.

"I'm goin'! I'm goin'!"

Bare feet slapping the rough-cut floorboards, she sprinted toward the door, her pale, pear-shaped breasts jiggling. She didn't so much as glance at Shepherd as she lunged for the doorknob, threw the door open, and ran into the hall, leaving the door standing wide behind her.

"Shut the goddamn door!"

Oldenberg's deep voice boomed around the room like the echoes of crashing boulders. His heart leaping, Shepherd turned abruptly and slammed the door. When he turned back to the desk, his boss was stumbling to his feet as he wrestled his longhandles and jeans up his hips, his big, silver belt buckle clanking against the desk.

His little mean pig eyes burned into Shepherd's quivering chest. His long, stringy hair continued dancing about his cheeks as he wrestled with his pants. "Now, let me get this straight—you're all that's left of the six I sent out?"

Shepherd dipped his chin and swallowed down the large, dry knot in his throat. "I reckon that's right, Boss.

Pepper had his girl with him, and she mighta made it. I don't know . . ."

"Goddamnit!"

"I apologize, Boss, but . . ."

"You were bushwhacked?"

"By some big, towheaded fella. Built like a boxer or wrestler. Blond-headed. Come runnin' down that mountain in deerskins, slingin' lead every which way. We'd sent ole Manover to flank the old marshal, and the blond-headed fella—"

"So Bob, Simms, and Blackburn are still in the jail wagon?"

Shepherd drew a deep breath. "That does seem to be the sum total of it, Boss. I knew I couldn't do much with this here neck of mine, so I hurried back fast as I could. Knew you'd want to put a new posse together, go after that wagon."

Oldenberg grunted as, with his pants finally up, he leaned forward to buckle his belt and stare under his bushy brows at Shepherd. "I don't suppose you got close enough to the wagon to find out where Bob and the others hid the strongbox?"

Shepherd sighed again and wagged his head sadly. "'Fraid not, Boss. Sorry about that. Ain't likely any o' them fellas woulda told us, anyway." He tried a laugh but it came out sounding more like the squawk of a rusty hinge. "They prob'ly woulda figured—"

"Woulda figured, being the suspicious sons o' bitches they are, that if they told us where the strongbox was before we sprung 'em, we wouldn't spring 'em." Oldenberg shook his head. "If ya can't trust members of your own group, who can you trust?"

Eyes snapping like Mexican firecrackers, Oldenberg walked out stiffly from behind his desk, which had little on it but a lamp, a pen, a corked stone jug, a shot glass, and one leather-bound account book. "Goddamnit, Lyle. I thought I was sendin' two of my best men. How in the hell did Pepper and McDonald let this happen, anyways?"

Before Shepherd could open his mouth to respond, Oldenberg said through gritted teeth, his eyes shiny with unfettered emotion, "You realize what'll happen if that goddamn jail wagon makes it Crow Feather?"

"I reckon . . . I reckon . . ."

"You reckon right. They'll hang those bastards without my ever learnin' where they hid the strongbox holding the most money we ever took down in a single job in this country, Canada, or Mexico."

"Want I should pull a posse together, round up some o' the fellas from the ranch?"

"Why don't you do that."

"Would it . . . would it be all right if I got a drink and had my neck sewed first? I don't know how much blood a man holds to begin with, but I think I mighta lost a good half of mine."

Oldenberg studied the underling, his fleshy, whiskery face menacingly inscrutable. Slowly, he dipped his head. "Sure, you just git yourself a drink. Sit down an' enjoy it. Hell, sit down and enjoy half a bottle while the pill roller sews you up. Maybe you'll want a girl, too?"

Shephered swallowed. His heart was pounding like the hooves of a dozen Cheyenne war ponies. He chuckled again though this time it sounded more like a sob. "Nah. I'll just have a drink and get my neck sewed. Then I'll fetch the boys from the ranch. The whole damn crew."

Clamping the bloody rag firmly against his neck, he turned slowly toward the door, keeping his eyes fixed on Oldenberg who stood in front of his desk, arms crossed on his broad chest.

When Shepherd had turned full around, he reached for the doorknob. His back crawled as though with a thousand scuttling spiders, and the hair along the back of his neck pricked straight up beneath his collar. Behind him, Oldenberg was horrifically silent.

Gritting his teeth, Lyle turned the doorknob. He wanted nothing more than to bound into the hall as quickly as the mangy, yellow cur had bolted toward Shepherd's ankle not fifteen minutes ago, but belly-churning fear and dread had turned his muscles as hard as new saddle leather.

He watched his hand wrap around the knob, turn it.

The door opened, squawking and brushing the top of a swollen floorboard. Before the door had cleared the threshold, a low, nearly silent grunt sounded behind him. At the same time, there was a soft snick and a rustle of heavy cloth.

Shepherd did not turn his head to see the Arkansas toothpick, which his boss had just shucked from the hard leather sheath dangling down his back, leave Oldenberg's flicking wrist to tumble through the air, end over head, and make a beeline for Shepherd's back.

But Shepherd heard the hornet-like whistle and, knowing it was coming, froze in his tracks and squeezed his eyes closed.

Fishhh-took!

The seven inches of razor-edged steel plunged hilt-deep in Shepherd's back, between his shoulder blades, just left of his spine.

Shepherd screamed and flew forward against the door, which his weight, in turn, slammed back into the frame with a bark of wood and a click of the latching bolt. He sagged against the door, groaning against the blistering sting of the blade embedded in his back and tickling his heart.

Cheek pressed against the wood, he dropped the rag and clawed with both hands at the solid door panel, as if to scratch his way through the wood and into the hall to freedom.

But he hung there, quivering like a bug on a pin, as Oldenberg's boots clomped across the floor behind him.

The burly, long-haired outlaw leader shucked his toothpick from Shepherd's back with his left hand and leaned close to Shepherd's quickly blanching face.

"On second thought," he rasped in the underling's ear, "I'll take care of it myself, Lyle. If there's one thing I've learned here this afternoon, it's never send a boy to do a man's work. You shoulda stayed with them fellas, kept fighting. They'd've done the same for you, you unforgivable wretch!"

He wiped the blood from the savage-looking blade on Shepherd's hat, then grabbed the man by his collar and yanked him brusquely back into the room. Shepherd hit the floor with a pinched sob drowned by a heavy thud.

Oldenberg spat on Shepherd's soon-to-be carcass as he went out, leaving the door open behind him, and clomped down the stairs.

The last words Shepherd heard, lying there belly up on the floor with his blood pooling all around him, were: "Betty, tell Dewey to fetch that mangy carcass out of my office, will you?"

"You mean Lyle?"

"That's the one."

Betty laughed her squealing, chortling laugh. Her laughter stopped abruptly. "Hey, did you see my bar rag?"

9

IT WAS GROWING dark by the time Cuno had buried the younger marshal, Chuck Svenson, in the hard, rocky soil away from the camp. Sweaty and exhausted from the hard labor, he tended his own horse and the mules, rubbing them down with dry grass, swabbing their ears and nostrils, and picketing them all together in deep grama along the box canyon's back wall.

He found several pounds of salt pork in one of the burlap bags on the wagon. When he had some of the pork and a pot of beans cooking over his glowing, popping cookfire, he scrounged around in the sleeping Bill Landers's pockets until he came up with a ring of three rusty keys.

After some fumbling to determine which key fit the cage's padlock, he opened the back of the jail wagon to let the shackled and manacled prisoners out to tend nature and to scrub their dusty, sweaty faces in the stream a ways down canyon from the pool.

"How 'bout you take off these cuffs and leg irons?" Blackburn said when he and the others had all worked their way out of the wagon, trailing the four-foot lengths of chain connecting their ankles.

When Cuno said nothing but merely stood back, aiming his .45 at the group from a good fifteen feet away, Blackburn flushed and held out his cuffed wrists. "Come on, junior. I wanna shit the way a man was meant to shit—*alone*. Get it?"

Cuno narrowed an eye and thumbed back the Colt's hammer with a dry click that sounded inordinately loud in the green evening silence. "If you don't shut up and hurry along into the grass, mister, you're gonna be shit outta luck."

Simms chuckled. Colorado Bob snorted. Blackburn cursed and hardened his jaws, but he clomped and clanked along with the others into the high brush away from the stream.

Cuno's peppering the jail wagon with hot lead had had the magical effect of turning the prisoners, for the most part, sullen and pensive rather than loud and belligerent. Blackburn's mini-tirade was the last spoken about the chains.

The four prisoners contented themselves with giving Cuno hard looks as, finishing their ablutions and fumbling their trousers back up to their hips, they clanked down to the creek to wash and drink before Cuno hazed them all back into the jail wagon.

Rather, three of the prisoners contented themselves with hard looks and muttered curses. The bald, one-eared half-breed—Fuego—continued to smile mildly, almost serenely, as he wandered along with the others in a dreamlike trance, regarding Cuno occasionally as though he had a secret he couldn't quite bring himself to share.

Cuno had to admit the man's attempt at putting him on edge was successful. The blond freighter kept the man in front of him and in total view at all times. The marshals had probably frisked each prisoner thoroughly—likely strip-searched them, in fact—but Cuno had the feeling Fuego was concealing a weapon of some kind.

Or maybe that's only what the big, kill-crazy half-breed wanted him to think, in hopes that Cuno would get close enough to search him.

He exhaled a silent sigh of relief when he'd finally slammed the cage door and had thrown the locking bolt home. Holstering his .45, he went back to the fire and checked on the sleeping marshal. The man's wound appeared to have stopped bleeding, and his breathing was regular though sweat beaded his forehead, glistening in the glowing light of the nearby fire.

Cuno drew the blanket up tight to the man's neck once more, then tended the beans and the salt pork sizzling in a large, cast-iron pan. When the food was done, he shoveled it onto four plates and hauled the steaming plates with spoons over to the jail wagon, handing each through the slit in the door.

He had to make a separate trip for the coffee, silently grumbling to himself over having to play nursemaid to four killers due to hang by the end of the week, with Serenity waiting for him and the bank loan in Crow Feather.

When Cuno had passed the last cup through the bars, Blackburn glanced toward the fading sky above the canyon's steep stone walls. "Gettin' dark soon." Then, as if he were only speaking to his two companions, he added, "Shepherd shoulda got back to Helldorado by now—don't ya think, fellas?"

Colorado Bob and Simms sat side by side, spooning beans into their mouths. "Oh, yeah," Bob said between chews. "He's there, all right. And I'd bet my right nut that Karl Oldenberg is putting a posse together even as we speak."

Chewing, Colorado Bob grinned at Cuno, those bobcat-like eyes slitting and flashing yellow in the last light angling down over the canyon walls.

"Eat up," Cuno said. "We'll be turnin' in soon. Early day tomorrow."

He glanced once more at Fuego. The man was staring at him over his steaming plate, that dark look of bemused menace in his eyes. He was like a perpetually coiled snake, rattles hissing softly.

Again, Cuno remembered the mountain-sized bounty

hunter, Ruben Pacheca, who'd followed him across two
territories. The bearlike savage had been on the hunt for the
bounty a rancher from Julesburg had put on Cuno's head
after Cuno had killed the man's son to save a sporting girl.

Cuno turned away, feeling an invisible knife tickle his
loins as he tramped back to the fire. He plopped a few
sticks on the dying flames, shoveled food onto a plate,
poured coffee, and sat on a rock bench back near the falls.

Stretching his legs out before him, he crossed his boots
and rested his back against a flat-edged boulder. He ate
while listening to the oddly melodic rattle of the falls behind him, staring out across the fire, the pool, the marshal
sleeping left of the pool, to the narrow mouth of the canyon
a hundred yards beyond.

The rolling sage-covered hills, scarps, and rocky-sloped
mesas were turning deep purple, and several stars kindled
dully. Good dark would close down, black as a leather
glove, in less than an hour. Soon, the hunt would be on all
across the dark, silent land—night predators versus their
anxious, scuttling prey.

Cuno should be halfway to Crow Feather by now, angling down through Squaw Butte, heading for the Cheyenne Drum Hills and the little town nestled on the sage flats
between the Crow Feather Mountains and the Little Snowy
Range.

Thirty yards beyond the pool, the jail wagon sat, tongue
drooping, near the narrow brush-sheathed gully through
which the stream snaked. Cuno saw the silhouettes of the
four prisoners lounging against the barred walls. He could
see only Fuego's legs stretched out from the wagon's front
wall, against which the big half-breed reclined.

They were all done eating, and the three Oldenberg
Gang members were talking. Cuno couldn't hear them
above the falls, but he could see their heads turning and
jaws moving, teeth showing intermittently between their
lips.

Probably planning a way out of their predicament. If
their gang didn't reach them soon . . .

Annoyance reared up again inside of Cuno. How in the hell had he gotten into this bailiwick? These men were destined to die and he, because of the tricky winds of fate, had drawn the unpaid job of hauling their smelly asses through the Mexican Mountains to the hangman in Crow Feather.

Even if he pushed the mules as fast as they could go, and didn't have to worry about tending the wounded marshal as well as the four prisoners, and watching his back trail, Cuno would make Crow Feather at least forty-eight hours later than he'd intended.

At least a day too late for the coveted freighting contract.

He and old Serenity would end up spending the winter in loud, smelly Denver, swamping saloons and whorehouses or shoveling shit from livery barns.

When he finished his meal, which he had no taste for, he threw out the last of his coffee and walked back down to the fire. The old marshal had rolled onto his side and, in the thickening darkness relieved by the umber light of the flickering flames, he shivered slightly, grunting and groaning softly.

Cuno went over to the wagon for the prisoners' plates and spoons, which they gave up without argument, regarding him owlishly through the bars. Fuego lay on his side, but it was too dark for Cuno to tell whether the man's eyes were open or closed. Something told him they were open.

When he'd washed all the plates, cups, and spoons in the stream, Cuno laid several heavy logs on the fire to keep the old marshal as warm as he could. Then he picked up his Winchester and tramped back out along the chuckling stream to the canyon's mouth.

He stood for a long time, staring across the high-desert plateau jogging out to distant peaks jutting along the horizon like the sharpened teeth of a saw blade.

The sun was down in the west, but several arrows of green-salmon light still streaked the plum-purple sky, small clouds like sand scallops silhouetted against it, and several stars like distant candles were beginning to spark. In the east, good dark had already pushed up from the horizon, the stars bold and lucid.

A breath of cool breeze rustled the rabbit brush and wild mahogany. Beyond that, the night was eerily silent, like the calm before a storm though there was no sign of bad weather.

Cuno spent the night hunkered atop a hogback just outside the canyon's mouth, watching and listening. He doubted the gang would be able to track him this soon, but he wasn't taking any chances.

He dozed occasionally between long stretches of looking around and listening for any unnatural sound or movement. Several times he returned to the canyon to check on the marshal and to add wood to the fire. Both times, the old marshal shivered in a restless sleep, limbs jerking and teeth faintly clattering.

Cuno mopped the man's face with a cold rag soaked in the pool below the falls, drank coffee, then returned to his sentinel perch. He woke from a doze, his back snugged against a rock humping out of the hogback's crest, to see a faint pearl wash over the eastern bluffs.

He returned to the canyon and had just put a fresh pot of coffee on the fire and started breakfast when the old marshal, still cloaked in dusky shadows, said in a clear, crisp voice, "Marliss?"

The man had lifted his head and was peering at Cuno from the other side of the fire. The flames leapt in his wide, glistening eyes.

Cuno set the salt pork and pan aside and went over and shoved the oldster back down on his bedroll. "Cuno Massey. Remember?"

Landers stared up at him, squinting, as though he were trying to remember not only who Cuno was but where they were and what had got them here.

"I pulled into a canyon to tend your shoulder. Think I got the bleeding stopped." A deep pang of frustration racked him as he voiced what he'd feared all along. "Looks like you might need another day or two of rest before we hit the trail for Crow Feather. Wouldn't want you opening up that shoulder again."

The old man rolled his eyes around in their leathery sockets, then turned his head to glance at the waterfall. "Shit!" He rammed his fists into the ground on either side of him. "I ain't in the Golden Garter in Tuscaloosa?"

"Sorry."

Landers lifted his head and turned it slightly to see behind Cuno and down canyon. Snorting, he grumbled, "That's the damn jail wagon, ain't it?"

"It is."

"Christ."

"How you feelin'?"

Landers pushed up on his elbows and drew a deep breath. "Like I been yanked in every which direction by a herd of green-broke broncs."

"Who's Marliss?"

Landers looked up at Cuno wryly. "You ain't old enough to hear *that* story." He glanced again at the wagon. "How's the boys?"

"Mean and ugly."

"Yeah? Well, just wait and see how mean 'n' ugly they get when we pull into Crow Feather and they see the gallows waitin' for 'em, nooses just a-swingin' in the wind, and the wives of their victims dancin' around in their widows' weeds!"

Landers grunted and his face twisted with pain as he pushed up to a sitting position.

"Hold on there," Cuno said.

"I'm fit as a fiddle." The old marshal reached over for the whiskey jug and popped the cork. "Well, maybe one with a few broken strings, but"—he threw back a liberal swig and sighed—"a fiddle just the same. You go ahead and make breakfast, then we'll get the wagon and mules ready to pull out. Gettin' late already, an' I gotta piss like a Prussian plow horse."

Cuno watched skeptically as the old marshal ran a greasy sleeve across his ragged gray beard, flung the blankets aside, and pushed himself to his feet, his creaky bones cracking like air bubbles in a frozen lake.

He tramped off into the brush, and Cuno went back to fixing breakfast. Soon he and the old marshal were letting the prisoners out of the wagon to perform their ablutions, and then handing the surly foursome their breakfast, which was the same as last night's supper, through the slit in the cage door.

Cuno was amazed by Landers's recovery. Of course, he could tell the old man was aching right down to his heels, as he drank as much whiskey as coffee with his breakfast, and his eyes were pinched, his cheeks pale and hollow. But if he could bull his way through his misery and help Cuno out with the prisoners and the wagon, they might make it to Crow Feather faster than Cuno had thought.

When Cuno had finished his food and coffee, he hustled off to grain the mules and Renegade and to hitch the mules to the wagon.

"While you do that, I'll grease the wheel hubs," Landers said, taking one more pull from his bottle as he grabbed the wooden grease bucket and stick from beside a boulder, and began ambling off toward the wagon.

Cuno said nothing as he headed into the brush along the canyon's back wall, but he was half conscious of a vague misgiving. He didn't realize what the basis of the worry was until it was too late.

He'd rigged up the mules and had just thrown his saddle blanket onto Renegade's back—he intended to keep the horse saddled for scouting and possibly hunting purposes—when he heard a muffled choking sound from down canyon. Then there was the rattling thud of something slammed against the jail wagon.

The choking sounded again, punctuated with a throaty gasp.

Cuno stared into the thick brush and boulders between himself and the wagon, an inner alarm screaming at him. He had his saddle by the horn in one hand. Dropping it suddenly, he bolted forward so quickly that Renegade whinnied and sidestepped away from him, and one of the mules brayed.

"Landers!"

Cuno palmed his .45 and bounded through the brush, weaving around boulders and large shrubs, angling down canyon. Ahead, the jail wagon appeared at the bottom of the gradual slope, the growing light defining it against the far, rocky, pine-clad ridge wall.

Cuno stopped.

Landers, standing near the rear wheel, had his back to the cage. He was slumped against the wagon, knees bent and dangling above the ground, and he was flailing with both arms, holding the grease stick in his right hand. A thick, brown arm angled out from between the cage's bars.

Landers snarled and grunted, his cheeks balled, teeth showing inside his greasy, gray beard.

The arm was snaked around Landers's neck, the bicep bulging as Fuego, grinning down near the top of the old marshal's head, jerked his muscular arm up and back sharply. There was a popping sound that sent pulse beats of horror shooting down all the frayed nerves in Cuno's body.

"*No!*" he shouted again, bounding off his heels and hoofing it down the slope.

"*Christ . . . nooo!*"

Too late.

Fuego released his grip on the old marshal's neck and drew his arm back through the bars. Landers, staring wide-eyed straight ahead, dropped his arms to his sides. The stick fell from his fingers to hit the ground with a thud.

Then Landers himself dropped straight down to his knees and knelt there, head wobbling unnaturally, until his chin dipped to his chest, and he fell over sideways.

There was a grisly bulge in the back of his neck where the half-breed, now grinning at Cuno through the bars, had snapped it.

10

CUNO STARED DOWN at the old marshal's quivering body. The man opened and closed his mouth and poked his tongue in and out, as though he were trying to say something.

But he was dead. There was nothing Cuno could do for him.

Shock freezing Cuno in place, he looked up from the marshal to Fuego, hunkered on his haunches, hands to the bars, and smiling out at Cuno with that mild, taunting smile. He shuttled and lowered his blue-green gaze between the dead marshal and Cuno, and the meaning was clear.

Cuno would end up the same.

The other men, lounging against the barred wall on the far side of the wagon, were grinning, too, like amused, faintly chagrined schoolboys.

"Jesus, Fuego," Blackburn chuckled. "What'd you go an' do that for?"

Colorado Bob King leaned forward to peer over the edge of the wagon. "Is he dead?"

"Didn't ya hear the snap?" said Simms. "Sounded like a

dry branch when the breed broke the poor old bastard's neck."

His chest rising and falling sharply, Cuno stared into Fuego's insolent, grinning eyes. His jaws hardened painfully as he raised the cocked Colt to the half-breed's broad, flat face. As he drew a bead on the big man's forehead, something like apprehension dropped over the half-breed's eyes, like a shadowy inner lid.

Slowly, Fuego unwrapped his fingers from the cage's bars and straightened his legs, raising his hands chest high, palms out. The mocking grin continued drawing up the corners of his thick-lipped mouth as he held Cuno's enraged stare.

Cuno held his gun on the man's forehead. Rage seared him from the tips of his toes to the top of his head. He felt his index finger draw back against the Colt's trigger.

"Easy, kid," warned Colorado Bob. "You wouldn't kill an unarmed man, would ya?"

"Yeah, kid," Blackburn said, shuttling his bemused gaze between Cuno and the big half-breed standing like a subdued grizzly before him. "Can't blame Fuego here for what he was born to. It was the old marshal's fault. Shouldn't have gotten so close to the wagon."

Cuno only half heard them. His own rage was screaming in his ears, howling across every nerve ending like a pack of raging wolves. As his own eyes bored holes into Fuego's, he slid his .45 slightly to the left, and squeezed the trigger.

As the gun's roar shattered the morning quiet, Fuego's head jerked straight back, and the skin above the bridge of his nose wrinkled. He slapped a hand to where his right earlobe and silver ring had been a moment before, then held the bloody hand in front of his face.

His lower jaw dropped and his eyes, totally lacking the mockery that had been in them when his sole remaining ear had been intact, flashed like rifle fire.

"I kill you for that, man!" Fuego slapped his hand to his

ear once more and looked at the even bloodier hand as though he couldn't believe what the first swipe had told him. "I kill you for that, you know? You hear me?" He bolted forward, making the wagon rock and squawk, and curled his hands around the bars. "I tear your *heart* out with my *hands*, and I take a bite as you *die*, you bastard son of a tiny-titted *whore!*"

Cuno grinned acidly as he thumbed the Colt's hammer back and raised the gun once more. The half-breed's eyes grew as wide as two fresh cow plops as the bore of the .45 stared down at him. The killer gave a terrified yowl and ducked, stumbling straight back.

Cuno's Colt roared, and the slug glanced off the bar where Fuego's face had been a quarter-second before. It screeched off another bar on the other side of the wagon, then dug into the ground with an angry plunk.

Cuno twirled the Colt on one finger and dropped the smoking iron into its holster. He narrowed an eye as he stared through the bars at Fuego, who'd fallen on his back and now lay propped on an elbow, his hat off, the grisly scars of his olive pate showing above the wide, white-and-blue bandanna wrapped around his forehead.

Blood dribbled from where his right earlobe had been.

"The only reason I'm not gonna blow your ugly head off right here and now," Cuno growled, "is to save me the pleasure of watching you dance three feet off the ground in Crow Feather. Now, I liked you a whole lot better when you were keeping your mouth shout. I strongly suggest, unless you want some other parts to go missing pronto, you get mute again fast."

Fuego stared back at him, his jaw hinges twitching. But his eyes, still glowing lime green with rage, had softened considerably under a hazy fear shadow. The others stared through the bars with similar expressions—all except Colorado Bob.

The notorious regulator lifted his chin and narrowed his slanted, Viking-like eyes, and the yellow orbs flashed in the growing dawn light filtering into the canyon, his broad, thin mouth spreading with a grin that said his initial estimation of the brawny blond lad before him had been correct.

Keeping his six-shooter clear of the wagon—he knew any one of these jaspers was waiting for an opportunity to reach through the bars and snag the weapon from his holster—Cuno reached down and pulled the dead Landers up by one arm. Stooping, he drew the man up over his shoulder, then backed away from the wagon, keeping his eyes on the prisoners still glaring through the bars at him.

Then he turned and tramped off to where he'd buried Chuck Svenson, intending to plant the second dead lawman beside the first.

He knew that burning daylight for a dead man might cost him his own life, but he couldn't leave the tough, old Landers to the coyotes and magpies. If for only not having foreseen the danger of letting the marshal, in his pain-racked, inebriated state, get within arm's length of the jail wagon, he owed him at least the gesture of a burial.

Quickly, he dug the hole, hacking away at the flinty clay with the shovel he'd found behind the wagon seat. When the hole was just deep enough to cover the old marshal's body, Cuno lay the man in the hole, covered him with the dirt and gravel he'd mounded beside it, then covered the grave with stones heavy enough that coyotes or bobcats couldn't get at him.

As he'd done with Svenson, he'd buried the man with everything he'd had on him but his guns, ammunition, and badge. The badge he'd save for Landers's widow. Soon, when Karl Oldenberg sent out more men from his devil's lair—wherever it may be—Cuno might need all the weaponry he could get his hands on. Oldenberg was known throughout Wyoming Territory and Colorado Territory for riding with only seasoned thieves and killers, the kind of men not even the wiliest of bounty hunters dared track.

The kind of men it would take plenty of cold steel and hot lead to hold off . . .

Cuno didn't take time to build another crude cross like

the one he'd fashioned for Svenson. The lone cross—two pine branches joined with rawhide—would have to serve both graves. He simply moved it to the front center of the two rock mounds and hammered it into the ground with the flat side of his shovel. He wasted no time with words, only a silent apology that he hadn't gotten to the wagon in time to save the old marshal's life.

Fifteen minutes later, perched in the driver's box and with Renegade saddled and tethered to the rear, Cuno drove the wagon back toward the valley. At the box canyon's mouth he paused to study the rising and falling hogbacks and stony shelves pushing up around him, across the valley's broad bowl, which was now bathed in golden morning sunshine glistening off the dew-beaded brome and grama grass.

Behind him, Renegade blew. The prisoners sat silently entangled in their cuffs, leg irons, and chains. Cuno could sense their drum-taut expectation, hoping and waiting and watching for Oldenberg.

Fuego sat against the wall directly behind Cuno. The freighter could hear the half-breed's clipped, guttural grunts as he dabbed at his ruined ear with his neckerchief and no doubt vowed to exact payment for the missing lobe soon.

Spying no movement across the valley, Cuno pulled the wagon on through the box canyon's mouth, gritting his teeth at the thunderous rattle of the bars and the wide, shod wheels as he put the mules through the winding ravine.

There was nothing he could do about the racket except hope Oldenberg wasn't yet close enough to hear it. If the gang descended on the wagon, Cuno would climb aboard Renegade and hightail it for the nearest high ground or fortification. From there he'd either hold the gang off with his .45 and Winchester, or, failing that, shoot the prisoners through the jail wagon's bars.

Better to kill them in cold blood than to allow the jackals to be freed to resume their depredations—especially the rapist and child killer, Fuego.

He pulled the wagon onto the main trail and headed

southwest, rattling and clattering, the prisoners for the most part sullen and silent behind him. The trail forked in several places, and signs for ranches stood at each fork, but he continued on the trace that headed toward Crow Feather and Sand River, a small mining camp at the edge of the Cheyenne Drum Hills.

There were several other small towns in the Mexicans but it was doubtful there were any with a telegraph office or even any law beyond a local marshal likely handier with a beer schooner than a .45.

Cuno would keep to the main trail for as long as he could. That the trail was pocked and grooved with other wagon traffic meant that Oldenberg would have a tougher time tracking him than if Cuno's was the only wagon out here. If he could find a side trail to Crow Feather, he'd take it.

The sun was nearly straight up in the clear, blue, high-country sky, beating mercilessly down on the sage and rabbit brush. Cuno suddenly drew back on the mule's reins. Scanning the low hills to the west, he'd seen a horseback rider meandering around sparsely scattered pines along a hill shoulder.

As he stared now, the wagon's dust catching up to him, his brows hooded his keen blue eyes. The rider he'd seen for maybe a single second was gone. Probably dropped into one of the several ravines troughing the low, dun hills bristling with pines, cedars, and a smattering of aspen.

At least, he thought he'd seen a rider. Maybe it was only a phantom conjured by his nettled, anxious mind.

He was about to flick the reins over the mules' backs when movement again caught his eye, and he returned his gaze to the slope ahead and right. A long, cinnamon tail swished on the other side of a ravine, between two pines. As the tail swished back in the opposite direction, catching the light, the horse continued into the trees, and disappeared.

Cuno's heart quickened.

He grabbed his Winchester off the seat beside him and took a long, steady look around, casting his gaze into every brush snag and depression around, trying to sear through the pines and scattered, sage-colored boulders.

Nothing.

He looked into the denser forest on the left side of the trail. Finding nothing there, either, he glanced back through the barred cage at Renegade standing passively hang-headed behind the wagon. Obviously, the horse had picked up no foreign scents.

Colorado Bob was sitting with his back to the barred door, smoking a quirley. A sneer etched itself on his thin, pink lips.

"What's the matter, Widow Maker? They closin' in?"

Cuno turned his head forward and, setting the Winchester back onto the seat beside him, flicked the reins over the mules' backs. When the bank along the left side of the trail became less sheer, he turned the team off the trail and into the heavy pines, bulling through low branches and sending pinecones cascading onto the cage.

The mules brayed angrily and Renegade chimed in with several indignant snorts as he thumped along behind. Squirrels chittered raucously and a magpie screeched as it winged up from a fir.

Cuno pulled the wagon up behind two boulders in a slight clearing opening onto a brush-sheathed stream. Setting the brake, he grabbed his rifle, jumped out of the wagon box, and tramped back to where Renegade stood, eyeing him skeptically.

"Easy, boy."

He grabbed the stallion's reins off the tailgate, and wrapped his right hand around the horn.

"'Bout time you wised up." Blackburn stood, looking disheveled from the rough ride and peering at Cuno through the bars. A self-satisfied expression flashed in his wintery gray eyes beneath the flat-brimmed hat shading his tanned, stubbled cheeks. "Before you go, throw open the door, will ya? Save the boys a bullet shootin' the lock off."

Cuno pulled himself into the saddle and reined Renegade away from the wagon. "Don't fret, Blackburn." He touched spurs to the stallion's loins and started off through the pines, heading back toward the trail. "I'll be back."

11

RENEGADE LUNGED ACROSS the wagon trail and into the gently rising meadow beyond, his great lungs heaving and his heart thudding beneath the saddle. When they made the forest, Cuno lowered his head to keep from being hammered from the saddle by low-hanging branches.

The slope grew steeper. The skewbald, enjoying the workout, shook his head and drew deep, clean breaths. Hooves thumped in the tall, sun-cured grass and rattled in occasional patches of slide rock.

Cuno drew rein at the lip of the shallow ravine where he'd spied the rider. He cast his gaze into the scattered conifers on the ravine's other side, where he'd seen the cinnamon horse tail. Swinging down, he dropped to a knee and traced a clearly defined hoofprint in the exposed dirt with one gloved finger. A crooked line ran along the right side of the print. The shoe was cracked.

Cuno stared into the trees once more, in the direction in which the rider had disappeared. Could be a range rider from one of the nearby ranches, but the skulking way of the man bespoke someone of more furtive intent.

Probably an Oldenberg scout. At least, Cuno would have to assume so.

Rising, he looked up at the crest of the ridge he was on, then reached into his saddlebags for his cavalry binoculars and looped them over his neck. He shucked his Winchester, dropped Renegade's reins in the grass, and patted the horse's rump.

"Stay, boy."

He tramped up the slope through scattered cedars and occasional rocks, keeping his ears pricked and his eyes skinned. Ten feet from the crest, he dropped to his knees, doffed his hat, and crabbed the rest of the way.

Keeping his head low, he cast a look over the ridge and into another, narrower valley down the other side. Beyond, countless rocky, pine-studded ridges rolled off toward high, blue mountains, several of the toothy crests flocked with old snow.

To the right, a slender stream snaked through a wide drainage running perpendicular to the others. He was running his gaze along the stream when he spied movement—three deer splashing across the stream and disappearing into another ravine to Cuno's left, hidden by the next ridge west.

Grown deer didn't run for fun. Something had spooked them.

Cuno stretched his gaze upstream from where the deer had crossed, until he saw what appeared, from a mile as the crow flies away, a disjointed brown worm snaking across a tan hillside.

He raised the field glasses and, adjusting the focus, brought the dozen or so riders up in the single sphere of magnification. The group was trotting across the gently sloping shoulder of a pine-capped bluff, following the trail Cuno had been following. They were angling down toward the stream where Cuno had watered the mules and his prisoners only an hour ago.

Cuno's forehead ridged as he held the glasses on the motley, bearded group in shirtsleeves and chaps, fur coats tied over bedrolls behind their cantles. Rifles jutted from saddle boots, and pistols and knives bristled about the men's hips and torsos.

The lead rider was a big, blocky chunk of flesh in red-and-black-checked trousers, and with long, sandy hair dancing about sloping shoulders from beneath the brim of a brown bowler hat trimmed with a silver-studded band.

Bandoliers crossed his broad chest, atop a shabby linsey tunic. Two big, cream-gripped pistols jutted from holsters on his hips, one in the cross-draw position. A broad knife was sheathed under his shoulder, the handle jutting up from the V of his cartridge belts.

As he approached the stream, the others following in a ragged line, a sun ray speared from the water to flash off one of the riders' silver-roweled spurs. Oldenberg and the others leaned out from their saddles, scrutinizing the ground around them.

"Found my trail, did ya?"

Cuno chewed his lip as he stared through the binoculars at the group of well-armed desperadoes looking around carefully as they swung down from their saddles to slip their bits to let their mounts drink. A couple loosened saddle cinches; several stared up the trail toward where Cuno hunkered atop the ridge.

He hooded his hands over the lenses to prevent sun flashes.

Finally, he lowered the glasses and turned to look down the slope he'd climbed, toward the wagon concealed in the pines on the other side of the valley. His mind shuffled through his options, few as they were.

Obviously, he couldn't outrun the gang in the wagon. He'd have to outmaneuver them.

He crawled back away from the ridge crest, doffed his hat, and climbed to his feet. Holding the Winchester low in his right hand, he jogged back down the ridge, returned the binoculars to the saddlebags, swung onto Renegade's back, and put the horse down the grassy slope through the pines.

"What'd you see, kid?" Blackburn asked as Cuno approached the wagon. "The devil's hounds, maybe, huh?"

"The devil's hounds," Colorado Bob said, sitting against the cage, one knee drawn up, a self-satisfied smile on his face. "They're an evil lot of demons. Have no mercy whatsoever. Hell, when they get ahold o' you, you're gonna be wailin' for your dear momma."

Simms chuckled as he stared at Cuno, his mouth a knife slash straight across his lower face. "They're back there, ain't they? You seen 'em. I can read it in your eyes, Widow Maker."

Simms laughed as Cuno swung down from Renegade and tied the stallion to the wagon's tailgate. Simms threw his head back on his shoulders and loosed a coyote-like howl.

"Come on, Boss!" he shouted as the howl echoed around the valley and set blackbirds to cawing angrily. "Come and join the party, Oldenberg. We're over here!"

He threw his back against the cage and clapped his hands.

"Go ahead," Cuno grunted as he climbed into the wagon. "Shout yourself hoarse."

Oldenberg couldn't hear the man from this distance and over the high western ridge. Besides, the wagon itself made more of a racket than all four prisoners could lift at the same time. Cuno had to stay out of hearing range or prepare to fight a dozen seasoned killers.

Unwrapping the reins from the brake handle, Cuno glanced across the stream, looked back at the brake handle, then looked across the stream again. A wagon was coming along through the adjacent canyon, a half mile away and closing on the creek a hundred yards downstream from Cuno.

A deep frown cut across Cuno's forehead as he studied it—a beat-up-looking ore wagon drawn by a beefy, black mule and driven by a lean gent in blue jeans and a steeple-crowned sombrero. From this angle it was hard to tell, but Cuno thought he could make out a cream-colored line de-marking a trail running before, behind, and below the churning wheels.

"Hay-ah!"

With a savage flick of the reins, he put the mules ahead and into the stream, the water splashing up along the rims. The wagon barked and clattered over the rocks. It bounced violently as the mules drew it up the low, opposite bank.

Water dripped from the mules' hocks as they continued angling across the sloping meadow, on an interception course with the ore wagon. Cuno could see the trail clearly now, jogging back away from the ore wagon and disappearing into aspens where the valley's walls steepened and drew together, forming a rocky gorge.

As the jail wagon closed on the ore wagon, the driver pulled back on his reins, then, holding the ribbons in one hand, reached stiffly beneath the seat for an old Spencer repeater with a weathered-gray stock. He held the rifle across his lap as he sat the stopped wagon, scowling toward Cuno, lines spoking his wary, deep-set eyes.

"Afternoon." Cuno drew the jail wagon up beside the ore wagon, and glanced again at the two-track trail disappearing into the wooded gorge. "This trail lead anywhere?"

The gaunt, bearded gent in the ore wagon tipped his head this way and that to inspect the prisoners sullenly sitting the cage behind Cuno. Distracted by the peculiar-looking contraption hauling the four obvious cutthroats, he said, "Depends on what ya call anywhere. Say, what you got there, anyways?"

"Anywhere up yonder I might find some saddle horses and another trail to Crow Feather?"

"What's wrong with the one you just left?"

"Snake-ridden."

The man shuttled his dark, knowing gaze back to Cuno. "Friends of their'n?"

Cuno nodded.

The old man looked back over his right shoulder. "Trail here rises up to Petersburg. Mine camp. Vein done petered out two years ago, but there's a hotel–saloon and a few hard-rock Rooshians holdin' on. Don't know about saddle hosses. I broke them rocks up to the gorge there till a few months ago. Now I cut and haul wood for them too busy searching for El Dorado."

"The trail circle back to the one leadin' to Crow Feather?"

"In a long hogleg through rough country." The woodcutter frowned at the jail wagon. "Too rough for that devil's contraption."

"Obliged."

Cuno shook the ribbons over the mules' backs. The wagon pulled up onto the narrow trace. As the mules turned eastward, Cuno glanced behind him, at the woodcutter still staring at him from over the bed of his sawdust-and-bark-littered ore wagon.

"If you run into a herd of hard cases lookin' for me, I'd appreciate it if you hadn't seen hide nor hair . . ."

The woodcutter pinched his own hat, and ran a sleeve across his mouth. "In Petersburg, beware of Tolstoy's whiskey. Turn ya blind as an old Injun mule!" He swung forward in his seat, shaking his reins and continuing west toward the stream crossing.

As the woodcutter pulled away, Cuno dropped his gaze to the jail cage rattling along behind him as the iron-shod wheels jounced through the chuckholes. Fuego sat with his back to him. The other three lounged against the other three walls, sneers on their lips and in their hard, belligerent eyes.

"Won't work," Colorado Bob said, poking at a hole in the knee of his black-and-gray-striped trousers. "You got the devil's hounds on your heels, boy, and there ain't no shakin' 'em short of turnin' us loose and hightailin' fer the tall and uncut!"

Cuno nodded. "'Preciate the advice, Bob. Now kindly close your loadin' gate 'fore I blow your ears off."

The sneering light left Colorado Bob's evil gaze as the lines in his broad, mottled forehead planed out, and his nostrils wrinkled indignantly. Cuno snorted.

He cozied to this situation no more than his prisoners did. But he kept remembering Landers's proud boasts about always finishing his jail-wagon routes.

Cuno vowed he'd finish this one for him, too, or go down in a hail of whistling lead.

The trail rose, fell, and snaked through one deep ravine after another. The pine-choked slopes often came right down to the trail, while at other times grassy meadows rose gently off to both sides before pitching sharply to high rock walls.

Cuno could tell they were gradually climbing, for his own lungs seemed to shrink as the air grew thinner, and the mules blew more often, shaking their heads indignantly. As much to rest the mules as to let the prisoners drink and tend nature, he pulled off the trace, in a broad horseshoe of a frothy creek rumbling over boulders at the base of a high granite wall.

Unhitching the mules, he led them and Renegade down to where the water curled back in a relatively placid pool. While the beasts drank and rolled, Cuno opened the cage and ushered the four prisoners out of the wagon by pistol point.

"You got five minutes," he said, casting an edgy glance back along the canyon toward the main trail they'd left two and a half hours ago. If Oldenberg savvied his detour, he and his dozen cutthroats would be heading this way soon.

"Don't know how you boys feel," Blackburn said as he and the others shuffled down the grassy slope in their leg irons, holding their cuffed hands down low before them, "but when Oldenberg catches up to us, I'm gonna take that kid's .45 and shove it up his ass."

The broad-faced redhead, Simms, snorted. "Would ya allow me the honor of pullin' the trigger?"

Cuno rammed his Colt into the man's back, shoving him forward.

The next second slowed to half a minute inside Cuno's head as Fuego, shuffling along to the right of Simms, wheeled suddenly. The half-breed gritted his teeth, jutted his jaws, and raised a big, red fist from which the manacle chain hung slack. One of the links was twisted where the man had somehow opened it.

Cuno watched the fist grow to the size of a russet Indian squash in front of him. He watched the deep, grime-encrusted lines around the man's scarred fingers widen until the fist plowed knuckle-first into his face and set a herd of bull moose bugling inside his head.

12

"YAHH!" THE HALF-BREED bellowed as Cuno's head jounced back on his shoulders.

Beyond his fluttering eyes, the pine tops wavered.

"Yahh!" Fuego grunted again as, again, he slammed the hammer-like fist into Cuno's left cheekbone.

The first blow had rocked him back but he'd been setting his heels beneath him when the second one, twice as powerful as the first and delivered with even more fury, had smashed him straight back again. Try as he might to set his boots, he flew a good half a foot in the air.

Both his arms whipped up and, as he flew straight back up the grassy, brushy slope, he saw his Colt fly high above his head, flashing in the sunlight against the spruce-green pines as it careened back in the direction of the wagon.

He hit the slope on his back, his right cheek screaming and his head feeling like an exposed nerve on a blacksmith's anvil, laid open by a stout steel hammer. Vaguely, he heard his revolver thump into the grass a good twenty feet upslope. Downslope, he heard the other prisoners yelling excitedly above the clanking of their cuffs and leg irons.

Blinking his blurry eyes, he stared straight up at the near-cloudless sky. The half-breed's enraged, wide-eyed countenance filled the field of his vision as the man, mewling like an enraged bull bison, flung his arms straight out in front of him and bolted off his heels.

Fuego's leather hat flew off his head, exposing the grisly pate above the wide fold of his bandanna and the blood-encrusted right ear. He landed on Cuno's chest. The air whooshed out of Cuno's lungs with the sound of a sudden, short-lived cyclone.

And then the man had his hands around Cuno's neck, bobbing his head and drawing his mouth wide with fury, bellowing loudly as he dug his beefy thumbs into Cuno's throat and instantly pinching off his wind.

Cuno, trained to sport box when he was only twelve years old, reacted instinctively, whipping his stout forearms straight up before him, hands clenched into one bulging, red fist. He rammed the fist up under Fuego's bulging arms to strike the underside of the man's chin with a dull clack, evoking an exasperated grunt from the half-breed's throat.

As Fuego's head jerked back as if shot through the forehead, Cuno's hands continued straight up, and he spread his swollen arms until, releasing his hands, he flung both straight out toward his shoulders, ripping the half-breed's hands from his throat.

As the man's arms flew out to his sides, as though he were trying to take flight, his chin dropped. Blood spurted from his mouth to spray against Cuno's face, and two bloody, broken teeth dribbled over Fuego's lower lip.

At nearly the same instant, bellowing himself now like an enraged puma, Cuno kicked his boots straight up in the air, levering his head off the turf and using the momentum to propel his clenched right fist in a slight arc up from his shoulder.

It slammed into Fuego's face with a solid, jaw-clattering smack. Fuego's head tipped sideways, blood continuing to froth from his lips. As Fuego's head tipped back the other way, Cuno hammered it again.

"Gnah!" the half-breed cried as he rolled off Cuno's left hip.

Cuno turned over, got his boots beneath him, and in spite of his pounding head and blurred vision, bolted to his feet. The other three prisoners, having sprung toward him and gotten tripped up by the chains connecting them, were sprawled in a grunting, cursing heap fifteen feet down slope.

"Get up, breed!" Blackburn shouted. "Get up! Get *up*!"

Fuego gained his knees, shouting, "You die, blondie!"

Cuno rammed the toe of his right boot into the man's ribs. Fuego screamed and dropped to a shoulder. In half a second, he was up again, grabbing Cuno's right boot as the freighter swung it forward again. Cuno flew up and sideways, hit the ground on his shoulder and hip with a snarling grunt.

Colorado Bob scrambled to his feet, then fell again, cursing, as the chain drew taut between himself and Blackburn. "Kill him, breed!" he shouted, chest down on the ground but raising his head and slitting his yellow Nordic eyes with exasperation. "Pluck his eyes out!"

Fuego bolted off his heels and hurled his big frame—he probably had a good four inches on Cuno though Cuno was more compactly and thickly built—into him as he again tried to rise. Cuno flew back, and as the back of his head hit the ground, causing two half-breeds to swim in and out of his blurring vision, he pivoted up and left.

Fuego had cocked his arm for a vicious punch, but the fist glanced off Cuno's left temple as the half-breed bellowed savagely and flew up and over Cuno's shoulder. Gritting his teeth, pent-up rage boiling up from deep inside him, Cuno scrambled onto his feet.

Clenching his fists, he moved on the half-breed like a bear closing on certain prey. His jaws appeared about to burst through his red-mottled face, and his blue eyes shone with a killing fire.

Fuego had just gained his knees and lifted his head when Cuno swung a right cross into the man's stout jaw.

As the half-breed jerked sideways, Cuno pivoted from the hips and put his entire 180 pounds into his left fist, which he swung from his thigh and rammed, thumb up, against the half-breed's bullet-torn ear.

Fuego's head jerked back in the other direction. His eyes snapped even wider than before, and his face turned nearly as white as that of a Scandinavian princess rarely exposed to the sun.

"*Nnnghhh,*" Fuego grunted, his features slackening as his gaze drifted off, a dull haze of misery dropping over his eyes.

Blood gushed from the ragged lower edge of his ear, dribbling down his neck and under his collarless calico shirt.

Cuno pivoted once more and rammed his left fist again into the man's ear.

Fuego's chin snapped up, and he looked as though he'd been hit with frigid snowmelt, eyes and mouth snapping wide once more.

As he began to fall to his left, Cuno grabbed the front of his shirt and pounded another left against Fuego's ear. Holding the man's slack body before him, Cuno hammered the ear again and again, hearing his own grunts rake out through gritted teeth, barely audible above the solid smacks of his knuckles pounding the half-breed's hideous ear like the regular blows of a blacksmith's hammer.

Wham! Wham! Wham! Wham!

Fuego's chin dropped to his chest in spasm-like jerks, shoulders slumping, a soft mewling issuing from his bloody lips.

Cuno released the man's shirt, and the half-breed fell over sideways, hitting the ground like a fifty-pound sack of cracked corn. He lay on his side, legs bent, unmoving.

Suddenly remembering the other prisoners, Cuno wheeled and raised his fists as though for another onslaught. His broad chest rose and fell sharply, his sweat-soaked tunic clinging to his torso like a second skin, his neckerchief turned backward and hanging down behind his neck.

The three other prisoners lay six feet away, immobilized by the chains connecting them. Blackburn was on his hands and knees. Simms was on his side. Colorado Bob was on his butt, one arm thrown ahead toward Blackburn's, the links connecting them drawn taut.

All three stared up the slope at Cuno, snarling, Blackburn muttering sharp curses, Simms merely wagging his head with the fateful chagrin of a man who'd missed his train.

"Ah, fer Pete's sake!" Blackburn grunted. "Shit! Shit! Shit!"

Cuno looked at the chain trailing from Fuego's ankle. Somehow the half-breed had pried a manacle link loose as well as a cuff link. Cuno should have expected that. Turning upslope, he grabbed his .45. Mopping sweat from his brow with his forearm, he swung the gun toward the wagon. "Back inside."

"I gotta take a piss," said Colorado Bob.

"Simms'll show you how to do it through the bars."

Cuno cocked the Colt and spread his feet. The rage hadn't died in him yet. His boiling blood still churned. He had to make a conscious effort not to draw his finger back against the .45's trigger and blow them all back to the demon that had spawned them.

"Inside. Pronto. Unless you want some o' what ole Half-Ear got."

When Cuno had the three gang members back in the cage, he strode downslope to where Fuego lay sprawled, unconscious and groaning like a dog squashed by a lumber dray. A few kicks drew the half-breed back to consciousness, and a few more got him crawling back up the slope to the jail wagon, cursing and snarling like a wolf in a leg trap.

The man was as white as Dakota snow and shaking like a leaf in a Texas windstorm, but the threat of more abuse to his badly shredded ear compelled him to crawl back up through the open cage door on his own.

While the others watched grimly, he crabbed to the far

end of the wagon, where he reclined on a shoulder and, with shaking hands, removed his already bloody kerchief from around his neck and pressed it to his ear. Groaning deep in his throat, he spread his bloody lips back from his bloody, gapped teeth in a tortured wince.

"Now, then . . ."

Cuno slammed and padlocked the door, then tramped out to fetch the mules and Renegade dining on the rich bluestem growing along the roiling stream. Cuno cursed as he probed his face with a thumb. His jaw and cheek ached fiercely, and a small heart hammered inside his head, but he didn't think anything was broken.

His vision was still semi-blurred, but all in all, he was damn lucky to have come out of the brawl intact. The look in Fuego's eyes had warned him such a move was coming, and he should have been ready for it. You had to expect the unexpected from yellow-toothed, child-killing demons like the half-breed.

Any more carelessness, and Cuno would be snuggling with snakes at the bottom of a deep ravine.

When he had the mules hitched and Renegade tied to the back of the wagon, he mounted the driver's box and cast a long, cautious glance behind him. Relieved not to see twelve green-broke killers galloping up his back trail, he shook the reins over the mules and resumed his trek toward the fir-studded slopes of the eastern Mexicans.

If he could have seen through the hills and forests behind him, he would have seen the brown mass of thirteen riders, led by the beefy Karl Oldenberg, galloping along the north-south trail Cuno had left two hours ago.

As the group approached the fork in the trail, on the west side of Spring Creek, they paused, dust billowing around them, horses stomping and chewing bridle bits as the men turned this way and that, looking around and conferring.

A few dug around in shirt or duster pockets for tobacco sacks and leaned back in their saddles, building smokes.

A few minutes later, while one of the riders was still

hunched forward, lighting his hastily rolled quirley, the mass continued straight along the trail toward Crow Feather, while four riders branched eastward, splashing along the stream and putting their sweaty mounts into long strides along the trail to Petersburg.

13

THE LEANING WOODEN sign along the road read in burned black letters: PETERSBURG, WYO TERR—POP 223. A line carved with a dull knife had been drawn through the 223, and above it had been scrawled with the same knife—4.

From what Cuno could see, sitting on the wooded, rocky hillside above a deep, dark gorge, the town—if even a town remained aside from a few abandoned log shacks huddled in the rocks and firs of the steep slopes rising and falling around him—was deserted. Crows cawed in the gorge, the cries sheathed in the steady murmur of a late-year stream tumbling down a steep, boulder-lined bed.

In the distance, thunder rumbled.

Cuno looked up at the sky, which was plum-colored in the north. The mass of bruised, ragged-edged clouds was slowly moving toward him.

He'd reached the town, or what remained of it, just in time. It was monsoon season in the high country, and while the storms rarely lasted longer than a half hour or so, the amount of moisture and lightning they could hammer

earthward, and the amount of wind they could kick up,
was often deadly.

Such a tempest could drown you, fry you, or blow you
into the next territory.

You didn't want to experience it without a roof over
your head if you could help it. And the iron bars of the jail
wagon would attract lightning like a cougar to a three-
legged rabbit. Cuno had to snort at the thought of his
problem being solved by all four of his prisoners fried to
cinders with one quick witch's fork of a lightning strike,
turning the wagon into a blue-white ball of howling elec-
tricity.

Problem was, he'd be turned into a hush puppy, as well.

Intending to locate a barn in which he could shelter himself and the wagon, he urged the mules on down the curving slope pocked with rocks, roots, and boulders heaving
up from below. The trail dropped steeply and, standing
with one foot braced against the dashboard and holding the
reins taut, he checked the skittery mules back as more
thunder rumbled like crashing boulders and a pitchfork of
bright white lightning flicked over the bald crags looming
on the north side of the gorge.

As the wagon gained the gorge's bottom, dilapidated log
shacks shoved up on both sides of the narrow trail. Over
rough plank bridges, the trace twisted back and forth across
a deep creek bed through which water gurgled and
troughed over rocks and mossy shelves.

Thunder continued to rumble, growing louder as the
mass of purple clouds approached. The mules brayed and
shook their heads. Behind the wagon, Renegade whinnied.

Someone rapped angrily on the cage's bars. "Stop this
heap before we're all toasted blacker'n Bob's soul!"
Blackburn yelled.

Cuno kept the mules moving along the trail, swinging
his head from side to side as he looked for a stable with a
complete roof. Virtually all the shacks appeared to have
been abandoned for a good length of time. Birds winged
in and out of the glassless, shutterless windows. Porches

drooped into the street or the creek bed. Chimney pipes were rusting, shingles were missing from gapped roofs.

Flanking the hovels, corrals and stables were partly dismantled, dilapidated, overgrown, or partly crushed by boulders fallen from the steep, sheer ridges.

At the far edge of town, smoke ribboned from a large fieldstone chimney on the canyon's right side. Cuno headed toward it, following the street across a gap-boarded bridge and having to hoorah the jittery mules, frightened by the oncoming storm, over the hazardous bridges with the rush of tea-colored water churning through the creek bed.

He pulled up in front of a sprawling, three-story, log, gambrel-roofed affair with a large front porch and real glass windows trimmed in white. Over the porch a large sign announced TOLSTOY'S TAVERN in blocky green letters. Piano and fiddle music emanated from over the batwings, as did the succulent aroma of spicy stew.

"A bar—now you're talkin'!" Colorado Bob whooped above the rumbling thunder. "Hooch and pussy. Just what a man needs after bein' locked up in a clatterin' damn gut wagon for nigh on a week with these smelly curs."

Cuno wrapped the reins around the brake handle, then leapt off the wagon and, taking another glance at the gunmetal-blue clouds now almost entirely filling the sky over the canyon, took the tavern's porch steps two at a time. From inside he could hear heavy-heeled boots and thigh-slapping hands keeping time to the jaunty dance tune being played by a scratchy fiddle and an out-of-tune piano.

He pushed through the batwings and poked his hat brim off his forehead, squinting into the heavy-beamed, cavernous room's deep, smoky shadows.

Several silhouettes were clustered around a piano near the back and around a brown-haired girl in a wine-red dress dancing in a circle with her arms thrown out, skipping and kicking between leaps and quick spins. Such a vigorous, fast-moving step Cuno had never seen. He'd have liked to have seen more if he hadn't been trying to outrun an angry mountain gale.

As several masculine faces turned toward Cuno and the fiddle and piano music dwindled, the young woman stopped suddenly, her back to Cuno and her long, wavy hair flopping against her slender back. Arms still thrown straight out to both sides, frozen in motion, she looked over her right shoulder toward the front of the room, frowning curiously, her liquid blue eyes glistening in the wan light angling through the windows.

The violin scratched out another note, and then the old man in the black cloth hat and sweeping gray mustache, sitting near the piano player, lowered it. Frosty gray eyes drilled through the shadows at Cuno. "Drink? Eat?"

Before Cuno could reply the girl swung full around to him and began striding forward on red-slippered feet showing beneath the pleats of her billowing dress. She said something in a foreign tongue, which Cuno assumed was Russian.

The old man with the fiddle stretched a smile beneath his mustache, set the fiddle on a table beside him, and leaned back in his chair, digging in the pocket of his duck shirt for a makings sack.

As the girl continued toward Cuno, the husky blond freighter felt a hitch in his chest. The girl's heart-shaped, blue-eyed face glistened with perspiration, and her red lips spread a bemused, welcoming, faintly curious smile.

In her false eyelashes, lightly applied rouge, and eyeliner, all of which served to accentuate the exoticness of her features rather than to obscure them, she appeared like some wraithlike conjuring from an imaginative young man's erotic dream. Polished silver rings danced beneath her ears, half concealed by curls of her thick, chestnut hair. The hair continued down to frame an ample bosom only half hidden by the lace edges of her low-cut dress, the wine red of which, relieved by stitched black stars, glistened with a faint metallic sheen.

Outside, the increasing wind moaned. Thunder rumbled, punctuated by a vicious, whiplike crack. A fire snapped and cracked in the large, stone hearth on the room's far right wall.

The girl moved as she looked, dreamlike, as though she weren't quite touching the floor. "You've probably heard about the whiskey." Her accent was thick, bespeaking stone huts in snowy glens in an ancient, mysterious world. "How 'bout an ale? My uncle brews it here the way he brewed it at home. We get orders from as far away as Bismarck in Dakota Territory."

She stood before Cuno, only two feet away, her head canted up toward his. Her teeth were fine and white between the rich, cherry lips, the stream-blue eyes primitively alluring.

Cuno was conscious of his bruised cheek and jaw, both of which he knew were liberally swollen. Remembering his hat, he doffed it quickly and cleared his throat. "I'm lookin' for a shelter for my wagon."

Her eyes flicked across his wide, thick shoulders. "Freighter?"

"That's right."

"How precious is your cargo?"

"A locked shed would be nice, but any solid roof will do."

The girl spun on a heel, floated over toward the horseshoe-shaped mahogany bar to Cuno's left. Propping a foot on the brass rail running along the base of the bar, she leaned across the mahogany and dropped a hand below. She floated back to Cuno holding a ring with two dangling keys in her long-fingered olive hand.

"This is for the lock on a red shed straight across the canyon, behind the green cabin with the falling-in roof. Park your wagon there . . . then come back for ale and stew." She dropped her chin, and her eyes glistened as she added with a slightly coquettish air, "It is elk, and it is very good."

She pronounced "good" like "goot."

She ran her soft, caressing gaze across his swollen cheek and jaw. "And I will find some raw meat for your face."

Another thunder crack made the whole room leap. Outside, Blackburn shouted something inaudible beneath the groaning wind and the rain beginning to fleck against the saloon's log walls.

"Obliged," Cuno said, his voice thick.

He held the gaze of the dark-haired waif smiling smokily up at him for another stretched second before he plucked the keys from her hand and found himself reluctantly turning away and tramping back out through the batwings.

"Come on, goddamnit!" shouted Colorado Bob from the jail cage. "Get us outta here before we're sent to our rewards in furry cinders!"

He and his two cohorts stood squeezing the bars in their hands, facing the saloon and glaring up at the ragged, angry sky. Fuego was lying on his side, unmoving except for the slow rise and fall of his shoulders, his head toward the partition dividing the cage from the driver's box.

As a lightning bolt shot out of the northern sky, flashing blue-white and hammering the stony ridge crest, and the accompanying thunder boomed like planets colliding, Cuno bounded down the saloon's broad steps and circled the skitter-hopping mules. Behind the wagon, Renegade loosed a bugling, angry whinny, his bit jangling as he shook his head.

"Hold on, boy," Cuno muttered to the horse as he climbed into the driver's box, released the brake, and started the mules forward.

He hadn't rolled two feet before the rain started slashing down. The drops were so large they sounded like small-caliber slugs plunking into the wagon and ticking loudly against Cuno's snugged-down hat, lifting a veritable cacophony in his ears.

By the time he'd pulled the mules past the green cabin that a wooden shingle dangling from a rusty chain identified as a former bakery, Cuno was soaked to the skin. He pulled the wagon into the shed rife with the smell of hay and the barley, malt, and hops fermenting in several large oak casks. Then he unhitched the mules to the rumble of hail hammering the roof over the hayloft. When he'd rubbed the animals down, and watered and hayed them, he checked the jail wagon's padlock.

"Let us outta here, so we can get out of these wet clothes and get ourselves dry," Simms pleaded through the bars.

"Like hell," Cuno chuckled. He had already passed a couple of dry blankets, which he'd found in the stable's tack room, through the bars. "You try pullin' what ole Half-Ear did, they'll be hangin' you gut shot in Crow Feather."

"Jesus God!" bellowed Colorado Bob, slumping down against the bars, his wet silver hair plastered against his scalp and shoulders. "The bastard's gonna leave us in here smellin' that beer without givin' us a drop!"

As he and the other two pleaded with Cuno for hooch and dry clothes, Cuno looked between them at Fuego. The half-breed lay back with his head against the cage's front wall. He'd drawn his bandanna lower and angled it taut across his freshly ruined ear.

One eye was swollen nearly shut, and his lips were crusted with dry blood.

With his stout arms crossed on his chest, he met Cuno's gaze with a hard one of his own, hardening his jaws and flaring his nostrils. He opened his mouth to speak, but, reconsidering, he closed it again. His brows drew up, the deep lines in his forehead planed out, and his eyes dropped to the wagon's blood-splattered floor and stayed there.

Cuno gave the padlock another tug, then let it drop against the cage. As the other three prisoners cursed and pounded the bars, Cuno went out, closed and locked the stable door behind him, then, lifting his collar against the driving rain and pea-sized hail that whitened the muddy ground, he jogged back through the brush around an abandoned chicken coop and the bakery and into what remained of the boomtown's main drag.

The sky now broiled with low, dark clouds, lightning flashed sharply, and thunder set the ground to quivering. Hail and rain javelined out of the sky at a forty-five-degree angle. As Cuno crossed the bridge, he glanced down to see that the creek had already risen a good six inches, bubbling and churning with clay-colored water and floating hail.

He stumbled into the saloon in his wet boots, ice and rain dripping off his hat. The girl was waiting for him with towels draped over her arms, a wistful smile etched on her plump, apple-red lips.

"First thing we need to do is get you out of those wet clothes and into a hot bath." She laughed.

14

THE GIRL WITH the heart-shaped face and full, red lips gave Cuno a towel, then wheeled and started into the shadows at the back of the room, red pleats swishing about her finely curved hips and long legs. "Right this way, sir."

Holding the towel stiffly, puzzled and mesmerized, and not a little taken aback by the invitation from a girl whose name he didn't even know, Cuno stared after her.

To the right of the broad stairs at the back of the room, the men sat, looking between Cuno and the girl. All were smoking either cigars or pipes, lounging back in their chairs and chuckling and muttering amongst themselves. On a table nearby were plates crusted with stew leavings and bits of bread.

It was hard to tell from this distance, but Cuno didn't think any of the men were under forty. They were work-bowed, weather-wizened men in blue denims, work shirts, and suspenders, with billed cloth caps on their gray heads and lace-up boots on their feet. Their bright, flickering eyes betrayed an air of wry, hearty optimism.

As the girl approached the stairs, pinching her dress up

her thighs, she loosed a breathy "Oh!" as though remembering something. She let her dress fall to her ankles again as she padded around behind the bar. The shadows semi-concealed her as she rummaged around, turning this way and that.

There were several clattering sounds, a sharp thud, as of a cleaver driven into a cutting board, and then she padded out from behind the bar, heading for the stairs and glancing over her shoulder at Cuno. He was still standing in front of the door, holding his hat in one hand as he dabbed tentatively at his face with the towel and regarded the girl uncertainly, vaguely suspicious of her intentions.

"Come on!" she rasped, beckoning, then starting up the stairs, which she climbed quickly with a swish of her bunched skirts, her swirling chestnut hair dancing about her shoulders.

The storm seemed to be hovering directly over the building, like a massive Indian war party powwowing before an onslaught against an ancient enemy. The roof shook under the pounding rain like a giant rattle.

Cuno grunted skeptically and started across the room, running the towel over his chest and down his arms. As the girl disappeared into the darkness at the top of the stairs, he glanced at the four men lounging to his right, all grinning as they puffed their pipes or cigars.

The bib-bearded man who'd been playing the fiddle and who now held a loosely rolled, smoldering quirley in a hand propped atop the table beside him muttered something in Russian. The man to his right pulled an old, cracked briar out from between his teeth and chuckled.

He squinted an eye at Cuno. "Tolstoy says you better mind yourself around his niece, me lad," he warned in a thick Scottish or Irish accent, "as he's got a Greener under the bar."

As the others wheezed and snorted, shoulders jerking, Cuno started up the stairs, taking the steps one at a time, while the men's muttering continued behind him, barely audible above the rumbling storm. A keen male desire drove him, as did the prospect of a hot bath. At the same time, apprehension tied a hard knot at the base of his spine.

There was a chance that the beguiling girl's intentions weren't as pure as her dancing, stream-colored eyes wanted him to believe. According to stories he'd heard, he wouldn't be the first traveler ambushed and robbed in some out-of-the-way dive, his carcass fed to the bobcats in the nearest deep canyon.

But then, he doubted he appeared worth the trouble to any but an inexperienced and sorely desperate siren. Something told Cuno this girl was neither . . .

His wet boots squawking on the rough puncheons, his spurs trilling in time with the soggy heel thumps, Cuno followed her up another set of stairs to the third story where the storm was even louder.

Lightning flashed in the window on the hall's far end, silhouetting the girl against it as she paused before a door and glanced again at Cuno. It was too dark for him to see the expression on her face, if there was one. He sensed she was smiling the beguiling smile that probed his swelling loins like a dull, rusty knife. Then she pushed the door open with a slight squawk of rusty hinges and disappeared into the room beyond it.

Cuno felt his stride lengthening, his heart quickening as he headed for the door. The girl stood in the room's shadows, lightning flashing in the curtained windows behind her, holding the door open with one hand. Another lightning flash limned her smile, and she stepped back, beckoning with one hand.

"Come, come—it's all right. There's no trickery here. Aside from my uncle Leo's whiskey, that is."

Looking around, holding his hand down over the holster thonged low on his right thigh, Cuno stepped into the room.

The girl lit a lamp. "If you'd like whiskey to cut the chill, though, I know where he keeps the good stuff. It's called vodka, actually. Have you tried it?"

"I don't think so," Cuno said as she closed the door behind him.

Strange aromas pushed against his face—pine, maybe sandalwood, and another musky, tealike scent he couldn't specify. Besides the soft umber lamplight, the only light in the room was the intermittent lightning bursts in the rain-streaked, thunder-rattling windows.

"Come on, now—out of the clothes," the girl ordered in a soft, seductive, slightly mocking voice as she went to a high-standing chest between the room's two windows. "I'll prepare a nice, hot bath. I've had the water steaming. I was going to take one myself before Uncle and his friend co-erced me into dancing for them."

"Didn't look to me like it took much convincing."

"I love to dance." She casually flicked her gaze across Cuno's chest to which his rain-soaked tunic clung, then dragged a large copper bathtub out from where it sat against the wall on a red velvet rug, under the mounted head of a large mountain goat.

She placed the tub in the middle of the room, then swept her eyes across Cuno once more as she headed for the door, swinging her hips coquettishly and letting her thick, chest-nut waves dance across her slender back.

"I'll bring the water. Good 'n' hot!"

"I don't wanna be any trouble, Miss . . ."

At the door, she turned back to him. "Ulalia." She hiked a shoulder and opened the door. "It is no trouble. You're the only guest we've had here in weeks. A girl gets tired of dancing for men old enough to be her grandfather."

She went out. Cuno stared at the closed door with his pulse throbbing in his ears and his neck feeling as though a hot iron were laid against it. He should be keeping an eye on the prisoners, but the storm showed no sign of letup. Oldenberg and his men were doubtless holed up in a cave somewhere back in the previous canyon through which the main trail to Crow Feather snaked.

Besides, he couldn't very well guard his charges effec-tively with a bad case of chilblain. And after all he'd been through, a hot bath offered by a pretty girl was just what the doctor ordered, though he was probably only torturing himself. If he tried discovering what succulent wares were hidden beneath that alluring red dress, he'd no doubt receive a buckshot-peppered ass for his troubles, courtesy of the protective Uncle Tolstoy's Greener.

Cuno doffed his hat and ran his hand through his damp hair, looking around the room—the large, canopied bed piled high with colorful quilts and embroidered pillows, a mirrored dresser, several chests of fine, ornately scrolled wood, and steamer trunks. A well-appointed room in spite of the bare, whipsawed boards paneling the walls. Pewter-framed tintypes of mustachioed gentlemen and dour, thick-necked ladies in high, ruffled collars hung from rusty nails.

The lamp guttered as rain blasted the room's single window. The building creaked in the gusting wind.

Downstairs, old Tolstoy had resumed playing his fiddle—a snappy tune to which a couple of his compatriots stomped their feet. Female voices sounded beneath the music, and Cuno realized he hadn't undressed yet.

He looked around uncertainly, then dragged a spool-back chair out from in front of a cluttered dresser and set it near the tub. He kicked out of his boots and wrestled out of his soaked tunic, deerskin pants, socks, and longhandles, and piled everything but his boots on the chair. Then he looped his cartridge belt over the chair back, angling the holster toward the tub, so that the .45's ivory handle would be in easy reach if a passel of ill-intentioned bandits returned in the girl's stead.

The storm had dropped the temperature, already cool at this altitude, a good fifteen degrees and gooseflesh rose on his arms and legs. He felt the fine hair prick across the back of his neck and his shoulders.

Still, looking down toward his crotch, he saw that the girl's warming effect had drilled through the chill and, hearing footsteps on the stairs and women's voices echoing around the cavernous halls, he stepped quickly into the tub and hunkered low, dropping his hand to hide the evidence of his automatic, carnal aspirations.

No sooner had his bare ass touched the tapered tub's icy

seat than the footpads in the hall were replaced by the click of the door latch. The door swung open, revealing the beguiling, alluring countenance of the dark-haired Ulalia. As she stepped into the room, crouching over the steaming wooden bucket she carried in both hands, another dark-haired girl flanking her, Cuno pressed his hands down tighter over his crotch, thrusting his shoulders forward and curling his toes with embarrassment.

Exposed to one woman was awkward enough. But two?

"Ready or not!" trilled Ulalia, laughing as she moved toward the tub, with the other woman—a round-bodied Indian with tobacco-dark skin and a pronounced limp—shuffling along behind her, dour-faced, eyes respectfully averted.

Ulalia walked around behind Cuno and grunted, laughing, as she lifted the bucket above his head. The steaming water hit his scalp and slithered down his face and back, spilling over his thighs and knees. The soothing contrast to the chill room and tub made him shiver and loose an involuntary howl drowned by a thunderclap that made the floor jump.

"That good, yes?" Ulalia laughed as she handed the empty bucket to the Indian and took the second one.

"Not bad," Cuno said, sucking in a sharp breath as the second bucket was dumped over his head, swathing his body in the soothing, womb-like warmth. "Oooh, yeah. Not bad."

"These," she said, grabbing Cuno's clothes off the chair and dropping the entire pile except for his hat and boots into the second empty bucket, "Lame Fawn will wash and dry before the fire."

"Jeepers," Cuno exclaimed, cupping the steaming water across his chest, "this is better service than you get at the Larimer Hotel in Denver!" He glanced at Ulalia ushering the Indian girl out the door. "Not that I know from firsthand experience, ya understand."

The girl looked at him as she closed the door. "You've never been to Denver?"

"Oh, I've been to Denver. Never been to the *Larimer*."
Cuno continued splashing the water up over his shoulders
and knees, chuckling now with the feeling of well-being in
the unexpected presence of this charming foreign waif and
the hot bath, energetic fiddle music leaping up through the
floorboards to be drowned occasionally by another thunderclap. His problems were a hundred miles away, on the
other side of the storm. "Doubt I ever will."

"I was to Denver once," Ulalia said, opening a drawer of
the chest between the windows. "But only once . . . when
we first came here from Russia. It was a dusty city, with the
smells of the cows." She wrinkled her nose as she moved to
the tub, a cake of blue-speckled white soap in one hand, a
stout scrub brush in the other. "But I heard the hotels and
restaurants are wonderful!"

"Overrated. I swamped a few." Cuno set his hand over
the hand in which she held the soap. "But I'll bet you'll get
back there and see for yourself someday."

He tried to take the soap, but she moved her hand away
and dipped the brush into the water beside his right thigh.
"I wash your back."

"You don't have to . . ." Cuno let the sentence die on his
lips and gave an audible groan as Ulalia ran the brush
across his back, between his shoulder blades, where his
muscles had grown taut as rawhide from tension and riding
stooped in the driver's box of the jail wagon. "Well, I
reckon . . . if you insist . . ."

He leaned forward, letting his shoulders hang slack as
the girl worked the brush over his back gently at first, in a
swirling motion. When she'd worked up a heavy lather, she
scrubbed harder, and he could see her buffeting hair in the
periphery of his vision, hear her soft grunts and sighs as she
worked.

"You come here to prospect the rocks?" she said, dip-
ping the brush in the water once more and making him
even more conscious of the erection he was trying to keep
hidden between his thighs. "Some say the gold is pinched
out, but Uncle doesn't think so. As quickly as the others

came and went, he thinks, after someone has followed another feeder creek to the mother lode, Petersburg will boom again."

"Just passin' through," Cuno said, the girl's question unfortunately reminding him of what he was doing here in the first place. "You know if this trail hooks up with the main one to Crow Feather—farther east, I mean?"

"You must ask my uncle. He goes to Crow Feather for supplies." Ulalia rubbed the soap across the brush again, and kneeling behind him, leaned forward to run the brush down over his shoulder and begin slowly scrubbing his chest. Her long hair brushed against his ear. "The main trail over the passes is six miles west. It goes south."

"Been through there," Cuno said, tipping his head up to look into the girl's pretty face. "I was lookin' for a more scenic route." He reached up and ran his thumb against her cheek. "I reckon I found it."

As she ran the brush in long, slow strokes across his chest, her eyes dropped to the soapy water between his thighs. The corners of her mouth quirked up, and Cuno followed her gaze.

His red shaft jutted boldly, proudly, above the suds.

He sucked a sharp breath, dropped his hands down to cover himself once more, and closed his knees. "Uh . . . whoa. Now, that there is . . ."

Ulalia dropped the brush into the water and rose. "Why don't you finish washing yourself?"

She walked away from the tub, and Cuno thought she was going to leave the room—possibly to hail her uncle and his shotgun—but then swerved off to a chair in the corner near the door. It was a high-backed, brocade chair beside an accordion privacy screen—cherrywood frames covered with black velvet in which large yellow moons and stars were stitched and over which several articles of women's undergarments were draped.

Keeping her eyes on Cuno, who stared back at her skeptically, she slowly lifted one of her feet to the edge of the chair, peeled off the bright red slipper, and dropped it to the floor. Her eyes were round and smoky, and her lips were frozen in that same beguiling half smile.

When she'd removed the other slipper, she rose and stepped behind the screen, which covered her only chest high. She wrinkled the skin above her nose and looked at him from under her thin chestnut brows, between the flowing wings of her chestnut hair, with mock reproof. "You finish washing. No lingering." She chuckled huskily. "I bring you towel."

As the storm continued to pummel the saloon with rain and thunder, Cuno resumed scrubbing himself with the brush more vigorously than necessary, his blood boiling in his veins. He hadn't been with a woman in many months, and his loins, he suddenly realized, were ready to burst.

Uncle Leo's ominous threat had retreated to the far back shadows of his heated mind.

Partly concealed by the black velvet screen, holding Cuno's heated gaze, the girl unbuttoned the front of her dress and leaned sideways to let if fall down one arm. She leaned the other way, and the dress fell down the other arm, leaving her creamy shoulders bare and accenting the pale length of her neck sheathed in the thick curls of her hair.

Her smile broadened, and she dropped her arms straight down in front of her. A moment later, they came up lifting a gauzy camisole. The lacy, white garment rose up over her face, taking her hair with it, and when she tossed it aside, her hair cascaded in a wonderfully messy mass about her cheeks and shoulders.

She stooped, her head and shoulders jerking this way and that as, obviously, she removed her stockings and other sundry unmentionables. Cuno had finished his hasty scrubbing by the time the girl turned away from the partition for a moment, grabbed something from down low by the back wall, then emerged wrapped in a thick, purple towel that covered her from the bottoms of her ripe breasts to the tops of her thighs.

As Ulalia strode toward him, holding the towel with one hand and grinning like the cat that ate the canary, Cuno

bounded up out of the soapy water so quickly that he got
his feet tangled and nearly fell. Ulalia laughed as, placing
one hand on the edge of the tub, he righted himself and, no
longer caring if she saw how engorged he was, straightened
and regarded the half-naked girl boldly.

Her eyes flicked down to his crotch, and her cheeks
turned rosy. As Cuno leaned toward her, reaching out with
his big hands, the girl stepped back, chuckling softly. With
the grace of a practiced dancer, she wheeled off to his left,
peeling the towel from around her with one hand and holding it up to Cuno, still partly concealing herself with it as
she twirled over to the bed.

In a blur of a single motion, she swept the covers back
and scuttled beneath them, drawing them up to her chin as
Cuno, drying himself quickly, stepped out of the tub and
moved toward her. He was breathing hard, and there was a
low scream of wanton lust in his ears, fairly drowning out
the storm.

Umber lamplight and blue lightning flickered across the
shadowy bed, illuminating the girl reclining on one side
and regarding him impishly, biting her lower lip as she slid
the covers down to her waist, revealing the two healthy,
pink-tipped globes of her succulent breasts.

15

NAT AVERY DIDN'T like folks pulling on his ears.

It rubbed him the wrong way, made him more conscious of how big the damn things were—large as a man's hand, some said, hanging off the sides of his long, horsy, red-haired head.

But the other gang members, especially Bo Creel, gave Avery's earlobes a tug every chance they got. Creel got such a chance when, caught in the rainstorm not long after leaving Oldenberg and the rest of the gang on the main trail to Crow Feather, Nat Avery, Bo Creel himself, and the two others in the foursome, whom Oldenberg had sent to scout the trail to Petersburg, sought shelter from the wicked gale in a cave close to the road.

Avery had turned his back on the others for only a second to loosen the saddle cinch of his lineback dun, frightened by the crashing thunder and hail the size of gumdrops, when Creel slipped up behind him and gave both of Avery's lobes a hard, painful jerk at the same time.

Adding insult to injury, Creel loosed two loud, mocking whoops—a poor but grating imitation of a train whistle—

then stumbled back away from Avery's swinging fists,
laughing as though at the funniest joke he'd ever heard.

The mockery grated Avery no end, and he wanted to
pummel Bo Creel's face till it looked like a pumpkin
smashed by a heavy-wheeled ore dray. But before he could
lay a lick on the big, cow-eyed son of a bitch, one of the
other two men—Stan Kitchen—rushed in behind Avery
and pinned his arms behind his back.

Then all three of his cohorts added more insult to injury
by accusing Avery of being unable to take a joke!

It didn't help that Avery, at five-five and a hundred and
thirty pounds, was the smallest of the four. He was the
smallest of Oldenberg's entire gang, in fact. Quick as he
was with his pistols, with his fists he was all bony, swinging knuckles, hoarse cries of blinding fury, and flying spit.
Whenever he retaliated—which was most of the time—he
ended up on his back or with his arms twisted painfully
behind him.

Avery tended his seething anger in brooding silence
while he and the others waited out the storm in the cave,
sipping coffee around a smoky fire, with the horses stomping and blowing in the shadows behind them. When an
especially loud thunderclap rocked the cave, one or all four
of the horses would loose an echoing whinny that pricked
the hair on the back of his neck, and twanged his fury-
frayed nerves.

After nearly an hour and a half of the pounding, earth-
shaking torrent, the rain petered out and the sky began to
lighten like a second dawn. Bruce Callaghan tossed his
coffee dregs on the fire, ran a greasy sleeve across his thin
brown mustache, and heaved his heavy bulk to his feet.
"Well, looks like it's clearin', fellers. Let's get a move on.
That jail wagon's gotta be holed up somewheres near."

They'd become certain they were close behind the jail
wagon not long after branching off on the trail to Petersburg, as the furrows and shoe marks they were following
matched those that had scored the main trail to Crow
Feather.

"Come on, Avery—grab your horse," said Bo Creel, nudging the little, horse-faced, big-eared man with an elbow. "Less'n you wanna stay here and sulk like a schoolgirl."

Snarling, Avery tossed the last of his coffee into the fire. He shoved his cup into his saddlebags, then stalked off into the shadows with the snickering others to retrieve his still-jittery mount.

Though his ears had long since recovered from Creel's assault, humiliation and anger continued to gnaw Nat Avery's gut and make the back of his eyes ache, as though mice were nipping at them, while he rode with the others along the muddy trail toward Petersburg.

The horses clomped wetly along the trace. Birds chattered in the pines and aspens, the stream gushed in its narrow bank, and a rain-fresh breeze wafted, tanged with wet sage and pine.

A mile out from the cave, Callaghan, riding point with Stan Kitchen—an Ozark Mountains–trained cold-steel artist and the fastest draw in the entire gang—stopped his big Appaloosa and raised his gloved hand. Avery checked his own mount down beside Creel.

"Yessir," Callaghan said, scrutinizing the ground beneath his horse. "That wagon came through here short time ago. Not even the rain and hail scoured those wide, deep tracks from the trail."

"He's holed up in Petersburg," Stan Kitchen said, rolling a three-for-a-nickel cheroot from one side of his mouth to the other. "I'd bet my left nut on it."

"Of course he's holed up in Petersburg," Bo Creel said, shifting around in his saddle. "He'll be holed up there a good long time. And if he's still headed fer Crow Feather, he'll either have to backtrack or head cross-country. Them creeks'll be broiling up around the tops of their cutbanks till nigh on nightfall."

His anger suddenly receding, his thoughts slowing and clarifying, Nat Avery poked the brim of his feathered bowler hat back off his forehead and lifted his chin toward

Callaghan. "Oldenberg said it was only one man tendin' the wagon. Correct?"

Callaghan spat a wad of chew into the still-dripping brush beside the trail. "Done said that, all right."

Avery's heart thudded. He could hear his blood singing in his ears like a choir of cherub-cheeked virgins.

The thought that had just occurred to him—half formed but a thought just the same—had really *started* occurring to him after Bo Creel had pulled his ears that last time, back in the cave.

Only, he hadn't realized it until now.

Stan Kitchen turned a snide look over his shoulder. He was a tall, gaunt man with close-set, hazel eyes and a mustache that covered his mouth like a dead beaver. "What the hell you gittin' at, Nat?"

"This very thing right here, Stan."

Avery's eyes didn't leave Stan's as he slapped leather and brought up his silver-plated Schofield, which he'd won off a Mexican pistoleer in Juarez last fall, and aimed it at Stan's right eye. He'd drawn so quickly that the sneer never left Kitchen's furred lips before the Schofield bucked and roared in Avery's gloved right hand.

Kitchen's right eye was punched back into the Texan's skull, where it was shredded amongst the man's pulpy brain matter before the bullet tore out the back of his head in a broad, visceral spray before plunking into a pine trunk behind him. Kitchen sat up straighter in his saddle, jerking a little from right to left as his horse started with the pistol shot.

Avery ratcheted back the Schofield's hammer as he slid the gun slightly left, lining up the sights on Callaghan's wide-open mouth. The man's horrified yell died stillborn on his tongue as Avery's second bullet careened between his lips and into his throat. It jerked Callaghan's head so brusquely back on his shoulders that his neck snapped like a dry twig under a heavy heel.

The bullet must have exited the back of Callaghan's head at a low angle and grazed his horse's rump; the horse's eyes snapped wide as it reared suddenly and pivoted with a shrill whinny.

The eye-shot Kitchen was just beginning to roll down his horse's hip, and Callaghan's dead, swaying carcass was being carried off across the canyon by his indignant Appaloosa, when Avery swung his smoking Schofield toward Bo Creel. Creel was staring wide-eyed at Kitchen and Callaghan.

His lower jaw hung down against his billowy red neckerchief. His usually sneering eyes were wide as two mounds of fresh bear plop, and they were glazed with disbelieving horror.

Creel leaned forward over his horn as though he were trying to catch his breath while trying to speak.

He held his frightened horse's reins taut as he shifted his gaze to Avery, who sat smugly back in his saddle, aiming the Schofield casually from his belly. He looked as though he'd just shared a good joke he'd been saving up for a long time, and like he was thrilled to have told it just the way he'd rehearsed it in his head.

"What the *fuck*?" Creel exclaimed, shifting his gaze between Avery and Kitchen, who lay in the soaked brush beside the trail, a rivulet of muddy runoff carving a new trough around his limp body. "What the fuck are you doin', Nat? Them's *our* boys!"

"I just got to thinkin'," Avery said slowly. "It ain't gonna take four men to take down that one tendin' the jail wagon. And, hell, when Blackburn and ole Colorado Bob see what I done fer 'em, they might just throw some o' that hidden loot my way."

Creel slid his nervous gaze back and forth between Avery's Schofield and the big-eared redhead's eyes. Creel held his hands chest high while drawing back on the reins of his jittery mount. "If you think Blackburn and Colorado Bob are thinkin' of double-crossin' Oldenberg, you got another think comin', Nat. They . . . they ain't that way. Besides, it'd be pure foolish to cross Karl. Shit, he . . ."

"He can't send men down every canyon between here

and Mexico," Avery said in that same, slow, self-assured drawl. He was enjoying the casual, fearless sound of his voice almost as much as he'd enjoyed popping two pills into Callaghan and Kitchen.

Almost as much as he was going to enjoy snapping another one or two into Creel.

They were far enough from Petersburg that if anyone there had heard the shots, they'd probably only think them lingering thunder.

"Besides, I do know that's what they had planned. Heard 'em talkin' one night over to the hog pen run by the English lady in Helldorado."

Creel didn't seem to know how to respond to that. He moved his lips several times, raised and lowered his eyes between Avery's own ominously mild gaze and the Schofield he held casually out in front of his flat belly.

Sweat glistened on the prankster's forehead. A bead as thick as a rhinestone dribbled down his unshaven right cheek.

He quirked a self-effacing grin and wrinkled his brows. "Nat . . . you ain't sore cause I jerked your ears, now, are ye? I mean, I was just kiddin'."

"You were laughin' *with* me."

"That's right. You know how I am—always doin' somethin' stupid to lighten the mood."

"Well, goddamnit, Bo, why didn't you say so?"

"I—I'm sorry, Nat. I shoulda—"

"Because that not only hurt, Bo," Avery yelled, rising up in his saddle now, his blood rushing hotly once more, forked veins standing out in his forehead. The saucer-sized ears sticking out from both sides of his head were as red as a New Mexican sunset. "It made me feel knee-high to a damn cricket!"

Creel flung his arm up, raised his hand palm out in front of his face. "No, wait, Nat! Don't shoot me!"

Pow!

A quarter-sized hole appeared in Creel's palm, just below the V of his middle and ring fingers. The hand flopped down to Creel's thigh, revealing the bullet's path through the man's left cheek. As the prankster's startled horse backed up, nickering and twitching its ears, Creel's head jerked forward over his saddle horn, and he dropped his reins. Both arms flopped like cooked noodles over his stirrups.

"There you go, you fun-lovin' bastard," Avery grated through gritted teeth.

He drilled another round through the top of Creel's hat.

Then, as Creel's horse bucked the dead man from the saddle and lurched back up the trail, screaming, Avery snarled another satisfied curse and enjoyed the sound of his own laughter.

He took a minute to reload the Schofield, then flicked the loading gate closed, holstered the piece, and reined his own horse down trail toward Petersburg.

16

NAT AVERY ROSE up in his saddle as the town pushed down the slopes around him and the rotting boards of a narrow bridge thudded beneath his horse's slow-plodding hooves.

He shuttled his cautious gaze from the dark, silent, dilapidated shacks on both sides of the trail to the faint furrows of shod wagon wheels, intermittently visible in the sopping mud of the narrow, winding street. When he'd threaded his way between the rows of mostly closed and forlorn-looking business establishments to the other side of town, he halted his horse before the only building he'd seen issuing smoke from its chimney.

Tolstoy's Tavern was a tall, sprawling log affair on the other side of the creek. The sky had nearly cleared for a time, but more clouds had moved in from the direction of the last ones, and rain had started spitting again, thunder rumbling in the north. The tavern looked darkly wet and ominous, its windows black as missing teeth.

Avery thought he'd heard fiddle music when he'd first ridden into the canyon. But now there was only the tick of the rain on the wet mud, the rush of the creek under the bridge, the distant thunder, and the soft sighs of his tired horse.

The wagon's intermittent trail led across another wood bridge, heading toward the tavern, but it returned again over the same bridge. Clods of mud from caked shoes and wheel spokes littered the bridge planks. It crossed in front of Avery and angled down a side street, disappearing in a soupy low area in which the light rain splashed the standing water like handfuls of thrown pellets.

Avery caressed the hammer of his Winchester with a gloved thumb and studied the saloon once more. A cunning half smile etched itself on his thin mouth, lifting his gaunt, pale, pimpled cheeks. He neck-reined his gelding left, in the direction the wagon had gone, keeping a cautious eye on the saloon behind him and scrutinizing the roofs and sodden woodpiles and trash heaps around him for signs of a possible ambush.

The tracks appeared again on the other side of the standing water, angling off across a weedy lot toward a dull red stable sheathed in cedars, with a solid shake roof. A stout padlock was looped through the iron handles of the two front doors.

Continuing to look around cautiously, his pulse quickening, Avery rode over to the stable and swung down from the saddle. He held his rifle high across his chest as he backed up to the doors, keeping his eyes on his back trail in case he'd been followed out from the saloon, and scrutinized the ground in front of the stable.

The broad wheel troughs disappeared under the doors.

Avery's head grew as light as a virgin's on her wedding night. The wagon was locked up tight behind these doors. And whoever had locked it up was outside somewhere with the padlock key. Probably wetting his whistle and drying his ass in Tolstoy's Tavern . . .

Avery lowered his hat brim against the pelting rain, ran the back of his hand against his nose, and turned his head toward the half-inch gap between the doors. He kept his voice just loud enough to be heard in the immediate vicinity. "Pssst! Blackburn! Colorado Bob! You fellas in there?"

A wooden squawk rose from inside the stable, and a low murmur of conversation.

"Blackburn? Bob?" Avery repeated. "You in there?"

Silence but for the rain and ratcheting thunder.

A voice that Avery recognized as Colorado Bob's said, "Who's there?"

Avery squeezed his rifle and swallowed the enervated knot in his throat. He'd found them!

"Howdy, Bob! It's Nat Avery!"

"Well, I'll be goddamned." This from Frank Blackburn.

"Avery?" one of the others whispered. It sounded like Brush Simms. "Who the hell's Avery?"

"Nat Avery. The late Louis's kid brother."

"Who—?"

"Shut up!" Colorado Bob rasped. Then he yelled, "Oldenberg out there, Avery?"

Avery shook his head as he regarded the crack between the stable doors, both doors buffeting slightly when the wind lashed them. "It's just me. Oldenberg and the others continued on toward Crow Feather. Couldn't tell if you'd branched off the main trail or not. Long story how it came to be only me out here, but rest assured I'm gonna get you outta there!" He was wondering when he should broach the subject of the hidden strongbox and his right to some of the money—before or after he'd let the three double-crossing cutthroats out of their cage? "Gimme a second and I'll blow the lock off!"

"No!" Colorado Bob said. "I seen the size of that lock. It'll take several shots, and a ricochet might take your head off!"

"Well, just what in the hell do you propose, Bob?" Avery heard Blackburn growl inside the stable, the clink of manacle chains reaching his ears, as well.

"Christ, shoot the fucking lock off!" Brush Simms bellowed in frustration.

"Shut up!" In a calmer but louder voice, Colorado Bob

said, "Avery, by the time you shoot that lock off and then start tryin' to shoot the lock off the jail wagon, that big, blond son of a bitch'll be on you like a duck on a june bug! You're gonna have to take care o' him *first*!"

Avery looked around beyond his horse standing hang-headed in the rain and pressed the back of his head against the door behind him. He could hear the men arguing inside the stable though he couldn't make out much of what they were saying above the rain and the occasional, echoing thunder.

Then, loud and clear, Frank Blackburn shouted hoarsely, "That bastard Widow Maker took out four of our best men and beat Fuego here to a bloody red pulp—not to mention he blew the poor man's only remaining ear off with a single shot!—and you expect that jug-eared little weasel out there to go in all by his lonesome and *kill* him?"

Avery felt a hot poker of blue fury push up from his asshole to the back of his throat. He set his teeth, but before he could say anything about how it was him running around out here, free, and it was them locked up in there, at *his* mercy—the conversation inside the stable tapered off.

"Avery?"

"What?"

"You're gonna have to dry-gulch the son of a bitch."

Cuno pressed his face against the back of Ulalia's head, burying his nose in the thick tresses of her wavy, chestnut hair. Belly down, she groaned into the deep feather mattress as Cuno toiled against her soft, round rump, which was driven up taut against his belly.

"Oh, Jesus," the girl said in her beguiling, Old World accent, as Cuno used the tips of his toes to lever himself slowly back and forth and in and out while she writhed beneath him, making the bed's leather springs squawk and the headboard knock the wall. "Oh, Christ."

She added a short, throaty string of half-whispered, half-sighed Russian, grinding her cheek into the mattress and raising her arms to wrap her hands around his neck and run them brusquely up the back of his head through his long, blond, still-damp hair.

It had dawned on him halfway through their first bout of lovemaking that the girl, whom he had at first thought as pure as the driven Siberian snow, was actually a nubile young lady of the evening ... and, obviously, a stormy afternoon. He'd been too busy enjoying the girl's supple, squirming flesh and the bewitching, moist caress of her rich lips across his nether regions to feel foolish. He was, after all—in spite of a brief, ill-fated marriage—new to the game of women and the dark, thrilling secrets of the boudoir.

And he was enjoying this reprieve from his four mangy charges in the jail wagon more than he could have imagined ...

"Cuno ... Cuno ... Jesus Christ ... why torture me so ... ?"

She drew his head down and twisted her own around. Wisps of sweat-damp hair were pasted to her flushed cheeks. Her eyes were grave. She parted her moist lips before giving a little, animal-like grunt and closing her mouth over his, ramming her tongue halfway down his throat and groaning.

At the same time, the volcano inside Cuno's loins finally blew its top.

The girl's face tightened and her mouth drew wide, and she chortled deep in her chest as Cuno rammed against her rump once more, harder than before, and froze there on the tips of his toes, powerful legs straight, chin aimed nearly straight up at the dark, wainscoted ceiling as he spasmed amidst the final, feral throes of their union.

He grunted as he gave a final thrust. The headboard knocked against the wall.

"Ahhhh," the girl moaned and let her head fall facedown against the mattress, as though she'd been mortally wounded in an attack of screaming Utes.

In the hall outside the room, there was the groan of a floorboard straining under a heavy foot.

Cuno had been about to pull away from the girl, but he

held still now, staring at the vertical planks of the wall before him. Ulalia wiggled her butt and gave a luxurious, satisfied sigh.

"Shh."

She frowned, turned her face to one side. "What is it?"

Cuno continued straining his ears, picking up a slight tap on the other side of the wall.

"Your uncle," Cuno said quietly. "He don't harbor no ill feelings about . . ." In light of his realization about the girl's profession, he assumed the old man's earlier admonition hadn't precluded a healthy romp.

"Of course not." Ulalia chuckled huskily. "We are Cossacks. We women as well as the men have extraordinary desires."

Cuno pulled away from her, and she grumbled in protest as she rolled around on the pillow she'd placed beneath her hips. Cuno slid his .45 from the holster hanging from the bedpost, shuffled quietly out of the bed, and padded barefoot to the door. He tipped his head against the varnished pine panel, listening.

Another tap sounded. Then another. A board squawked slightly, and he thought he detected a strained, raspy breath.

He looked down.

Two oblong shadows angled under the door from the other side.

Cuno glanced toward the bed. Ulalia lay on one hip, facing him, her rumpled hair framing her face still flushed from lovemaking. Her full, pale breasts rose and fell heavily while her smooth, soft belly expanded and contracted.

"Don't move," Cuno whispered in the sudden, heavy silence that had filled the room after the second storm's passing.

He stepped to the far side of the door, in case the sport in the hall triggered shots through the door panels. Gooseflesh rose across the backs of his shoulders, and he squeezed the .45's ivory grips as he held the revolver straight down by his side.

Had Oldenberg caught up to him? Damn foolish, taking

time to carouse. Here he stood in a candlelit room, naked as the day he was born, while Oldenberg's men were likely combing the town for him.

There was a slight chirping sound. He glanced at the porcelain doorknob. It was turning slowly.

Cuno raised the gun, pressed his shoulder against the wall, and gestured to Ulalia. The comely Russian dropped facedown on the bed and drew the covers up over her hair.

The door latch clicked. Cuno watched the door open slowly in front of him, the hinges squeaking softly.

When the door was open a foot, the barrel of a pistol slid through the crack, a foot above the knob. When the entire gun was inside the room, as well as the gloved hand wrapped around the cocked Schofield's walnut grips, the door began opening wider.

Cuno stepped forward and rammed his right shoulder against the door panels.

A shrill cry sounded as the door slammed into the wrist of the hand holding the gun. The hand opened, the gun fell with a thud, and Cuno jerked the door open to reveal a wiry, long-faced kid stumbling back and groaning, his pimpled face with wide-set eyes creased with pain.

He had ears so large that they looked like hands clamped against both sides of his head, the lobes hanging like fleshy pendulums.

As the big-eared kid stumbled back against the opposite wall, he screamed, "Son of a bitch broke my wrist!" and fumbled for a second gun wedged behind his cartridge belt, over his belly.

Never feeling as naked as he felt standing in that doorway without a stitch on, Cuno extended his Colt and fired. The kid screamed again savagely as, lowering the old Remington he'd just brought up when Cuno's slug had taken him through his belly, he jerked sideways and dropped to a knee.

Raging like an ox in an abattoir and holding the Remington over his belly, the kid heaved himself back to his feet and ran stumbling toward the stairs opening off the hall's right side.

"Gawddammit!" His shout echoed loudly as he dropped to both knees at the top of the stairs and jerked his head back toward Cuno. *"Why don't nothin' never work out right for me?"*

The Remington flashed in the dawn-like light from a nearby window, the maw angling toward Cuno, beneath the kid's gritted teeth and fury-bright eyes.

Cuno paused as he moved toward the kid, and fired another round.

The slug plunked into the kid's left temple, twisting him around and throwing him back against a stout rail post. Cuno thumbed back his Colt's hammer once more as he stood staring at his attacker through the wafting powder smoke.

The kid hung up against the post behind him, eyes blinking rapidly. He dropped the Remington to the hall floor, and sighed as though deeply tired. His legs jerked. His eyelids froze open, eyes staring opaquely. He slid left, tumbling down the stairs and out of sight, the rumbling thumps of his fall making the floor quiver beneath Cuno's bare feet.

There was a pause as the kid hit the second-floor landing. Then the cacophony continued, albeit more quietly, as the corpse continued rolling on down toward the main saloon hall until it hit the bottom floor with a final, resounding boom.

17

COVERING HIS NAKED privates with his free
hand, holding his cocked Colt straight out before him,
Cuno bounded down the steps on his bare feet. He paused
on the second-story landing, looking into the hall on both
sides, expecting rifles and pistols to blossom in the stormy
shadows.

Nothing moved in the near-vacant building that had no
doubt hopped every day and night during the height of the
boom. There was only the sound of rain dripping off the
eaves outside.

Cuno continued down the stairs. The jug-eared kid lay at
the bottom in a ragged, rumpled heap—still, silent, and
bleeding, his neck tipped at a weird angle. Ulalia's Uncle
Tolstoy was on one knee beside the body, leaning on a
long-barreled, double-bore shotgun. The man's thick, silver
mustache shown against his dark, angular face as he stared
up toward Cuno.

The slap of bare feet sounded on the stairs. Cuno
turned to see Ulalia, clad in a short, red satin shift, pad
down the stairs behind him, one hand on the banister, hair
bouncing on her shoulders. Brows arched, she shuttled her

gaze between Cuno and the dead man at the bottom of the
stairs.

Uncle Tolstoy shook his head gravely at Cuno. "He no
friend of your like he tole?"

"Nope." Holding his gun out, slightly crouched, Cuno
looked around the room.

Tolstoy's companions had apparently left, returned to
their cabins and maybe their women. The young freighter
stretched his gaze out the gray windows at the front and
sides of the deep room. "He the only one here?"

"*Da.*" The old Russian nodded and straightened his
bowed legs. "Him the only one rode in town. I seen from
window. What his beef with you, hah?"

Cuno continued on down the stairs and stepped across
the kid's body, the sightless eyes gleaming dully up in the
vagrant light. "He was after the men in the jail wagon I
have parked in your shed yonder."

Continuing to hold his hand across his privates, feeling
foolish but wanting to see how many others lay waiting for
him outside before he took the time to get dressed, Cuno
padded toward the front of the saloon's main hall.

He looked out the three front windows and peered over
the batwings. There was nothing but the forlorn, abandoned
buildings of the mostly deserted town hunkering wetly in
the dripping aftermath of the storm. Cuno could make out
no hoofprints in the puddle-pocked street before the saloon.

That didn't mean no more men were out there, hidden
behind rain barrels or hunkered inside the nearby shacks,
possibly in the gully through which the enervated creek
was churning. But the town looked and felt as abandoned
as when Cuno had first ridden in.

Had the jug-eared kid been alone?

Cuno had to make sure. But first he had to find some
clothes to wear until his own were dry.

As he made his way back to the rear of the room, Tolstoy was going through the dead man's pockets, grunting
disapprovingly at the few coins and single crumpled paper
dollar he found in a pocket. He was handing a tarnished

pocket watch up to Ulalia, standing barefoot on the bottom step, when Cuno came up.

"There a back door to this place?" Cuno asked.

Tolstoy stopped counting the dead kid's coins to tip his head back and look up at Cuno as though he hadn't quite heard what he'd said.

Ulalia shook the pocket watch and held it up to her ear. "We keep it barred when we're not hauling in wood." She seemed oddly unperturbed by the attack and the killing, as though such dustups were part and parcel of life in Petersburg—or had been before most everyone had left.

Maybe it was a welcome break from the recent boredom, Cuno speculated vaguely. He himself could have done without it. But then, he was damn lucky it had just been the kid . . . so far.

Cuno looked around once more, listening. When he turned toward the stairs, he saw that Ulalia's eyes had dropped to his red dong peeking out from behind his hand. She chuckled. "If you're going to fight, my blond Cossack, you better get some clothes on first."

She dropped the watch on the kid's lifeless chest. "Come."

She turned and headed back up the stairs and, in spite of nearly having been greased for the proverbial frying pan only a few minutes ago, Cuno enjoyed the view as the red satin shift, trimmed with black velvet, drifted up to reveal the shifting twin ovals of her smooth bottom, and the naked backs of her full but well-turned thighs.

As he followed her back to her room, continuing to look around for more attackers, he wondered if he should offer payment for her services. Then again, he didn't want to offend her. Here was where his lack of experience caused undue perplexity, and he had enough problems with his four prisoners and likely a dozen swollen creeks in the back country between here and Crow Feather.

He'd just drop a few coins on the dresser on his way out.

Ulalia rummaged around her own room and another room down the hall, until she'd come up with an armful of men's clothes—longhandles, faded and slightly torn denim jeans, and a heavy gray workshirt that appeared large enough for his burly frame. She even found a neckerchief, as well, but he left the kerchief on the bed, as she'd assured him the Indian girl was drying his own duds before a hot fire even as they spoke, and that they'd be ready in another hour.

Cuno couldn't help wondering where the clothes had come from. Why wouldn't the men who'd worn them into the saloon have worn them out? But he had enough on his mind without looking a gift horse in the mouth. No sooner had he stepped into his boots, which had been gently dried in front of the downstairs hearth, than he donned his hat and headed outside.

It had occurred to him that the kid had possibly only been a diversion while others sprang the four prisoners from the stable. So it was with a palpable lightening of his chest that he saw the padlock still looped through the handles of the stable doors.

"Avery, that you?" Frank Blackburn's cautious query echoed in the musty shadows as Cuno turned the key in the padlock. He didn't think he'd ever feel relieved to hear the pugnacious little bastard's voice again, but relieved he was.

Blackburn and the others obviously were not relieved to see him, however.

As Cuno threw the doors open, Simms sagged against the bars, lower jaw sagging. "Ah, shit!"

Cuno closed the doors behind him and moved into the shadows relieved by the blue-gray light angling through several sashed windows.

"Let me guess," drawled Colorado Bob through the bars, blinking his snaky, crestfallen eyes. "You've added another notch to your pistol grips."

"Don't see the kid's big ears hanging off his belt." Blackburn slumped down against the cage's far wall with a sigh. "If I was you, Widow Maker, I woulda taken them ears. You coulda preserved 'em in vinegar and sold peeks for quarters on any street corner in Denver."

Cuno peered over a stable halfway down the alley's right side. A saddled blue roan looked at him over its right shoulder, twitching its ears and waving its tail. A local's horse, obviously.

"At least he had *both* of his ears." Cuno, having grabbed his rifle from his saddle sheath, stepped into the stall of the saddled horse. He intended to follow his jug-eared would-be assassin's back trail for a ways, to make sure no one else was out here. Faster to take the already saddled horse than to waste time saddling Renegade.

"Hear that, Fuego?" Colorado Bob chuckled as Cuno grabbed the roan's reins. "Widow Maker's makin' fun of your condition."

Cuno backed the horse out of the stall and glanced at the jail wagon.

Fuego, sitting in his customary place against the cage's front wall, hacked phlegm from his throat, then turned his head to spit it through the bars. He muttered something so softly in Spanish that Cuno couldn't have made it out even if he'd understood the tongue. He doubted the half-breed was praying for Cuno's continued good health.

"Easy, easy," he told the horse as it bobbed its head rest-lessly, wary of the stranger.

He led the gelding back through the open doors and into the weedy lot fronting the stable.

As he threw the doors closed behind him, Simms yelled, "Hey, we're hungry, ya son of a bitch!"

The doors thudded closed, rocking the stable's front wall. Holding his Winchester in one hand, Cuno swung into the leather and reined the jittery mount back toward the main trail, the roan's hooves splashing up water around the stirrups.

Though more rain had fallen since the kid had ridden into town, his water-filled tracks still shone in the muddy caliche. Cuno racked a shell into the Winchester's breech one-handed as he put the horse up the trail rising and twist-ing up out of the canyon's west end.

The sky was clearing, and the sun was peeking out

between high, ragged clouds, when Cuno checked the roan down suddenly. He lowered the Winchester over the horse's head and rose up in the saddle.

A body lay belly down along the left side of the trail, parallel to it, head on the downslope, boots on the upslope. The water had dug shallow troughs to either side, and chunks of clay and stones had washed up against the man's arms and legs and against the base of his chin, damming up against his open lips and mustache.

His hat lay farther off the trail and a gaping hole shone in the back of his head, blood and white flecks of brain and bone congealing in his thin brown hair. More of the same viscera had spewed off into the rocks and grass and against a bullet-pocked pine trunk.

Cuno looked around warily, then quickly slid off the roan's back. Holding the reins in one hand and the rifle in the other, he crouched over the dead man and turned him over.

Cuno's mouth quirked up on one side. The man's right eye socket was a grisly mess of liver-colored blood flecked with lice-like bits of brain tissue. The other eyelid rested lightly shut, as though the man were only dozing.

Cuno straightened slowly, swinging his head this way and that. His gaze held on the opposite side of the trail. Hefting the rifle, he crossed the trail and tramped into the brush, stopping before a dense chokecherry thicket over which another dead man lay, back down, legs and arms dangling across the gray, spindly branches, as though he'd been dropped from the sky.

His upside-down head faced Cuno. One bullet had bored a clean hole through his cheek. Cuno couldn't see it from this angle, but apparently the man had taken another slug through the top of his head. Blood as thick as molasses webbed down from his scalp, pooling in the wet yellow grass beneath.

His eyes were wide and bloodshot. His thin, mustached lips were drawn far back from his teeth, in a perpetual agonized scream.

Cuno sucked air between his two front teeth. "Christ."

Both this man and the one by the trail were well-armed. Cuno had seen enough cutthroats to know these two fit the bill. Oldenberg's men, without a doubt. But how had they ended up dead?

He scoured the trail and saw where four horses had held up amidst a mess of scuffed sand, dirt, and blood, and one horse—the kid's, from the hoofprints—had ridden on down canyon toward Petersburg. Straightening after examining the blood-washed trail, he heard a whinny from down the northern slope. The roan answered, rippling its withers.

Cuno walked to the edge of the steep slope and peered down into scattered pines and deadfall. A quarter mile away, two saddled horses—a buckskin and an Appaloosa— stood at the base of the far canyon wall, facing each other as though conferring upon a serious dilemma.

They were swishing their tails. The Appy turned toward Cuno, lifted another whinny, and shook its head belligerently.

"I'll be damned."

Cuno mounted the roan and gigged the horse down the steep bank and gently sloping meadow. Not far from the two horses, he found the third body—another cutthroat deader than last year's Christmas goose.

This one had been shot through the mouth. The bullet had exited the back of his neck. He was rolled up against the boulder he'd apparently fallen against, judging by the blood smear, and upon which he'd apparently cracked his head open. He lay in a twisted heap, one knee up, one arm bent behind him, his chin pointed at the eastern horizon. Blood dribbled down his scalp and into his eyes. More thick, half-congealed blood flowed from his mouth like oil from a spring.

Cuno didn't know what to make of the three dead men. That the jug-eared kid might have shot his three compadres was too preposterous for Cuno's rational mind. He stopped worrying about it when he realized that he'd suddenly been blessed with exactly what he needed to outrun the rest of the gang and cut cross-country to Crow Feather.

Four saddled horses . . . after he located the kid's.

He adjusted the saddles and bridles of his two new mounts—one of which, the steeldust, had a relatively fresh bullet burn across its rump—then gathered up the reins and began leading them back along the trail to Petersburg, cutting cautious glances behind him.

He hoped Oldenberg didn't get too curious about where his four outriders had disappeared to before Cuno and his motley chain gang had put some nicely rough mountain country between them and Petersburg. Cuno had had a nice reprieve in the dying town. He'd no doubt remember the lithe, curvaceous figure of the beguiling Cossack girl on his deathbed.

But it was time to split ass for Crow Feather.

18

"KID, YOUR LUCK'S on a short, *short* leash. You realize that?"

"I don't know—I'm startin' to feel pretty lucky."

They were a couple of miles east of Petersburg, cutting cross-country through heavy timber, climbing a steep slope toward a saddleback ridge. The sun, what little of it shone through the high clouds remaining after the storm, was falling quickly behind the western, snow-spotted mountains.

"Oldenberg's done got him nigh on a dozen riders, and he'll be combin' this country like he's checking fer lice on a warthog's ass!"

"Well, he's short another four," Cuno said with a speculative air. "That makes him down to nine or less. At this rate, I like how my odds look, say, day after tomorrow."

He was scanning the darkening ridge ahead and above him. The food sack that Ulalia had prepared for him, before he'd abandoned the jail wagon and forced his shackled prisoners onto the saddled horses of their own dead gang members, flopped down Renegade's left shoulder.

The prisoners' horses, tied tail to tail, were strung out

behind him single file. The prisoners themselves, hands cuffed, were tied to the saddle horns and stirrups.

"He's right, Bob," Blackburn said from the back of the line. "This ain't lookin' none too good. Kid's tougher than he looks—a hell-thumbin' widow maker, sure enough—and this is big country. Hell, Karl may never even find us way out here on this pimple on the devil's ass."

"What're you sayin', Frank?" Bob said, riding directly behind Cuno.

"I'm sayin' let's cut the bastard in. Give him a full quarter of the payroll loot."

Simms whistled. "Let me see—a fourth of twenty-five grand . . . that's . . ."

"Six thousand two hundred and fifty dollars." Blackburn raised his voice. "Hey, kid, did you ever think you'd see that kind of money? I know I never did at your age. How old are ya, anyways? Nineteen? Twenty?" He clucked just loudly enough for Cuno to hear above the hoof thuds. "That kind of money, invested right, could set you up for life. You like to ranch, run stock, do ya?"

Cuno said nothing as he continued urging Renegade up the grassy slope, keeping his eyes on the ridges around him—not only for Oldenberg but, as this was Indian country, for Utes and Crows, as well.

"Big son of a bitch like yourself—obviously used to hard work—could double that sixty-two hundred in a couple years."

"No, Frank," Colorado Bob said, directing his words at Cuno's back, "he didn't learn how to shoot that forty-five diggin' ditches. The kid's a pistoleer. I'd say he probably rode our side of the law, time or two. Tell you what, kid—you turn us loose, we'll let you throw in with us. We'll double that little nest egg for you in two months down Texas way. Banks in Texas, you know, they're just like everything else in Texas—big and filled with big money!"

Simms said, "Big whores, too. Big in all the right places!"

As his charges—all but Fuego, riding in customary,

brooding silence behind King and in front of Simms—
continued to try to convince Cuno that he'd be far better off
if he'd turn them loose, Cuno studied what looked like a
small cabin sitting just below the conifer forest draped
raggedly across the saddleback ridge. The shack—if it was
a shack and not just a large, dark brown dimple in the
mountainside—lay about a hundred yards up the slope and
another hundred yards to Cuno's left.

The blond freighter studied the brown blotch, which
seemed to shift ever so slightly as the waning, saffron light
edged across the slope. He needed a place to hole up for the
night, and an unoccupied cabin would do nicely.

"I seen you had your eye on that comely Russian lass
back in Petersburg," Colorado Bob was saying. "Well, if
you like the brown-eyed, chocolate-haired fillies, Mexico is
just the place—"

"Stow it." Cuno had stopped Renegade at the edge of
aspen woods straggling down from the ridge. He swung
down from his saddle and tied the big skewbald to a stout
branch.

"What're you doin', Widow Maker?" Simms asked.
Like the others, he was crouched slightly over his saddle
horn, to which his wrists were firmly tethered with rawhide.
The man's feet were tied to the stirrups so he couldn't grind
his heels into his horse's flanks and gallop away if he got
the chance. Much of his greasy, dark red hair had come
loose from its queue, giving his head a tumbleweed look.

"Shut up." Cuno looked down the ragged line of his four
charges, all regarding him with dull interest. "I'm gonna
take a little walk. On the off chance you should somehow
free your horse from the others and decide to hightail it,
keep in mind I can make a long shot with my Winchester."

"You can't leave us here tied to these beasts," grouched
Colorado Bob. "Suppose a griz or a cougar comes along?
We're defenseless!"

"I've been lucky but not that lucky." Cuno chuffed as he
wheeled and started tramping off across the shoulder of the
slope, slanting upward toward the cabin.

The sun disappeared behind the western ridges as Cuno tramped through the short brown grass and sage. Almost instantly, the air cooled. Purple shadows tanged with sage and juniper washed across the slope, turning the jack pines on his right the color of India ink.

Cuno hunkered down behind a low shelf and peered over the top at what he'd concluded several yards back was indeed a rough hewn, log, brush-roofed cabin dug partway into the slope. He studied the cabin for some time before he detected a thin skein of smoke unfurling from a long, rusty chimney pipe. There was a heavy thud and resounding ping, as though someone had dropped a cast-iron skillet on a wooden floor.

Peering across his Winchester's receiver, Cuno muttered a frustrated curse. He'd hoped the place was abandoned. He couldn't very well ask some lone prospector to share his hovel with four cutthroats, nor risk the possibility that the cutthroats might convince the man to help free them for a share of the loot.

Cuno started to turn away to head back to his prisoners—he'd have to look for another place to throw down for the night—but snapped his head back toward the cabin. He'd heard a woman's clipped yell. A man laughed—a pinched, barely audible sound emanating from within those stout walls.

Several seconds later, there was a ratcheting scrape of a chair or table kicked across a rough board floor.

Cuno pricked his ears to listen more closely, his curiosity piqued, but then the night wind rose, ruffling the grass and sighing in the pines and drowning all other sound. He wanted to head back to the horses and continue on up and over the ridge, find a camping place on the other side.

But before he knew it, he found himself striding straight up the slope, then, once inside the trees, heading toward the cabin's rear corner, where the brush and the angle would conceal his approach from the door and the single window in which wan umber lamplight shone in the west wall.

He trod more carefully as he closed on the cabin, clearly

hearing the scuffs, thumps, and clipped, angry yells of a struggle. It sounded like two men and a woman. Pressing his shoulder against the cabin wall and holding his rifle in both hands, Cuno stole forward. One shutter was missing from the window, while the one nearest Cuno was partway open, blocking his view of the inside.

"Damn you!" the girl screamed.

"Hold her, Albert!" There was a thud and the rattle of boot spurs. "I said *hold* her!"

"I *am* holdin' her!" The other man laughed, his voice trembling with labored breaths. "Go to it, Harrel!"

With one quick swipe of his arm, Cuno drew the shutter back against the cabin wall and edged a look across the frame.

Inside, one man in a long, fur coat and leather hat was holding a slender, blonde girl on a table in the middle of the room. Another man, his buckskin breeches and long underwear bunched around his ankles, was trying to position himself between the girl's bare knees. Her denim trousers and frilly pink underpants were drawn down to her boots, and she was squirming around on the table, trying to close her knees.

"Damn you." The girl spat between gritted teeth, her cheeks red with fury. "I'll see you sons o' bitches in hell, you do this! I'll cut your damn *peckers* off!"

She'd barely got the last word out before she jerked her left arm free of the grasp of the man in the long fur coat and raked her fingers across the bearded cheek of the man trying to impale her with his jutting, brown dong.

"Ach!" The man clapped a hand against his cheek, yowling and cursing.

Cuno ducked under the window and ran around the front of the cabin.

"I told you to hold the bitch down, Albert, you brain-pickled son of a she-griz!"

The man bellowed another curse, and there was a sharp slapping sound as Cuno squared his shoulders in front of the cabin's plank-board door that hung slightly askew from rotting leather latches.

Cuno stepped back, raised his right foot, and slammed his boot into the door just left of the steel-and-wire latch. The door burst open and slammed against the inside front wall. Cuno stepped into the room just as the man trying to impale the girl swung the back of his hand against her cheek with a crack that was drowned out by the door's impact with the wall.

He had his back to Cuno, while his partner faced the freighter from the other side of the table. Both men reacted to the kicked-in door at the same time—the man between the girl's flailing knees twisting around and reaching toward his shoulder holster. The man facing Cuno stumbled straight back from the table, snapping his eyes wide with surprise and whipping his right hand across his waist to the walnut-butted hogleg angled across his belly.

"Hold it!"

Neither one stayed their reaching hands.

Cuno slammed the Winchester's butt against his shoulder. He fired and cocked, fired and cocked, the cabin leaping under the blasting echoes and powder smoke wafting in the shuttling shadows as empty cartridge casings clattered to the spongy puncheon floor and rolled in circles.

When four brass casings had been ejected, smoking, from the Winchester's breech, the two would-be rapists lay in twisted heaps on opposite sides of the sparsely furnished cabin.

"Oh . . . Jesus . . ." rasped the one who'd been holding the girl down, as he lifted his head from the floor near a cot, wincing, blood welling up in his mouth and dribbling down over his pendulous lower lip. He dipped his chin to peer down at the two ragged holes in his baggy calico blouse, between the flaps of a smoke-stained deerskin vest trimmed with Indian beads.

His eyes closed and his head fell back to hit the floor with a hollow thud.

When Cuno had started firing, the girl had twisted around on the table, raising a shielding arm over her head and scissoring her naked legs together, slightly bent at the knees, her jeans and panties hanging down over her stock-man's spurred boots.

Now Cuno shuttled his gaze to her. She was staring up at him from beneath her raised right arm, her tusseled, tawny hair fanned out around her oval face. She had a nasty, purple gash on her right temple, and fresh blood dribbled down from it.

Cuno started to look away, in deference to the fact that she was naked, but then he returned his eyes to hers once more. Recognition mantled his brow.

"You get around," he grunted.

It was the pretty, slender, tawny-haired girl whom Joe Pepper had slapped around in the Buffalo Flats Saloon, and whom Cuno had last seen in the valley where her party had ambushed the marshals. Apparently, she mistook Cuno's last comment for a moral judgment instead of literal obser-vation.

As she dropped down off the table in a huff, she told him to go diddle a goat. Then, her blue eyes pinched with fury, her lips pooched angrily, she hauled up her panties and jeans in one swift jerk, brushed a sleeve across her bloody temple, and stomped past him and out the cabin door.

19

CUNO TURNED TO the open door and watched the haughty girl stomp off across the flat, hard-packed area in front of the cabin. She knelt down where water trickled up through a rocky shelf, and, throwing her straight, tawny hair back over one shoulder, cupped the water to her face, dabbing her right cheek and bloody forehead tenderly.

Cuno turned to the man who'd been trying to savage the girl. He lay on his side, half under a dusty shelf littered with rusty pans, a half dozen airtight tins, and mouse droppings. His bloodstained buckskins and longhandles were bunched around his boot moccasins, and his limp dong had curled up against his thigh like a sleeping snake.

A trapper or market hunter, most likely.

Grunting his disapproval at having stepped unsuspecting into another in a series of proverbial bear traps, Cuno set his Winchester across the table, grabbed the man's ankles, turned like a mule in the yoke, and dragged him unceremoniously out the door and into the yard.

He slid the half-naked body up against the bole of a pine

about fifty yards from the cabin. Seeing no point in allowing him in death a dignity he obviously didn't subscribe to
in life, Cuno didn't bother pulling his pants up.

The girl was sitting beside the spring when Cuno approached the cabin. She held a damp handkerchief to her
cheek. Knees drawn up to her chest, the points of her boots
aimed toward the fast-darkening sky, she watched Cuno
skeptically.

The light night wind tussled her hair about her pretty
face that was no less pretty for a slight tomboy quality—a
firm practicality around the eyes and the frank line of her
broad mouth.

For an instant, Cuno thought she was going to remind
him of July. But he'd become an old hand at turning
quickly, almost painlessly away from such memories.

When he'd dragged the other dead man over to where
the first one lay, he grabbed his rifle out of the cabin, then
walked over to where the girl sat near the spring, still regarding him like a wolf who'd wandered into her camp and
she was still trying to decide if he was wild or only half
wild.

He set the rifle over his shoulder and tucked a thumb
behind his cartridge belt. "Put some mud on it. Take the
swelling down."

"Ain't you just a man of the land." She had a sexy,
raspy voice, but he didn't doubt, judging by her eyes, that
she'd core him with a well-concealed pigsticker if he got
too close or said the wrong thing.

The market hunters had sauntered into a wildcat's lair.
She might not have needed Cuno's help in the long run.

Cuno glanced off to where he'd left his prisoners, feeling the urgency to get back to them and traipse up and over
the mountain to find a camping spot before good dark. "I
only meant you cover a lot of country fast."

The girl looked down and waggled her boots. "So do
you. I seen you comin' through my field glass. That's when
those two jumped me from out of the trees."

"Who are they?"

"I seen 'em at a lean-to during the storm. They was in Bailey Gulch. They musta followed me when the rain cleared."

Cuno glanced at the shack hunkered down against the black line of the forest. "That yours?"

"Just hole up here, time to time, when I'm on my own." She drew the wet handkerchief away from her cheek and squeezed it in her small, strong fist.

"You alone now?"

"What's it look like?"

Cuno turned away. "Luck."

"Where you goin'?"

"Over the mountain."

Cuno continued heading back the way he'd come.

"Hole up here if you want."

Rifle on his shoulder, Cuno turned to her. "If you saw me comin', you know I'm not alone."

"Got 'em on a leash, don't ya?" She glanced at the cabin. "You can lock 'em in there. I was gonna sleep out under the stars, anyways. Too much mouse and squirrel shit in the cabin."

She must have read the suspicion in Cuno's eyes, because, turning her back to him and soaking the handkerchief in the spring, she added, "Just 'cause I rode with coyotes, don't mean I'm a coyote. Suit yourself."

She pushed to her feet and, whipping the handkerchief over her shoulder, strode over to the dead men. She toed one of them, tipping his head this way and that with her boot, then gave a caustic chuff and walked off into the pines.

Cuno stared after her. Then he wheeled and tramped up and over the bench as a mourning dove cooed softly from a nearby aspen and coyotes yammered in the distance. The western horizon was a painter's palette of mixed colors behind black, toothy peaks.

"Well, well, well," Blackburn groused as Cuno approached the horses. "Back so soon?"

"Heard the shootin'," said Colorado Bob, slumped over

his apple-tied wrists. "Who'd you beef now, Widow Maker?"

Cuno burned at the handle they'd given him. A killer was the last thing he wanted to be. He aspired to a peaceful albeit hardworking life hauling freight—like he and his old man had done before his old man was killed by Rolf Anderson and the half-breed Sammy Spoon.

Was that too much to ask? He'd been given every indication that it was. Still, it was the direction he intended to continue traveling.

He said nothing, gave no indication of how the name chafed him. Letting the cutthroats know they'd riled him would only keep it going.

Untying Renegade from the aspen branch, he climbed into the saddle and set out toward the cabin.

"You find shelter?" Simms called from behind him. "It's monsoon season in the high country. Clear now but liable to rain again soon."

"Worried about a little rain?" Colorado Bob laughed. "Hell, Simms, you're due to have your neck stretched in three days!"

"Yeah, but I want mine dry-stretched," quipped Simms. "Besides, me an' Fuego got us a bet."

"Oh, yeah," Blackburn said. "What'd you two fellas bet on, pray tell?"

"I bet Fuego a hundred dollars of the stolen loot that by this time tomorrow, we was all gonna be headed back up to Helldorado with Oldenberg and the fellers."

Simms laughed toward Cuno's back—a grating, mocking laugh that hardened Cuno's jaws and made him wonder why he was doing this. He'd already killed a half dozen men since leaving Buffalo Flats. What difference would four more make?

Four more who were due to hang anyway.

"What about the strongbox?" Blackburn said, directing the question at Colorado Bob. He was speaking more quietly now. "If Oldenberg springs us, we're gonna have to lead him to the loot. If he ever got wind that we . . ."

"A bridge we'll cross when we come to it, Frank," Bob said.

As Cuno led the horses over the bench and down the other side, he saw that the girl had set a fire in a large, stone-lined pit in front of the cabin. She'd led a couple of horses up to the fire—rangy mustangs heavily rigged with saddles, rifle boots, bedrolls, and bulging saddlebags.

She had a pair of saddlebags and a rifle boot on the ground before her and was holding the rifle near the fire-light, working the cocking mechanism as she inspected the breech. She'd found the horses of the men who'd tried to ravage her and was seeing about some payback in fire-power and trail supplies.

Again, July drifted up to the edge of Cuno's consciousness. She'd have appreciated the frontier logic in that.

"Well, well—lookee here," said Colorado Bob. "Hello there, little miss. If I haven't seen you somewheres before, my name ain't Colorado Bob, killer of men and lover of women."

Simms said, "Ain't that the little number that ran with Joe Pepper?"

"A lot of little numbers ran with Pepper," grumbled Blackburn. "Shit, he had one in every jerkwater between here and Calgary."

The girl didn't look up at the motley newcomers, but continued to inspect the heavy Sharps rifle in her hands.

"You got a picket line?" Cuno asked her as he led the others past the fire.

"At the edge of the trees," she said. "Mind the pinto—he's a biter."

"Right."

When Cuno found the picket line, he made it long enough to hold his five horses, giving the pinto plenty of room. He noted that the pinto had a long, shaggy brown tail that, with the afternoon sun on it, might have looked chestnut from a distance. Like the one he'd seen on the ridge before the rainstorm.

He took his time cutting each of his cutthroat charges out of their saddles, leaving their wrists tied with a footlong strip of rawhide. When he had them all down, he ordered them to unsaddle and rub down their own mounts, then haul their gear back to the cabin.

"Shackin' up with another filly, eh, Widow Maker?" Simms laughed as Cuno shoved him down against a broad pine stump ten yards back from the fire. "You got another one lined up for tomorrow night?"

The girl had obviously gone through the dead men's gear, piling what she wanted near the cabin door. The saddleless horses were hobbled near the spring. There wasn't room for them on the picket line, and being mountain horses, they were no doubt accustomed to hobbles.

Now the girl was cutting deer meat on a board beside the fire while a pot of beans gurgled and churned on the low flames. A dented black coffeepot sat on a rock near the flames, and three tin cups sat around the burlap sack at her feet—more booty from the would-be rapists, Cuno figured.

"If you want any supper tonight," Cuno said, aiming his rifle out from his hip, "keep your mouths shut." He tossed the coiled rope in his hands at Colorado Bob, who sat in the middle of the group, with Simms on the left, Fuego on the far right. "Wrap that around your ankles. Tight. Any cheating, there'll be no grub for you."

"He's become right proddy," Blackburn grumbled as he coiled the rope around his ankles. "Reminds me of a teacher of mine."

"That the one you tossed in the privy pit?" Colorado Bob asked, leaning forward to coil the rope around his high-heeled, hand-tooled black boots stitched with red thread and into which the cuffs of his striped trousers were stuffed. His slanted, Nordic eyes shone yellow in the firelight.

"That's the one."

When the rope was coiled around the prisoners' ankles, Cuno tied the end nearest Simms to a stout branch protruding from another pine stump. Then, holding his rifle negligently out from his right hip, he sauntered over and stooped down beside Fuego. As he reached for the rope end, he looked at the big, bald, earless half-breed.

Fuego had been glowering at him. Cuno'd seen the fire-reflected gaze out of the corner of his eye. But now the man was staring at the ground between his raised knees with mock fascination. He was whistling very quietly between the gaps in his teeth.

"Hey, Widow Maker."

As Cuno grabbed the end of the rope, he looked at Colorado Bob. The gold-toothed, devil-eyed man nudged Fuego with his elbow. "You'll have to cut his meat up for him, don't you know. That'd be the polite thing, since you broke the last of the poor man's teeth."

Colorado Bob grinned, showing his own choppers glistening brightly in the firelight.

"He can gum it."

Cuno slid his gaze away from Bob, let it drag across the menacingly hang-headed Fuego, then moved off to tie the rope around a lump of granite poking up out of the ground to the right and slightly behind the seated prisoners.

In spite of his rejuvenating sojourn in the bed of Ulalia Tolstoy, his efforts with the four prisoners had fatigued him. With a weary sigh, he hunkered down on the north side of the fire, opposite the prisoners and from where he could keep a close eye on them, and drew his knees up.

He looked around, grinding the rifle butt into the ground between his boots and wondering how far away Oldenberg was.

The girl dropped a handful of venison into the churning, steaming stew pot and glanced at him. "Long ride?"

"Might say that."

"You a marshal?"

Cuno shook his head and reached into his shirt pocket for his makings pouch. He didn't smoke often, but occasionally, when he was tired, a cigarette went well with the cool air and the smell of pine. It helped him relax, take his mind off his troubles.

The girl, kneeling to his right, her back to the shadowed cabin, frowned and jerked her head toward the prisoners. "Why are you taking the trouble, then?"

"Because I'm a copper-riveted fool." Cuno slowly closed the brown paper cylinder between the thumb and index finger of both hands, then raised it to his mouth and licked the paper.

"Seems like it'd be a lot easier to turn 'em loose."

Cuno leaned back against a rock, stretching his legs out in front of him and, as he plucked a lucifer from the breast pocket of his tunic, studied her suspiciously. Was she savvy to the hidden strongbox? Was that why she was holed up here so conveniently on his way to Crow Feather?

He chuckled to himself. Now he had five possible cut-throats to keep track of . . . and one of them a girl of questionable allegiances.

"Yeah, it would be," Cuno said, firing a match on a rock. "But I've grown kind of fond of them four. I think I might get lonely without 'em." He touched the match to his quirley. "And I'd take it personally if anyone tried to get between us."

20

"BESIDES," CUNO ADDED to the girl glower-
ing at him over the leaping flames, "those four running
loose across the countryside would make the two that attacked you look like tail-wagging puppy dogs."

One of the prisoners laughed.

Blackburn said, "I'll take that as a compliment. Hope
the food's soon done. We're hungry over here. Miss, could
you put a little extra salt on mine?"

"What'd I tell you, Blackburn?"

Cuno blew cigarette smoke at the darkening sky in
which several stars winked brightly. He looked at the girl
biting a hunk of fat from a dark red chunk of venison before tossing the meat into the bubbling pot.

"What's your name?" he asked her.

"Johnnie."

She tossed the last handful of meat into the stew pot,
wiped her hands on a swatch of cloth, and leaned back on
her butt, drawing her knees up and wrapping her arms
around them.

She'd donned her man's tan hat, and it partially shaded
her face, its leather thong dangling beneath her chin. She

shook her hair back out of her eyes and regarded him soberly, defiantly, as though expecting a mocking retort.

"You're not gonna chuckle?"

"At that name? Nah. I'm used to girls with strange names." He was thinking of July Summer. "Got a strange one myself—Cuno Massey."

He took his quirley in his left hand and leaned toward her, extending his right. She looked at it suspiciously, then, haltingly, leaned over to place her own right hand in his.

"Johnnie Wade." Cuno squeezed her hand, half consciously probing the fine bones as though they might give some indication of her motives. She squeezed back slightly.

"Unusual, all right," she said, wrapping her arms around her knees again. "Where'd it come from?"

"An old family name. I think it was my great-grandfather's name on my ma's side."

The girl sniffed as she studied the fire, resting her chin on her knees. "Johnnie ain't my real name. It's Joanne, but Pa didn't know what to do with a girl after five boys, so he called me Johnnie, and I reckon it stuck. I was more like a Johnnie, anyways, than a Joanne."

A pine knot popped, throwing sparks over the bubbling stew pot. Cuno could hear a couple of the prisoners, silhouetted against the pines behind them, muttering to each other. He thought it was Blackburn and Colorado Bob, though their dark, hatted heads were turned toward the fire.

He couldn't help feeling the target of some treacherous scheme and found himself wincing again at the lousy luck of having his fate intertwined with that of the two dead marshals and the jail wagon.

Serenity would start looking for him tomorrow. But at the speed he was moving, he wouldn't pull into Crow Feather until the day after tomorrow. Too late, most likely, for the freight contract.

"From around here?" he asked the girl.

"Texas. You?"

"Nebraska, couple years back. Was freight haulin' around Denver till my money pinched out last year; had to close up shop and head for greener pastures. Or less crowded ones, anyways."

"Tough haulin' freight in these parts, with the mountains an' owlhoots an' all."

"You're tellin' me." Cuno looked at the prisoners and snorted.

The coffee smelled done, so he leaned forward and used a leather swatch to pick up the steaming coffeepot. He poured himself a cup and felt the girl's eyes on him.

"Like I said," she said, "just cause I run with lobos don't mean I'm a lobo."

"I reckon a lawman would feel different—especially the ones I buried up north. To tell you the truth, I don't know what to think about you. All I know is I'd like to make it back to Crow Feather with those four lobos over yonder, and I'd appreciate it if you didn't get in my way . . . no matter how much they offer you to backshoot me or ram a pigsticker in my neck." He held up the steaming coffeepot. "Belly wash?"

Johnnie reached for one of the cups beside her and, scowling at Cuno, extended it toward him. "Trustin' sort, ain't ya?"

"Nope." Cuno sipped the coffee. "It's none of my business, but how'd you end up with a son of a bitch like Pepper, anyways?"

"You're right," she said, as she swallowed some coffee and glowered into the flames. "It's none of your business."

Cuno leaned back on an elbow and hiked a shoulder. "Just makin' conversation."

They sat in silence broken only by the simmering coffee and the chugging beans. When the four prisoners, some of whom had obviously been dozing after the long ride, started caterwauling for coffee, Cuno fished a couple more cups out of the burlap sack near the girl's feet.

While the girl disappeared into the cabin, where he could hear her scuffing and moving furniture around, he picked up his rifle and slipped off to scout for interlopers.

The fire was well concealed beneath the bench at the

edge of the forest. And he doubted any of Oldenberg's men were within at least a couple of miles, but he saw no reason to get careless.

He dropped to a knee downhill from the cabin, on the north side of the bench, and looked around, listening. Nothing but the usual night sounds and the occasional rasp of weeds rustled by a vagrant breeze. An inky black mass of clouds shone in the northwest. They could bring rain in a few hours, or move on to the northwest. It all depended on which way the wind blew.

After a time, Cuno strode quietly back to the cabin and stopped near a boulder about thirty feet from the fire. He could see the girl kneeling by the fire, stirring the stew pot. The four prisoners were a ragged clump ahead of her and to her left.

Simms was saying something too softly for Cuno to make out. Apprehension nibbling at him, the freighter brought his Winchester up and caressed the hammer with his thumb. Near the fire the girl laughed caustically.

"That's right good money," Johnnie said, above the snapping, dancing flames. "But I know I'd never get my little finger on one stolen dollar before you blew my wick and tossed me in the nearest ravine. After you done what those other two fellas over yonder *planned* to do."

"Ah, honey," Colorado Bob said. "You gotta learn to trust folks in this ole life! Sooner or later, ya . . ."

The silver-haired desperado let his voice trail off as Cuno stepped out from behind the boulder and tramped toward the fire. "The girl's no fool, Bob." He shouldered the rifle and poked his hat brim back off his forehead. "I reckon she read your hand the moment she saw you."

"What about mine?" Blackburn asked, white teeth showing in the darkness. "I play an honest hand, honey. Why, sure. If you cut the young Widow Maker's throat while he sleeps this evenin', we'll cut ya in for a full fifth."

"Who says I'm gonna sleep?" Cuno set his rifle against his saddle and accepted the plate the girl had filled with smoking beans and venison.

"Gotta sleep sometime," Simms said.

"Besides, what about Oldenberg?" Cuno said, taking another filled plate from the girl and tramping around the fire to the cutthroats lounging like royalty in the shadows near the tree stumps. "Ain't he gonna be a little sore when he finds out you double-crossed him?"

"Who says he's gonna find out?" Colorado Bob took the plate from Cuno, bowed his silver head over it, and blew on it.

"I'll tell him."

"How you gonna do that?" Simms said. "He'll blow your wick long before you see him . . . or get close enough for chatter except maybe for you to beg him to put you out of your gut-shot misery."

Cuno handed over two more plates supplied with wood-handled forks to Fuego and Blackburn. "Suppose he does blow my wick. What're you gonna tell him about the money?"

"Don't need to tell him nothin'." Simms was digging into the food like a German bricklayer. "When we dig it up, we get the drop on him right quick-like. Karl—he's the trustin' type, you see. A big, mean son of a bitch. A master of organization and inspiration to boot. But, hell, he trusts us like we was all brothers. We'll kill him deader'n a drowned squirrel . . . and all the boys ridin' alongside him."

"Ain't too many o' them left, thanks to ole Widow Maker here!" Simms laughed, dribbling beans down his chin and back onto his plate.

"Sure enough, Karl's simpler than a Montana whore," said Colorado Bob, delicately spitting a fleck of charred meat from his lower lip. "He had us all take a blood oath. I swear the son of a bitch thinks we're all twelve years old and playin' bank robbers in the barn loft!"

When Cuno had delivered coffee to the prisoners, then sat down with his own plate and refilled coffee cup, he saw Colorado Bob looking at him from across the fire, yellow eyes glowing like a cat's. "Sure would be easier, though, if we could git shed of you, Widow Maker. Nothing personal, you understand."

"You can sleep on it," Cuno said, finding himself shoveling the tasty beans and meat into his mouth as quickly as Simms. He was so hungry he felt his ribs crowding his belly. "Just as soon as you boys are done eatin', you're turnin' in."

"Ah, come on, Pa!" Blackburn chuckled. "Just one more story?"

Even Fuego grunted a laugh at that one.

Cuno was dead-dog tired, but he kept a close eye on the men, over the barrel of his Winchester, as he freed them from their ropes and led them off into the trees to tend nature.

He kept an especially close watch on Fuego, from at least ten feet away, for the man's entire furtive manner and sinister silence, in spite of his never looking Cuno directly in the eye, bespoke another sudden attack.

One more of those, in Cuno's tired state, would most likely be the end of him.

When they'd washed and drank at the spring, Cuno ushered all four into the sparsely furnished cabin, from which the girl had hauled out her own gear and dropped it near the fire. Cuno had scoured the hovel for weapons, confiscating every fork, butter knife, and bottle, and when he had the men shut up inside, he nailed the shutters closed. He hammered a plank across the door, nailing the broken latch to it, barring every possible route of escape.

That done, he turned back to the fire with a weary sigh.

He had to hand it to the lawmen—hazing four cutthroats across the territory to certain death by the hangman was no task for old women or sissies. He had a pretty good idea, firsthand, why the life expectancy of a badge toter was little longer than that of a wolfer or a soldier stationed in Apacheria.

"More mud?" the girl said, stretched out against her saddle, hands crossed behind her head as she faced the fire.

"Don't mind if I do."

As he moseyed over to the fire and set his rifle against his saddle, the girl refilled his coffee cup, and they sat together in oddly comfortable silence, listening to the flames snap and pop and watching the stars. Cuno habitually listened for the sound—a weed or twig crunched beneath a boot—of unwanted visitors, but there was nothing but the occasional snort or hoof clomp of the horses back in the trees.

Finally, Johnnie tossed her grounds into the fire, turned onto her side, and drew the blanket up to her chin. She ground out a little place to accommodate her hip, then drew up her knees and closed her eyes, a wing of tawny hair falling over the exposed side of her face.

He watched her for a time, remembering July, his young, pregnant wife killed by ambushers who'd been gunning for Cuno. Not a day passed that he didn't think of her, racked with the same anguish and futile regret for the past he couldn't change any more than he could influence the spin of the stars above his head.

If she'd lived, they'd have had several children by now, a few horses with maybe a cutting pony or two, and a sizable herd. A dog running about the place. Cats for keeping down the mice. Some chickens and a milch cow. Ranching was how they'd intended to make their way together back then . . . nigh on three years ago now . . .

Freighting was a bachelor's life, July had told him.

He rolled another cigarette and strode off down the slope, into the blanketing darkness beneath the stars, feeling tired and gloomy and as alone as he'd ever been.

Everyone who'd ever loved him was dead. The thought was as raw as the chill night air.

He tramped a complete circle around the cabin, checking on the horses and adjusting a couple of tie ropes, then headed back to the fire, which had burned down to a soft, pulsating glow. It was cool, but he didn't bother building it up. He intended to doze for an hour or two, and he didn't want the fire attracting anyone to the camp.

Cuno spread his bedroll in front of his saddle, checked his rifle and his .45, then set the rifle against a nearby rock, within easy reach, and removed his cartridge belt. He coiled the belt around his holster, placing it between himself and the rifle, and pulled his blankets back.

On the cabin side of the fire, the girl whimpered softly. Cuno looked at her, the umber light flickering across her straight tawny hair and her lithe form mounded beneath the blankets. She turned her head slightly, groaning.

"No . . . don't . . . please, don't . . ."

She continued to fidget around and whimper, pleading with some phantom, likely the two men who'd attacked her, to leave her alone. Cuno left his bedroll and knelt beside her. He slid her hair back from her temple, running the backs of his fingers gently across her bruised cheek.

"It's only a dream," he whispered when her eyes opened and she stared up at him, fearful at first. The hard light left her glassy gaze and her chest rose and fell more slowly.

"Just a dream," Cuno said again. "You're all right. Go to sleep."

She closed her eyes and snugged her cheek against her saddle, drawing the blanket up to her chin once more. Cuno went back to his own saddle and crawled under his blankets. With a rock, he dug out a place for his hip, snugged into it, drew the blankets up, and glanced once more at the stars shimmering above the jack pines.

He closed his eyes. He'd sleep for only a couple of hours, then look around again and check on his prisoners.

He fell away into a deep, dreamless slumber he couldn't have fought off had he tried.

Something brushed his cheek. Keeping his eyes closed, he flicked it away with his hand.

It brushed his cheek again, an annoying tickle. It raked across his eyelid.

He opened his eyes, frowning. At first he thought he was dreaming that it was dawn and that Fuego knelt beside him, grinning down at him toothlessly and holding a single blade of bromegrass in one hand, a silver-chased Buntline Special in the other. Then he looked around and saw Simms, Blackburn, Colorado Bob, and the girl standing in a semicircle before him, the pink morning light falling through the dew-dappled pine boughs behind them.

The men smiled devilishly. They all held pistols or rifles, and knives jutted from their cartridge belts.

The girl stared down at Cuno, a pensive, troubled expression knotting her thin, blonde brow beneath her man's felt hat. Colorado Bob leaned against her, one arm draped casually over her shoulder, his head close to hers.

Cuno's blood sizzled through his veins, making his eardrums roar like a train whistle. He reached for his .45 but clawed only leather.

The gun was gone from its holster.

The Winchester no longer leaned against the rock. Sitting up quickly, Cuno saw Fuego straighten, draw his right boot back, and sling it forward.

With a savage laugh, the half-breed buried his foot in Cuno's gut.

21

CUNO DOUBLED OVER with a great *whush* of expelled air, blowing up dust and pine needles. He felt as though he'd been stabbed. Pain flooded his writhing guts. He opened his mouth but made only a gurgling sound as he tried in vain to draw air into his chest.

If he'd had any food in his belly, he would have spewed it all over Fuego's boots, the right one of which flew back once more. But before the half-breed could ram it forward again, Johnnie shouted, *"No!"*

The boot stopped, and Fuego set it slowly down beside the other one. Cuno stared at the boot's silver tips as he continued to writhe and grunt in holy agony and tried to squeeze some air into his lungs before he passed out.

"I told you—we ain't gonna kill him."

"Pshaw," Colorado Bob said. "Fuego ain't gonna kill him. Just gonna clean his clock for him, make him think twice about how poorly he done treated us all out on the trail!"

"What do you mean we ain't gonna kill him?" Blackburn stepped forward. Glancing up, Cuno saw that the stocky blond cutthroat was wearing his, Cuno's, cartridge belt and .45. "After all he done to us? And if you think ole Widow Maker ain't gonna come after us, you got another—"

"I done told you, Frank," Johnnie said, jutting her jaws at the man whom she had a full inch on, "we ain't gonna kill him. If it wasn't for him, them two dung beetles over yonder woulda used me for a pincushion and slit my throat."

"It ain't our fault you can't watch your backside, Miss Purty-Ass!"

"Hey!" Colorado Bob yelled, turning to Blackburn and flushing. "You can't talk to my little sis like that, you pint-sized son of a bitch! If Johnnie says we don't kill him, we don't kill him. Simms, get some rope and—"

Just then Cuno managed to draw a half ounce of air down his throat. Rage and humiliation at having been caught with his veritable pants down—*Christ, they'd escaped the cabin and stripped him of his weapons while he'd been sawing logs!*—he propelled himself straight up off his knees, springing off his heels and plowing shoulder-first into Fuego's broad chest.

The half-breed flew back with a grunt. He hit the ground hard, Cuno on top of him.

"Cuno!" Johnnie cried.

Incensed, his face a mask of russet fury, Cuno gained his knees and wrapped his hands around the dazed half-breed's stout neck. He'd just started to grind his thumbs into the man's throat when a rifle butt slammed against his left temple, whipping his head sideways and throwing him off the half-breed and onto his back.

He stared up at the lightening sky stitched intermittently with birds flying, wings spread. Some were blurry. He felt as though a railroad spike had been hammered through one temple and out the other. The railroad whistle blaring in his ears had doubled in loudness.

A voice rose as though from the bottom of a long, metal tube. "Damnit, Cuno, you crazy son of a bitch. I'm trying to save your life."

Johnnie's angry face appeared in his field of vision, staring down at him. She held his rifle up high across her chest. Blood shone on the brass butt plate. Fuego had gained his feet, and his broad, flat face with slitted, blue-green eyes appeared in the same sphere of vision as Johnnie's. His nostrils flared as he raised a wide-bladed knife in his left hand.

"I cut his head off and wear it on my saddle horn!" he barked.

Johnnie stepped back and aimed Cuno's rifle at the half-breed's head. "Step down, breed, or buy a bullet from me!" Loudly, she jacked a live round into the Winchester's breech.

"Christ!" Blackburn groaned.

"I'm in charge," Johnnie grated out, still aiming the rifle at Fuego, who'd taken one step back, a skeptical look in his blue-green gaze. "Me and Brother Bob. And what we say goes. Simms, fetch that rope. Damnit, dig the fucking grease outta your ears, you deaf son of a bitch!"

"All right, all right," Simms exclaimed as he stomped out of Cuno's range of vision. "Heaven of mercy—outta the fryin' pan and into the fire! Never seen such a girl!"

Colorado Bob laughed and, stepping forward, shoved the rifle down. "That's my li'l sis. Step down now, girl. We're gonna need ole Fuego here. A fightin' man of his caliber—ahem, in spite of what ole Widow Maker did to his ear and his teeth—will prove valuable if Karl and the fellers start barkin' up our back trail."

Through the veil of pain over his eyes, Cuno studied the two—Johnnie and Colorado Bob—and, sure enough, he saw a vague resemblance in the curve of their cheeks. Johnnie's eyes were more slanted than Cuno had noticed before, and the two had vaguely similar body shapes. Obviously, they shared one parent if not two, though there was a good fifteen years between them.

"Just stay there, Cuno," Johnnie said, squatting down beside him as Simms came up with a couple of lengths of rope in his hands. "Don't make this any harder than it has to be."

Cuno was so enraged that he might have made a play for his Winchester, but Fuego stood behind the girl, aiming the big Buntline Special at Cuno's head, glaring down the long, silver-plated barrel, his broad nostrils expanding and contracting above his blood-crusted lips.

The girl must have taken weaponry off the dead men whom Cuno had beefed back up the trail, where they'd attacked the jail wagon.

She'd been dogging him ever since. There was no doubt in his mind that the horse he'd seen on the piney bench had been her brush-tailed pinto.

Cuno lowered his gaze to the girl, staring at her through the veil of pain over his eyes. Simms grabbed one of his wrists and wrapped one of the ropes around it.

"Turn over," Simms ordered.

"Not behind the back," Johnnie said. "He's gotta be able to get out of those ropes after we leave."

Simms jutted his jaws at her and spoke through gritted teeth. "What if he gets out of them *before* we leave?"

Johnnie kept her cool, blue gaze on Cuno. "Then we shoot him."

Simms chuckled caustically and finished tying Cuno's wrists together, leaving about two inches of rope between them.

"Better check his boots," Johnnie said.

After a quick inspection of Cuno's boots, Simms pulled a horn-gripped hunting knife from the freighter's right boot well. "Nice," Simms said, thrusting the knife into the ground beside him. "That'll come in handy."

When he'd tied Cuno's ankles together so tightly that Cuno's feet tingled inside his boots, he grabbed the knife out of the ground, stood, and threw his arms up like a calf roper trying to beat the competition's time at a Fourth of July rodeo celebration.

"There." Simms rammed his boot into Cuno's ribs. It wasn't as savage a blow as Fuego's but it rolled Cuno onto his side and set a new fire blazing in his ribs and curses snarling from his lips. "Take that, Widow Maker!"

"Simms!" Johnnie scolded. "Go get the gear together. We gotta pull foot!"

She straightened and turned to Fuego still aiming the Buntline at Cuno. "You, too."

Fuego was obviously not accustomed to taking orders from women. He cut his eyes at the girl, as though she were an annoying fly buzzing around his head. The other men must have made a damn good deal with the half-breed, because he turned back to Cuno, lowered the Buntline, and turned away and began hoofing it toward the picketed horses.

He barked over his shoulder, "We will meet again, blond man. And then I will twist your head off and mount it on my saddle."

Johnnie lowered her gaze to Cuno once more, and brushed a fleck of ash from her cheek. Her hair blew back in the rising morning breeze. "I know this ain't much thanks for what you done yesterday. Be grateful I didn't let them kill you."

"Thanks."

"You just lay still till we're outta here."

"Damn, here I'm in the mood for a barn dance."

"We're gonna take your guns and your horse. Even without your hideout knife, you'll find a way out of them ropes soon enough. When you do, head back to Petersburg."

She added archly, "You can rest up with Miss Ulalia—I know you'll enjoy that—and then you can get a horse and start on the trail to Crow Feather again. Whatever you do, don't try to follow us, Cuno. I appreciate your beefin' those two dogs yonder, but if I see you again, I'll let Bob or that mangy half-breed put a bullet in you."

Johnnie wheeled and started away, resting Cuno's Winchester on her shoulder. She stopped, turned back to him. "I'm just tryin' to get my life together, see. Me an' Bob's. He's my half brother, but he's old enough to be my pa. Once we get the payroll money and get shed of Oldenberg, we're walkin' the straight an' narrow, Bob an' me."

Cuno grunted against the ache in his ribs and watched

the girl stride off into the pines beyond the dead fire. Colorado Bob, on one knee, loaded a pistol from the cartridge
belt around his waist. He was chuckling softly to himself
and slitting those snaky eyes, as though thoroughly bemused by his own private joke.

Cuno spat grit from his lips and returned his gaze to
Johnnie's slender back and buffeting, tawny hair.

"Good luck with that."

Cuno rolled around snarling like a trapped, wounded wolf.
He'd never felt so humiliated, frustrated, and angry.

The ropes were tied too tight for him to work loose
without something sharp, however. Damn that bitch for
thinking about a knife.

Here he'd felt sorry for her—a poor little girl alone in
the world.

His ass.

He looked at the fire. The renegades hadn't built it up
since he'd let it go out last night. But if he dug deep down
in the ash pile, he'd probably find some coals hot enough to
burn through the hemp.

Hooves clomped. Cuno glanced beyond the fire ring,
toward the ragged edge of the forest dropping down from
the crest of the ridge. Simms and Blackburn were riding
toward him along the edge of the woods. Simms was
mounted on Renegade. The big skewbald didn't cotton to
strange riders, and he arched his neck, chomped his bit, and
twitched his ears, rage flashing in his wide eyes.

Fury welled up in Cuno once more. Simms must have
seen it. The hammer-faced, ponytailed cutthroat grinned
and jerked Renegade's head around sharply, whipping his
withers with his rein ends.

"Treat that horse right, you black-souled son of a bitch.
Better not be a mark on him when I come for him, or before I kill you I'll gut you first!"

Simms chuckled as he put the horse up close to Cuno,
Renegade's chopping hooves dangerously close to his master's face. "I'll be waitin'!"

With that, Simms reined Renegade in a complete circle, showering Cuno with dust, pinecones, and needles, then stabbed the skewbald's flanks with his spurs. Renegade loosed a furious, bugling whinny, lunged off his rear hooves, and bolted straight up over the bench, angling past the dark cabin and heading for the western ridge.

"You're damn lucky that girl took a shine to you, Widow Maker!" Blackburn grinned down at him, leaning forward on his saddle horn. "But not even she's gonna be able to save your hide if you get it into your thick head to track us."

More hooves thudded in the south. Cuno glanced that way. Fuego, Johnnie, and Colorado Bob were galloping toward him. As Blackburn turned and headed off in the same direction as Simms, Fuego directed his horse—one of the hunters' orphaned mounts—toward Cuno.

Shouting something in a strange argot Cuno didn't understand, the half-breed jumped his horse over Cuno and, laughing and slapping his horse's rump with one hand, galloped up and over the bench.

Colorado Bob tipped his hat to Cuno. "Good day, Widow Maker. I hope you get those ropes off before a cougar finds you. Thought I heard one mewling around last night . . . while you were sleepin'!"

"Diddle yourself," Cuno rasped as the silver-haired killer put his buckskin up the bench.

Johnnie reined up beside Cuno, who sat on the ground, wrists and ankles tied, scowling up at her. She tossed a canteen into the grass beside him. She reached back and pulled a small burlap sack from her saddlebags and tossed that down beside the canteen.

"Water and jerky," she said. "That should hold you until you make it back to Petersburg."

"Don't do me any more favors."

"Sorry you're takin' it so hard." The girl squirmed around in her saddle. "Keep in mind, you ain't the first man I've hornswoggled. I've had some practice."

"You hornswoggle Pepper, too?"

"I couldn't take down the marshals myself, could I? I knew Karl would send Pepper. Don't worry—he'd say I was worth it. I'm sorry you won't be able to find that out for yourself." She studied him smokily, knotting her brows. "We mighta had a good time."

"I'll be thinkin' about what coulda been while you and your cutthroat pals ride off with my horse and my guns, you crazy bitch."

"Bye." Johnnie reined her horse around and rode away.

Cuno watched her, feeling the reverberations of the hooves in the ground, until she was out of sight. Then, wincing at the raw, sawing pain in his ribs, he rolled onto his belly, pushed up on his knees, and crabbed awkwardly over to the fire ring.

He shoved his hands into the powdery coals, probing deep with his fingertips. The hottest ash he could feel was only warm. Nowhere near hot enough to burn through the rope.

He forgot himself and tried to stand, but his feet wouldn't separate, and he fell hard on his forearms, cursing.

Rolling onto one side, breathing hard and bunching his cheeks at the pain in his ribs, he looked around for something to cut the ropes with. Spying a rock, he wormed his way over to it, and inspected it closely. "Shit!" Its sides were too blunt.

He looked around again, saw another rock humping up out of the ground behind him, surrounded by wiry, blond grass. Rolling onto his other side, he wormed back in the opposite direction.

This rock was about the size and shape of a cow pie. Spotted with green-gold moss, it was dull on one side, fairly sharp on the other. It was embedded firmly enough in the ground that it shouldn't move when he scissored his wrists across the sharp side, which wasn't sharp by knife standards but the most he could hope for.

He grunted as he raised his arms and dug a boot into the ground for leverage. Draping his hands over the rock, he drew them back toward him, running the rope between his wrists across the rock's sharpest edge.

A couple of sawing motions told him the rock wasn't as sharp as it looked—at least, not sharp enough to make fast work of the rope. No point in wasting time looking around for something better. He continued drawing his wrists back and forth across the rock, pressing hard and gritting his teeth with the effort of sawing the tautly wound hemp.

Clish-scritch, clish-scritch. The rope began coming apart strand by strand, the ends of the cut sinews fraying and snapping away from the edge.

When he'd worked for a time, Cuno glanced up at the sky. The sun had risen, beating the shadows back into the forest and across the cabin. The air warmed, and the dew drops were quickly disappearing from the brown grass curling around him.

A breezy whiz sounded overhead, and he glanced up to see a rough-legged hawk careening over him and down the slope, hunting for mice and rabbits from about fifty feet in the air, tawny wings spread, feet tucked back against its downy belly and barred, fanlike tail.

Cuno sucked a breath and continued working at the rope—back and forth, back and forth across the rock, making sharp, quick cutting motions. He was encouraged by every strand that separated and snapped back away from the rock.

He hadn't given much thought to what he was going to do once he was free. He hadn't needed to.

He was going after the cutthroats and the girl. And god help them when he caught up to them.

22

CUNO TURNED HIS wrists away from each other as the last rope strand stretched, quivering with drum-taut tension, glistening in the climbing morning sun. He ran the strand across the rock's sharp edge, and it snapped easily, the two ends leaping like tiny snakes against the undersides of Cuno's callused palms.

Heart quickening, the burly young freighter clawed at the left rope with his right hand, peeling it up over his knuckles and mottling the sun-browned, work-toughened skin. When he got the left rope off, he worked at the right one, stretching his lips back from his white teeth as he lifted his gaze up the slope over which his prisoners and the girl had disappeared.

Finally, he flung the other rope away and, leaning forward, went to work on his ankles until he had both boots off, and grunting and sweating and cursing under his breath, he wrestled the ropes down his ankles and over his feet, ripping one worn white sock off with his vigorous effort.

When his ankles were free, he pulled his boots on and stood, taking only a moment to savor the free movement of his arms and legs. He took another hard gander up the slope. The cutthroats had headed west, straight up and over the ridge. Was there a trail heading in that direction that Cuno hadn't seen before, or were they heading cross-country to their rendezvous with the hidden loot?

He took a slug of water from the canteen, then corked it and hung it across his chest. He dug into the jerky sack, devoured a strip for sustenance though he was too full of bile to feel hunger, and hitched his pants higher on his hips, feeling naked without his .45.

No revolver. No Winchester. No knife.

And Renegade was headed west under the spurs of Brush Simms . . .

Cuno had been in some tight spots before, and if he would have thought it over, he would have decided it was about as tight a spot as he'd ever known. But he didn't think it over. He simply looped the jerky sack over his belt by its drawstring, drew a sleeve across his sweaty forehead, stuffed his hat down lower, and began tramping up the bench, taking long, ground-eating strides.

He couldn't move as fast as a horse, but his mounted quarry had to stop sometime.

The tracks of the eight horses weren't hard to follow in the blond grass covering the slope. They climbed straight up the ridge and dropped into the valley on the other side. Cuno did the same, descending through scattered aspens on the opposite slope and starting up the next ridge, which was rockier and sparsely studded with firs and Ponderosa pine.

Halfway up the next ridge, the gang released their spare horses. The tracks of the extras angled off to the north. Cuno considered tracking the spares down but nixed the idea. They could be miles away by now, and he'd probably only lose the trail of the gang.

Rage propelled him ahead too quickly, and when he'd crossed the second ridge he began to pace himself, slowing his stride, taking regular sips from the canteen. Every hour, he laid a small slab of jerky on his tongue and let it slowly melt, biting down occasionally and allowing the salty fluid to dribble down his throat, sustaining him.

An hour past noon, he stopped at a creek to refill his canteen. He took a breather on a rock, sucking another slab of jerky and flexing his feet to stretch his calves, which were beginning to tighten up on him. He was strong, and powerfully built, but he wasn't accustomed to long, sustained walks with bruised ribs.

His feet would look like hamburger after a few more hours, especially if he had more mountains to climb. Fortunately, the gang seemed to be sticking to draws and coulees, zigzagging relentlessly westward.

Cuno flexed his left foot again and winced. That calf was tighter than the other. What he wouldn't give to happen upon a horse or even a mule. Hell, a prospector's burro would do.

But, while he'd seen a few cattle—mostly white-faced stock crossed with longhorns—he had yet to stumble across a ranch. He'd spied one dilapidated cabin with a sagging, moss-encrusted roof hunkered in a hollow and a few mine holes, but no humans.

He stood, rose up on the balls of his feet, and threw his arms up high above his head, stretching his legs, back, and neck, wincing at the hitch in his ribs. He tipped his hat against the sun and continued forward through the grassy valley winding southwest through scattered aspens whose small, round leaves flashed silver in the early afternoon light.

An hour later, crossing a low saddle between grassy ridges, a cool blast of wind pushed against his sweaty back, chilling him instantly and making him shiver. He glanced behind. A purple mass of anvil-shaped clouds was moving toward him, shepherding a massive, dark shadow across the valley behind.

The wind wooshed. A dead branch was jostled out of a tree crown and hit the ground with a clatter.

"Shit!"

Cuno glanced at the hoof-pocked ground before him. A hard monsoon rain would likely erase the cutthroats' trail.

He glanced back at the curtain of rain wavering down

from the purple cloud bank, cursed again, teeth clattering as the chill wind shoved against him. Thunder rumbled. Lightning sparked over a rocky spur on the right side of the valley. A flock of mountain chickadees lit from an aspen copse to his left and, like a cloud of bees, careened up valley and away from the storm.

Cuno ran down the saddle, holding the jerky sack against his thigh, and looked around for cover. Rain began ticking off his hat and peppering his back as he jogged down between two rock escarpments bottlenecking the trail just below the saddle.

To his left, a cabin-sized, mushroom-shaped boulder loomed. The side facing the valley was concave, offering shelter. Cuno ran under it and, turning to face the valley and dropping to a knee, watched the storm move over the saddle like a lid closing on a box.

In the aspens and ash about a hundred yards beyond, he saw what appeared to be an old Indian burial scaffold stretched between two trunks and partially concealed by foliage. As the wind and rain hit the scaffold, several branches—or branches and bones and maybe some old sheepskin from a burial shroud—were blown out of the tree to tumble from branch to branch to the ground.

The sheepskin was whipped along the ground for several yards, like paper, before it hung up against a bole.

Cuno shivered from the damp cold stealing down his collar and pasting his icy, sweat-soaked tunic against his back, and from the ominous visage in the trees beyond, and dropped to his butt. He pushed himself back farther beneath the boulder, drew his knees up, and wrapped his arms around them, settling in to wait out the storm.

As thunder and lightning filled the valley, he silently prayed that the wind and rain wouldn't obliterate the tracks. He'd never considered himself a superstitious sort, but if he had, he'd take that ruined scaffold to be one hell of a bad omen.

Leaning back from the rain and wincing at the hammering thunder, he watched the monsoon gale slide on down the valley. It passed quickly—not as quickly as he'd have liked—but after twenty minutes the rain stopped abruptly. The thunder dwindled into the distance, and the sun's high-country rays slanted down once more—clearer and brighter than before and glistening like melted butter off the wet rocks and leaves.

Cuno took a drink from the canteen, and hearing the spatter of the rain tumbling off boulders and dripping off the trees, he rose from his makeshift shelter and moved down the slope to the valley bottom. He stared down at the grass for a long time, his expression implacable but his jaws set with frustration.

The tracks were all but gone—wiped out beneath the grass that had been bent by the wind and the rain.

Cuno moved forward, picking up occasional glimpses of the trail, but he found long stretches—one was over fifty yards long—where there was nothing but bent, sopping grass, occasional branches blown out of the trees, and leaves.

He continued down the valley, stretching his stride and suppressing the pain in his calves, feet, and ribs.

When he came to the confluence of three ravines, he lost precious time looking for sign. A few plops of still-warm horse apples finally pointed him down a narrow, rocky cut angling more south than west. But he soon came to another confluence, and then another, and by late afternoon he had no idea whether he was heading in the right direction.

Where the rain had not totally obliterated the group's tracks, it made it nearly impossible to distinguish them from those of other riders. Since the area was spotted with cattle, and he'd seen two line shacks from a distance, it was impossible to tell if the tracks he glimpsed were those of the cutthroats or merely brush-popping ranch hands.

By sundown, he was thoroughly frustrated, weary, and lost. He continued heading west down a broad valley spotted with large tracts of pine and aspen woods, and lined with steep limestone formations, like dinosaur teeth jutting straight up from the ridges to his right and left. Nearby, a creek curled, murmuring softly and filling the juniper-tanged air with a mineral scent. Mule deer grazed or lounged along the green apron slopes rising to the base of the limestone cliffs.

Hawks screeched as they hunted the rocky heights for gophers and rattlers. A lone wolf howled forlornly.

As the last light retreated before him, Cuno stopped suddenly. Ahead and slightly left, a gray skein of smoke rose from the trees to curl against the distant blackening ridge.

He bolted left from his course and dropped to a knee behind a scraggly cedar, looking around the shrub toward the trees from where the smoke rose. When he heard nothing and spied no movement except for the smoke, he rose and jogged quietly into the aspen woods, crouching, heading toward the smoke.

His heart hammered his breastbone.

Could he have stumbled onto the cutthroats? The fact that he had no weapon didn't bother him. Somehow, he'd get his hands on one.

Ahead, through the dark columns of the trees, the burned orange of a campfire shone. Cuno slowed, suppressing his urge to hurry, setting each tender foot down carefully. At the edge of the woods, he knelt and stared out into the slight clearing in the trees—not really a clearing but merely a thinning—where several hatted silhouettes were hunkered around the fire.

It was hard to tell in the dark, but Cuno figured there were eight or nine men out there.

A couple sat on rocks, a couple more on saddles. One tipped a coffeepot over a tin cup. The crimson light shone on leathery, bearded faces.

Cuno's heart sank. He hadn't stumbled onto the cutthroats, after all. Probably waddies from a nearby ranch gathering cattle from the surrounding canyons.

The men sat close together, turning their heads this way and that, their mouths opening and closing, deep in discussion. Cuno studied the group from beneath mantled brows.

Cow waddies would be lounging around more sedately, wouldn't they? With maybe one man strumming a guitar while the others laughed, played cards, and passed a bottle?

These men looked grim, serious, and they kept their voices low and grave.

Deciding to get close enough for a better assessment—if they were, indeed, cattlemen, they might spare him a horse and a six-shooter—he retreated back the way he'd come, then turned sharply right. He walked slowly, quietly for a couple hundred paces, then turned right again, tracing a broad half circle around the faintly glowing, flickering light of the cook fire.

Cuno crawled on hands and knees through the short grass, meandering around the slender trunks of aspens. Before him, the fire grew as did the silhouettes of the men gathered around it.

As he set each hand and knee down softly, the low voices grew louder. He began to hear the snaps and cracks of the flames, the occasional pop of pine sap and to see the flickering sparks rise.

A few minutes later, as he approached a fallen log, he caught a whiff of coffee on the cooling air and the smell of cooked beans and side pork. He was only half aware of his rumbling stomach. There was a long stretch of muttered conversation, which Cuno didn't dare crab any closer to eavesdrop on.

One of the men leaned back against a large log angled near the fire—a blocky gent in a fringed elk-skin jacket, with long hair, muttonchops, and a goatee—and crossed his stout arms on his broad chest. "I don't know," he said with a heavy sigh, just loudly enough for Cuno to clearly hear. "I can't believe ole Bob would do me that way."

Another man belched.

"Hard to believe," said a dark-haired man over the coffee cup raised to his mustached mouth. He had a twisted, knobby scar on his chin, and a Winchester leaned near his knee. "After all you done fer him, Karl. Sort of restarting his career for him, an' all. But it looks to me like they're headed west fer Alfred. If they was headed fer Helldorado, they'd have taken Sandy Draw."

"I'm pretty damn sure it was him." A tall, long-limbed man with a rifle across his knees tugged on his bib beard as he stared into the fire, his black eyes reflecting the dancing flames. "Like I said, they was a fair stretch away, but I glassed 'em with them good German binocs I took off an army lieutenant who tried doublin' me in a card game, and I'd swear on my pap's grave that was Bob, Frank Blackburn, and Simms—with a girl that looked a lot like Joe Pepper's little gal and some big, dark-skinned son of a bitch."

"Why the hell would he be goin' to Alfred?" inquired another member of the group.

The tall gent said, "Maybe he went stir-crazy in that jail wagon, decided to go get him some cooch before headin' back to Helldorado."

"He could get him cooch in Helldorado."

"Yeah, but it's a hundred miles farther—a day and a half longer. To red-blooded men, Dean, that's a hell of a long . . ."

He let his voice trail off as a Mexican in a bear coat and leather hat trimmed with silver conchos said between puffs on a briar pipe, "Maybe that's where he hid the payroll money. Maybe he intends to bring the money with him back to Helldorado."

The bulky gent with the long hair and goatee shook his head as he tugged at his beard. "The agreement was that if we had to ditch the money, we'd all go back for it. *Together*." Karl Oldenberg looked at the others around the fire. "It ain't that I don't trust you boys. You all took a blood oath to the clan. We're good as kin. But money has a way of workin' on a fella . . . 'specially a cached fortune like the one waitin' in the strongbox."

Cuno dropped his head and pressed his shoulder against the fallen log. He dug his fingers into the pine needles and rotting leaves, feeling his pulse in his fingertips.

He'd heard enough. Oldenberg's boys had spied the five Cuno was after. He'd never heard of a place called Alfred. In this country, looking for even a good-sized town could be like looking for a needle in a haystack. He had no choice but to follow the Oldenberg bunch.

But to keep up he'd need a horse.

As the gang continued to discuss the situation darkly, Cuno backed away from the fire and forted up behind another log, looking around. He'd spied no horses east or south of the fire. They had to be west or north.

Pausing to scoop up a barkless branch about four feet long and as big around as his upper arm—it would have to do for a weapon until he could get his hands on a gun—he scuttled west of the fire, stealing amongst the trees and looking around for horses while keeping one eye skinned on the camp.

Ten minutes later, after hearing a horselike snort, he found himself crawling up behind nine mounts tied to a long picket line between two tall pines. They were about fifty yards northwest of the fire, near the murmuring creek.

Cuno eased up left of the remuda, the nine mounts standing still as statues in the darkness, tails hanging straight down. A couple had their heads up, as though listening. Gritting his teeth, Cuno prayed that none loosed a warning whinny.

When he was wide of the group, he moved in slowly, holding out his hands placatingly and making low shushing sounds, setting each foot down softly. At the same time, he swung his head around, keeping an eye out for a night guard.

He moved in on a lineback buckskin tied at the left edge of the group. The horse gave him a wary, sidelong glance, its dark eyes reflecting starlight. The musk of the horses was sharp in Cuno's nostrils—a familiar, welcoming, hopeful smell.

Soon he'd be on the trail toward Renegade and the cutthroats for whom a reckoning was due.

"Easy, fella," Cuno said, reaching toward the horse's long neck. "Easy, now . . . easy . . ."

He'd no sooner stepped up beside the buckskin and set a hand down on its long, coarse mane than the horse lifted its head sharply and, glaring at Cuno indignantly, loosed a shrill, bugling whinny.

23

CUNO PULLED THE buckskin's snout down and snapped his head toward the camp. The silhouetted gang members jerked toward him, one dropping a coffee cup and cursing loudly.

Uttering shocked exclamations, several men heaved to their feet and stepped out away from the fire to peer into the darkness.

"Mountain lion, you think?" a man asked.

Cuno didn't hear the reply. His blood was rushing loudly in his ears as he grabbed a bridle from a branch jutting up from a nearby log. More voices and foot thuds rose from the direction of the fire. He wasted no time untying the buckskin from its picket line and slipping the bit between its teeth. The horse jerked its head up and whinnied once more, throwing the bit free.

Cuno glanced toward the fire. Several men were jogging this way, the firelight behind them reflecting off gun metal.

"Might be a bobcat," one of the gang members called.

"Might be a Crow, too! Or a Ute. Mind your hair, fellas!"

Cuno backed the buckskin away from the other jittery horses, wrestling its head down, and rammed the bit between its teeth. The horse fought the bit but Cuno, an old hand at harnessing stubborn mules, quickly slipped the bridle straps over its ears.

A man's indignant cry sounded above the loudening foot thuds and breath rasps. "Someone's got my buckskin! Son of a *bitch*!"

Cuno didn't look again over his shoulder. Holding the buckskin's reins in one hand, he swung up onto the horse's back.

"Get the bastard!"

A gun roared. The slug whistled about six inches off Cuno's right ear. Ducking, he reined the nickering, prancing horse around and ground his boots into its flanks. The buckskin whinnied again as it lunged with a start off its rear hooves. It bolted forward so suddenly that Cuno, accustomed to a saddle, nearly flew straight back over its ass.

"Yeah, that's right," he grumbled. "Steal a horse and let it throw you!"

Regaining his balance, he ducked low and continued batting his heels against the buckskin's ribs, urging more speed. Pistols cracked behind him, the slugs humming around him, a couple barking into trees or spanging off rocks.

The shouting continued behind Cuno, dwindling gradually beneath the thunder of the buckskin's hammering hooves. He didn't like running a horse in the dark. The dangers were obvious. Besides, he needed the Oldenberg bunch to lead him to Colorado Bob, Blackburn, Simms, Fuego, and the girl. He also needed a gun.

After a half a mile, he checked the buckskin down, and turned him back the way he'd come, listening and staring into the inky darkness. He was out of sight of the fire, and he could neither see nor hear anything of the gang. Surely, they'd send men after him. But it was doubtful the entire gang would come and risk their other horses or get caught in an ambush. They had no idea how many men were out here, and Cuno didn't think they'd gotten a good enough look at him to tell if he was white or Indian.

For all they knew, he was Colorado Bob King trying to

lure them into a trap, or renegade Indians with a taste for white-man blood.

But they wouldn't let someone run off with one of their horses without protest, either.

Cuno sat the nervous horse tensely, holding the reins taut against his chest, watching and listening. Finally, the thud of hooves rose in the direction of the camp, growing louder beneath the chitter of crickets and the gurgling of the nearby creek. One of the riders said something, but they were still too far away for Cuno to make it out.

He counted to ten slowly, hearing the hoof clomps grow. When he hit ten, he'd begun hearing the squawk and rattle of tack and seeing the jostling, dark figures behind him. Two, maybe three riders were closing.

He swung the buckskin around, gave a loud, mocking whoop, and ground his heels into the mount's flanks, grabbing a handful of mane as the horse bolted forward, stretching its stride into a ground-eating gallop.

Behind Cuno, a pistol cracked, barely audible beneath the thunder of his own hooves and those of the oncoming riders. He gave another whoop as he crossed a low saddle. About twenty strides down the other side of the saddle, he turned the buckskin right up a shallow rise amongst jutting rock outcroppings and pinyon pines.

He drew up beside a knob, slipped straight back off the horse's rump, and smacked the buckskin's right hip. The horse whinnied again and bounded up the slope, kicking rocks and gravel out behind him.

A yell rose above the sound of pounding hooves at the bottom of the slope. "Up there!"

Cuno stepped back behind the knob and looked around for a heavy branch as one of his pursuers—there were two, he saw now—ordered the other to spread out across the slope. Not finding any near branches, Cuno settled for a stone that fit easily in the palm of his hand. He pressed his back to the knob and squeezed the rock, his chest rising and falling heavily.

The hoof thuds rose, and he could hear the grunts and

rasps of his pursers, the rattle of the bit in his horse's teeth. If the rider hadn't seen Cuno dismount, he'd follow the buckskin on up the slope. Or he'd try to . . .

Cuno edged a peek around the knob. The rider was within ten feet and closing, his horse lunging straight up the slope, bounding off its back hooves, spraying gravel in the starlight.

The man's carbine winked, jutting up from the boot on the horse's right side. The man himself was crouched forward, holding the saddle horn with both hands to keep from being spilled, and his legs scissored back and forth across the horse's ribs.

When the horse was at about the same place Cuno had been when he'd slipped off the buckskin, he sprang out from behind the knob. He flung the rock aside as he saw his opportunity for a riskier but more resolute move. Bounding forward, he slammed his 180 muscular pounds against the side of the horse, putting his head down and bulling off his heels.

The horse whinnied. The rider loosed a shocked *"Oh!"*

As the horse began falling sideways, head turned toward Cuno with its flashing, terrified eyes, Cuno reversed his momentum while wrapping his right hand around the carbine's stock and jerking the rifle from its oiled boot.

When he had the Winchester firmly in his hand, he leapt back away from the fallen, screaming horse's flailing hooves. His left boot heel clipped a stone, and he gave his own startled grunt as he hit the ground on his butt.

He winced at the gnawing pain in his battered ribs and looked up. The horse was scrambling to its feet, tack squawking, empty stirrups flapping like wings.

As the pinto regained its feet and continued up the slope in a cloud of sifting black dust, Cuno saw the rider scrambling around on the ground beyond, about twenty feet away.

The man grunted and cursed. His shadow stopped moving.

There was a red flash followed by the pop of a .44.

The slug hammered a rock above Cuno's left shoulder, the ricochet echoing off across the valley. Cuno had levered a live round into the Winchester's breech. Throwing himself into a sitting position, he leveled the saddle-ring carbine and fired at the same time the man's revolver flashed again.

The man's slug whistled past Cuno's ear.

"Mee-yah!" the man screamed.

He fired once more, into the ground before his slumping silhouette, blowing up dust and gravel. Cuno levered and fired two more rounds, and when he saw through the wafting gun smoke the man's dark figure stretched out on his back, unmoving, he hauled himself to his feet and looked straight across the slope beyond the dead man.

The second rider was a jostling shadow before him, crouched low behind his horse's bobbing head. Steel glistened in the starlight just left of the mount's neck.

Cuno flung himself sideways and rolled back behind the escarpment, wincing at the rocks gouging his sore ribs. A revolver smashed once, twice, three times, its rolling echoes drowning the pounding hoof thuds. Then the man and horse were in front of Cuno, rocketing on across the slope to his right.

Cuno raised the rifle toward the mounted figure who had turned his head and angled the pistol back over his horse's right hip. As the man's pistol flashed and roared, Cuno's carbine loosed a reverberating whip-crack across the slope. He triggered two more hammering rounds as the horse continued galloping into the inky, vertical arrows of scattered timber.

The empty cartridge casings chinked off the escarpment to bounce off Cuno's hat.

When the horse had disappeared in the darkness, Cuno heaved himself to his feet and rammed another round into the carbine's smoking breech. He tramped heavy-footed up the slope, angling right, following the sound of the wounded rider's guttural groans.

He stopped.

The man lay on the rocks before him, a pinyon sapling bowed beneath his shoulder. With a curse, the man flopped over on his side and flung a hand out toward an ivory-handled .44 wedged between two stones.

Cuno released a weary breath, raised the carbine, and triggered a finishing shot into the back of the man's head. He picked up the revolver, dusted it off, and shoved it behind the waist band of his deerskin leggings. He removed the man's cartridge belt, shook the sand out of the holster, and wrapped it around his own waist, adjusting the buckle for his slightly narrower girth.

Shouldering the carbine, he headed up the slope in the direction the buckskin and the first rider's horse had fled.

The next morning, around ten o'clock, Colorado Bob King reined his horse to a halt on a low knoll in a broad bowl in the hills at the far west end of the Mexican Mountains.

The sun beat brassily down. The mountains appeared low, spruce-green humps in the far distance. A hundred yards below the knoll upon which the riders sat their weary mounts, the little whipsawed frame town of Alfred stretched along both sides of a broad, dusty, virtually deserted main street. It was an old hide hunter's camp that hadn't grown much beyond its original ten or twelve business establishments and flanking sod shanties and dugouts.

"Jesus H. Christ!" cried Brush Simms, slapping his dusty hat across his thigh. "Is that finally fuckin' *it*?"

"Finally?" said Colorado Bob. "We ain't been trailin' but a little over a day, Brush."

"Seems like a long damn time. After all we been through. First gettin' run down by that posse in the first place, then that damn Widow Maker and his bone-hard intent to keep our appointment with the hangman."

Sitting his roan on the far right edge of the group, beside the girl Johnnie Wade, Frank Blackburn hooked a leg over his saddle horn and leaned back in his saddle. "Well, it's all over now. I see the hill. You see it, Bob? I swear it's fairly gleaming like someone sprinkled diamonds over the top."

Colorado Bob chuckled and slowly blinked his snake-like eyes. He had two Colt Navy pistols bristling on his cartridge belt—both guns that he'd found in the saddlebags of the lusty hunters who'd tried to savage his half sister. He preferred the old cap and ball revolver to the newer models worn by Pepper and the other men who'd been greased by the Widow Maker—guns that Johnnie had appropriated and that were now worn by Blackburn, Simms, and their new partner, Fuego.

"You know, Frank," Bob said. "I do believe I see what you're talkin' about. You wanna go up and git the loot first, or git the cooch first and worry about the loot later?"

"Cooch?" Johnnie Wade scowled at her older brother. "We ain't takin' time for no cooch, Bob. We're gonna dig up that strongbox and hightail it south. Hell, Oldenberg's back there, scourin' those mountains fer us!"

"Yeah, he's back there," said Simms. "Way the hell back there, most like. Hell, we can rest up here a day, maybe even two days. Git some rest for us and our horses . . ."

"As well as some pussy," interjected Blackburn.

". . . as well as some pussy," Simms laughed, nodding.

"Might be wise to even ambush old Karl and them other boys," opined Colorado Bob, hipping around to look over their back trail. "Get 'em shed of our trail once and fer all."

Simms rubbed his hands together eagerly. "And then we can hit the trail for the southern regions of this fine country of ours!"

"We get money now, goddamnit," Fuego spat, sitting his mount at the far side of the group from Blackburn, slightly higher on the knoll.

The half-breed had been dabbing at his bullet-ruined ear again with a handkerchief. He'd scraped the ear on a rock wall earlier and opened it up. Two finger-sized blood dribbles had crusted on his neck, but the blood on his ear refused to clot again, and it was annoying the half-breed no end.

Close as he could tell, he was thirty years old, and a

mere five years ago, when he'd had a full head of hair and both ears, he'd been a handsome man who'd never had any trouble with women in spite of his penchant for meanness.

Now, on top of all his other problems, his freshly ruined ear wouldn't stop bleeding. He shook his head, ramming the handkerchief hard against the bloody knob. "I wanna see the loot. I want my cut, and then I want to get the hell shed of you crazy sons o' bitches."

"I hate to say it," said Johnnie. "But I agree with the half-breed. We got no time to waste on women."

"That ain't for you to say, Li'l Sis," Bob said with a strained, tolerant air. "Now, I done told you you can't go bossin' me. I won't have it. You an' me—we're gonna start a new life for ourselves farther south. But that life don't include old Colorado Bob King being kicked around by his little half sister from Abilene."

Bob dipped his chin and narrowed an eye sternly. "We done had this conversation, and I don't intend to have it again."

Bob sealed his reprimand with a look. And as an angry flush rose in Johnnie's smooth cheeks, the outlaw leader turned to the other men. "Let's go dig up the loot, split it up, and then go get us some cooch and hooch. What do you fellas say to that?"

"That sounds fine as frog hair to me!" howled Simms.

"Who'm I to argue?" shouted Blackburn.

He, Bob, and Simms spurred their mounts down the knoll and into the sun-beaten little town. After a moment's hesitation, and looking a little skeptical while pressing the bloody handkerchief to his ruined ear, Fuego gigged his own mount down the knoll.

At the rear of the pack, Johnnie Wade cursed as she pressed spurs to her pinto and cast a long, wary look along their back trail.

24

BRINGING UP THE rear of the pack, Johnnie Wade cast her gaze around the nearly deserted main drag of Alfred, Wyoming Territory, which a sign had told her was home to thirty-three souls.

A few dogs—one which looked like it had a good bit of coyote in it—sunned themselves on boardwalks before the weathered frame buildings forlornly lining both sides of the street, or sniffed through rotten, smelly trash piles in the gaps between them.

A ranch wagon was parked before the high loading dock of a mercantile on the right side of the street, and two men were silently tossing supplies into the wagon. Besides them and the dogs, the only others about were two men hammering new shingles on a livery barn on the street's right side, about halfway down, and another man standing atop a long ladder and adding fresh spruce-green paint to the sun-bleached sign over the barn's broad, open doors.

The staccato raps of the hammers echoed around the street.

Johnnie stared ahead at her group riding two by two toward a gaudily painted frame house on the left side of the street, sitting kitty-corner across from the livery barn. The pounding stopped as the hammer-wielding roofers turned to regard the newcomers, as did the two men loading the ranch wagon.

"I shoulda guessed," Johnnie breathed, her blue eyes incredulous as she watched Colorado Bob and Frank Blackburn pull up just short of the gaudily painted house. It was pink with white trim and a front porch with scrolled posts and gingerbread trim, and a freshly painted sign above the porch read simply MISS ALVA'S.

Bob and Blackburn angled their mounts down along the side of the whorehouse, heading toward the backyard while the others fell into line behind them.

"Yeah," Johnnie wheezed again. "I sure as shit shoulda known what I got myself into here. They say there ain't no savin' the devil . . ."

Her incredulous, angry expression remained in her eyes and in the set of her wide mouth as she followed the men around behind the whorehouse and along the edge of the backyard in which three girls clad in pantaloons, camisoles, and see-through shifts of nearly every color of the rainbow were hanging wash on several clotheslines stretched between the house, a woodshed, and a small enclosed stable at the back. The stable had been freshly painted the same gaudy pink as the house, making the sashed, flyspecked windows appear especially dark and shabby.

"Looks like Miss Alva's done spruced the place up a bit," Brush Simms said, grinning and tipping his hat to the wash-hanging whores.

The girls stared back at him and the others, the vaguely puzzled looks on their pale faces framed by unruly shocks of uncombed hair and multicolored night ribbons. Gauzy shifts and white silk camisoles buffeted in the dry breeze, and the wet sheets snapped and popped.

"'Bout time," said Blackburn at the head of the pack, riding to Bob's left. "It was gettin' so's I was embarrassed to stop here." He laughed and called out to one of the girls—a black-haired girl apparently named Wynona—to get a hot bath ready and to pop a bottle of the best hooch in the house. He'd be along shortly.

Colorado Bob and Blackburn led the procession around the stable and up a slight knoll, then down the other side, to a little cabin dug into the side of a hill. The grass grew thick atop the hovel and in the yard around it. The windows were boarded up, and the front door hung askew.

Likely, it was an old hider's hut, unlived in for years.

"Frank and I'll get the strongbox." Colorado Bob swung down from his horse, his coarse silver hair dangling over his shoulders from his shabby brown bowler.

"Why you get?" Fuego leapt Indian-like from his own horse, dropping the reins and narrowing an eye suspiciously. "Why don't *we* get?"

Colorado Bob regarded the half-breed with an ironic furrow of his pewter brows. "You realize, don't ya, Fuego, that there ain't nowhere for me and Frank to spend that gold between the dynamite hole in the cabin and out here?"

Fuego threw his shoulders back and pounded his chest with a clenched fist. At the same time, he wrapped his other hand around the walnut grips of the long-barreled Buntline Special jutting from the holster tied low on his right hip. "We get!"

"All right." Bob laughed. "*We* get! *We* get!" He glanced at Simms and Johnnie, who couldn't shake the spine-crawling feeling that Oldenberg was a lot closer than these idiot men were giving him credit for.

Chuckling, Bob shoved the door open and ducked into the cabin, Blackburn following but not needing to duck. Simms waved the half-breed on ahead of him with a courtly bow but Fuego snarled, refusing to give any man his back. Heedless of the girl, he ducked into the cabin behind Simms.

Johnnie found her own outlaw paranoia eating at her inexplicably. She'd been running cattle back and forth across the Texas–Mexico border with all her brothers except the much older Bob since she was ten years old and had learned to trust no one, even good old Bob. She dropped her reins and entered the dark, musty cabin.

"You boys stopped for pussy at Miss Alva's, with the posse on your tail?" she asked as Bob crouched at the back of the empty, dust-caked cabin.

"Oh, hush, Li'l Sis," Bob said. "Give us credit for an ounce of sense. We figured we'd lost 'em."

Johnnie just shook her head, cocked a hip, and folded her arms across her chest with exasperation. The money better be good. Ole Bob had gotten too cork-headed to pull any more jobs. The man just couldn't be trusted. It was time for her and him to retire down south somewhere other than Texas, where Johnnie herself was wanted by the law.

Her younger brothers were all dead—shot down by Texas Rangers. That's why nearly a year ago she'd drifted north to find her older half brother, Bob, who was all the kin she had left.

As the other men gathered in a semicircle around him, Bob used a knife to pry up the floorboards nearest the back wall. Eagerly, he tossed each half-rotten board aside, shredding cobwebs as he did. When he'd tossed away the third board, his face clouded up, pewter brows knotting with consternation. He pried up a fourth board quickly, continuing to scowl into the hole.

When he'd thrown the board aside he hardened his jaws, muttered a curse, doffed his hat, and dropped low to study the hole, turning his head this way and that and up and down.

"What's the matter?" There was a hitch in Blackburn's voice.

Bob stopped moving his head. He kept it lowered, staring into the hole. He didn't seem to be breathing.

Johnnie stepped forward, licking her lips. "What is it, Bob?"

Slowly, Colorado Bob lifted his head and looked around at the men staring down at him, blinking his eyes slowly. "It ain't there."

A silence descended so heavily that Johnnie thought she

could hear the black widow spiders stirring under the floor and in the ceiling. The breeze brushed across the open doorway behind her.

"You lie." Fuego backed up the low, taut accusation with his big Buntline, which he slipped from its holster and raised, rocking back the heavy hammer as he aimed the barrel at Bob's face. "You double-crossin' lobos!"

"Squeeze that trigger, Injun, and you're wolf bait!" Blackburn's ivory-gripped .45 was in his right hand in a blur, the quick ratcheting click of the hammer sounding inordinately loud in the close quarters.

"Nobody's bein' double-crossed here," said Colorado Bob, straightening his back and raising his hands chest high, palms out. He chuckled mirthlessly. "At least, no one here's doin' any double crossin'. Frank, Brush, an' me was all run down just seven miles north of here. None of us had time to double back for the loot. And, since we all been together since we was caught, we'd know if any of us *sent* someone back."

Fuego stepped back, angling the long-barreled, silver-chased pistol to and fro before him, covering the other three men. "You're liars. You think I'm a dumb half-breed. You keep me around in case Oldenberg comes and you need another gun, but you never intended to—"

"Oh, shut the fuck up, breed!" Johnnie fairly screamed. Her nerves were frayed and she just now realized that she'd drawn her own Colt .38 and was aiming at the big half-breed's flat belly. "You either holster that hogleg or take a pill from me. I'm tired of all this mooncalf *bullshit* from you fellas!"

The half-breed looked at Johnnie as though he'd never seen her before and was vaguely surprised to see her there in the cabin with him. He looked down at the revolver aimed at his belly, an additional problem, then let the Buntline wilt.

Finally, easing the hammer back against the firing pin, a pensive look in his dark eyes, he slid the revolver back into its holster.

"Where money, then, goddamnit, King?" he barked, his anger flaming again but without the killing fury.

Brush Simms stared desperately into the hole, fingering a faint scar on his chin. "Oldenberg?" He looked at Bob still kneeling beside the hole from which the faint scent of cordite rose. "You think he . . . ?"

"How could he?" grunted Blackburn. "When we separated after the holdup, he and his boys swung south and we headed north with the pack mule and the loot. Karl knew the posse would go after whoever they figured had the gold. That's why he didn't balk when we rode off with it . . . an' him bein' the trustin' sort, to boot."

"No way he could have known where we buried it," Bob said with a quietly confounded air. "The only ones behind us was the posse, but they weren't that close when we buried the strongbox. We knew they was comin'—we glassed 'em when we left Miss Alva's."

That last hung in the air like an especially loud hummingbird flickering around their faces. Colorado Bob glanced at Blackburn, who returned the meaningful look. Then both men turned to Brush Simms, who switched his gaze back and forth between them, the dawn of understanding growing in the wedge-nosed redhead's auburn eyes.

Simms grinned savagely. "Miss Alva's been fixin' the place up."

"Makin' it look right respectable," added Blackburn, turning again to Colorado Bob. He chuckled. "Where do you suppose she found the lucre to do all that?"

Bob rose slowly, breathing through his nostrils, his chest rising and falling heavily. He donned his hat, pushed between Blackburn and Simms, and didn't give Johnnie, standing in front of the door, so much as a glance. Fists balled at his sides, he headed back out into the sunlight and looked toward Miss Alva's place.

Johnnie followed him, her heart thudding dully. She'd had a bad feeling about all this for the past couple of hours. But that bad feeling was nothing compared to the new bad feeling she was feeling now.

There was going to be blood here. Not just a little blood, either. Things were gonna start getting nasty bloody real soon.

The other men including Fuego tramped out of the cabin behind her, moving slowly and with an air of barely restrained fury.

"Looked to me like Miss Alva done bought her girls some nice, new, colorful dress pretties." Running his hand under his nose, Blackburn turned to Simms. "Did you notice that, Brush?"

"I noticed," Simms said, nodding, as he stared toward the knoll separating the old miner's shack from the whorehouse. They could all see the house's roof peeking up from the top of the knoll. "Them girls . . . Wynona and Trinity and Sarah . . . they looked right nice in 'em, too."

"'Nough talk, boys," said Colorado Bob, grunting as he swung up onto his horse's back. "Time to see about our money."

"Bob," Johnnie said, shielding her eyes against the climbing morning sun. She didn't bother continuing, for Bob had just raked his heels against his horse's flanks, and the horse was lunging up the knoll, galloping toward the whorehouse.

The other men followed suit, grimly silent, their eyes hard as rocks. Only Fuego showed any emotion. The half-breed gave a rebel-like howl as he hazed his horse up the knoll alongside Blackburn and Simms.

The prospect of doing violence to working girls seemed to sit well with the big, bald, earless breed.

25

COLORADO BOB SPURRED his horse down the knoll, toward the backyard of the pink whorehouse in which bedding and ladies' unmentionables of every color imaginable—all looking fresh and bright and new—snapped and tossed in the light wind under a clear, blue Wyoming sky.

As Bob pulled around the stable he saw that the scantily clad girls had disappeared. He glanced at the whorehouse's back wall as the door closed with a dull bang but not before he'd caught a glimpse of a bulky figure clad in billowy white underwear and a night sock.

"Alva, that you?" Bob called as, about twenty feet from the door and surrounded by the buffeting frillies and silk sheets, he and the other men and his sister, Johnnie Wade, swung down from their saddles.

Bob poked his hat brim off his forehead and, flanked by the men and Johnnie, tramped to the door, which was of crude Z-frame construction, with its whipsawed planks freshly painted the same pink as the rest of the house and trimmed in white.

Bob stopped, turned an ear to listen through the planks

before glancing at the other men forming a half circle around him. He tried the metal latch but the door had been barred from inside. Muttering an oath and hardening his jaws, he rapped his knuckles against the pink planks.

"Alva? Bob King here. Colorado Bob. Got something we need to talk over, you an' me."

A woman's deep voice rose on the other side of the door. "Go away, Bob. I've taken sick."

"Sick?"

"Believe it might be the influenza. Right catching, it is. Several of the girls are down with it."

"Alva, I know you found the dynamite hole in the old shack back yonder."

"Dynamite hole?"

"The one some old prospector musta dug out of the floor."

"What on earth are you talkin' about, Bob King?"

"Alva!" Bob rammed the back of his hand against the door. "I'm missin' a passel of *dinero, comprende*? Me and the boys and my li'l sis have come for it, and we aim to get every penny that you ain't yet spent"—Bob's voice rose sharply, cracking with exasperation—"*and take the rest out of your ugly, rancid, fat hide!*"

"I'm warnin' you, Bob!" came the bugling retort from behind the door.

There was a faint, metallic click.

Colorado Bob stepped to one side, waving the others back. "Careful, now. Old Alva's rumored to keep an old Liverwright barn blaster on the—"

Ka-booooommmm!

A squash-sized dogget of wood was blown through the door from the other side, throwing wood splinters straight out into the yard, peppering the wiry brown grass and sage tufts.

"There's the first barrel."

Bob stepped in front of the door, shielding his eyes as he peeked through the ragged, smoking hole.

"Alva, I ain't gonna ask ya again!"

He bolted to the other side of the door.

Ka-booooommmm!

"There's two."

Bob jerked back in front of the door. Taking his pistol in his left hand, he thrust his right hand through the single, pumpkin-sized hole in the middle of the door. He pulled the wooden locking bar up out of its brackets, and tossed it aside.

A scream rose from the other side of the door, and through the gaping hole he saw a white-clad figure move.

"I'm gonna blow this place to hell and back, Alva!" Bob kicked what was left of the door open and bolted inside. "The devil's come a-callin', Alva. What'd you do with my money?"

The whorehouse madam was built like a rain barrel with short, curly blonde hair and a mottled fleshy face with little, colorless pig eyes. She wore a corset and pantaloons and a low-cut camisole over her two-hundred pounds of sagging suet that the skimpy clothes covered all too little of.

She sat on the floor against the kitchen's back wall, just left of the hallway leading to the front of the house, her fat, dimpled knees drawn up to her chest. The smoking, empty shotgun lay near her feet. Staring at Bob in horror, she was reaching through a slit in her pantaloons.

"Bob, you leave me be. I had no idea that money was yours!"

"You were prowlin' around out back when we done hid it, and we was too worried about the posse to figure on a fat little whorehouse madam stealin' us blind!"

Alva rose to her knees and thrust a six-inch blade toward Bob. Her lusterless eyes were pinched down to the size of buckshot pellets. "You come near me, I'll gut you like a fish, Bob King!"

Bob ground his teeth audibly and stepped toward her. "You stick me with that blade, whore, and I'll cut your head off, dry it, and hang it from my vest for a watch fob!"

In the doorway behind Colorado Bob, Blackburn shouted, "Where's the money, bitch?"

With a shrill scream, Alva tossed the knife. It careened over Bob's left shoulder and plunked hilt deep in the door frame, six inches right of Blackburn's fury-red face. With unusual agility for a woman her size, Alva bounded to her pink-slippered feet, the slippers decorated with small pink balls on each velvet toe, and bounded off down the dark hall, throwing her head back on her shoulders and bellowing like a calf in a panhandle thunderstorm.

"Goddamnit!" Colorado Bob railed as he lunged after the woman, taking long strides down the dim hall and bunching his cheeks with fury. "You can run, Alva, but you couldn't hide if you was no bigger than a dung beetle! Not from me!"

As he stomped out of the hall and into a large, well-appointed parlor—a room he had frequented several times on his journey through this part of the territory—he could hear the terrified peeps and hushed screams of the girls cowering upstairs in their rooms.

Ahead, Alva was fumbling with the front-door handle, casting wide-eyed looks over her shoulder at Colorado Bob marching toward her, fury sparking in his slanted, Viking eyes.

A single glance around the red-papered room told him that the madam had added a new piano to the premises, as well as a gilt-edged mirror and a brocade-upholstered fainting couch shoved against the wall beneath the carpeted stairs.

"Really deckin' the place out on ole Bob an' the boys, ain't ya, Alva?" As the woman fumbled the door open and lurched onto the porch with a continuous cry rumbling up from deep in her well-padded belly, Bob shouted, "Where's the rest of it, bitch? I know you ain't had time to spend the whole twenty-five grand!"

He bolted out the front door and tramped down the porch steps to the dusty little yard spotted with sage and yucca. Ahead, Alva ran out of the yard and into the street, lifting her knees and arms high, the balls on her pink slippers bouncing bizarrely around her toes.

"I just took half!" she screamed.

Halfway across the yard, Bob stopped and raised his octagonal-barreled Navy .44. He slitted one eye as he aimed.

The gun leapt and roared.

Alva loosed a shrill yowl and flew straight forward, hitting the street on her face and chest, then rolling in a churning cloud of tan dust, straw, and horse manure. On her belly, facedown in the dust, Alva moaned and reached back with one hand toward the blood staining her pantaloons over her large, round left butt cheek.

"Oh," she sobbed. "Oh, you bastard, Bob . . ."

Bob lowered the smoking Colt and continued striding purposefully forward. The men who'd been hammering new shingles on the roof of the livery barn on the other side of the street had stopped their work to stare slack-jawed into the street where the fat whore lay sprawled and bleeding.

Colorado Bob strode grimly toward the butt-shot madam, his chin lowered, coarse silver hair buffeting out behind him in the breeze, his slanted yellow eyes pinched down to slits.

Alva looked at him over her shoulder. Sobbing, she heaved herself up onto her hands and knees and began crawling forward, mewling and crying and working up some speed as she neared the livery barn's open doors.

Bob stopped and raised the pistol once more.

K-pow!

Alva stopped crawling to throw her head back with an echoing, coyote-like howl. Bob's second bullet had drilled a matching hole in the woman's right butt cheek, and as on the left side, blood issued thickly, staining the crisp white pantaloons as it dribbled down the back of her thigh.

She dropped belly down in the dirt, reaching back with her arms to cup her pudgy, white hands over the twin holes in her bleeding ass. She kicked, sobbed, and shook, her wet lips caked with dirt from the street.

Unaware of the other men filing out of the yard behind him, his eyes glued like twin rifle sights on the quivering woman in the street before him, Bob continued over to Alva, stopped, and stared gravely down. He thumbed back the Colt's hammer and angled the barrel toward the tufts of blond, curly hair poking out around her night sock.

"Where's the other half?"

Still holding her hands over her bloody butt, Alva lifted her chin toward the open doors of the livery barn. The tall, hollow-eyed man in suspenders who'd been adding the fresh paint to the sign over the doors now stood on the ground, beneath the ladder, using it to shield him from the trouble his dark eyes were now riveted to.

He held a paint can in one hand, his brush in the other.

"Billy Borden!" Alva bellowed. "Him an' me both found it. He took half!"

The woman's words were like grapeshot peppering the dumbfounded man standing behind the ladder. He jerked back, wincing, eyes widening, and dropped his paintbrush in the dirt.

Bob glanced at the freshly painted sign, which read WM. L. BORDEN LIVERY AND FEED, then up at the new roof. He dropped his gaze once more to drill a withering stare at the man still stumbling straight back into the barn shadows.

"Where's the money?" Bob grumbled.

He'd taken one step toward the barn, raising his gun, when something hot hammered into his upper right arm. The whip-crack of a rifle echoed from down the street to his right.

Racked with sudden, excruciating misery that dimmed his vision and set bells tolling in his head, Bob stumbled left and grabbed his arm with the hand still holding the gun. His knee shook uncontrollably and for a moment he thought it would buckle. He felt the thick, heavy wetness of blood pouring from the ragged hole in his shirtsleeve.

"That's right, Bob!" a man shouted. There was the metallic rasp of a cocking lever ejecting a spent cartridge and seating a fresh one. "Where's the *money*?"

Bob trailed the voice with his eyes, to the heavy bulk of Karl Oldenberg standing atop the mercantile's loading dock. The two ranch hands and their wagon were nowhere to be seen, likely having lit a shuck out of town. It was only Oldenberg up there, staring down his Winchester's barrel, the stock pressed to his cheek, his long sandy hair falling from the brim of his shabby black bowler hat.

Wincing and breathing hard as the blood from his wounded arm leaked out through his fingers, Colorado Bob glanced at Simms and Blackburn standing about thirty yards behind him, in front of the whorehouse. Both men were frozen, crouching and staring at Oldenberg, hands on their holstered revolvers.

Behind them, the screams of several girls emanated from the upstairs whorehouse windows.

Fuego.

Blackburn kept his head turned toward Oldenberg but rolled his eyes sharply, inquiringly toward Colorado Bob.

The fat madam, Alva, lay belly down in the street, cupping her hands over her wounded butt cheeks, groaning.

There was another loud, tooth-gnashing rasp of a cocking lever. Bob jerked his head toward the left front corner of the barn. A man he recognized as Dewey Ordinary stood there, half concealed by the barn wall, his red neckerchief blowing out in the wind as he squinted one light blue eye down the Winchester's oiled barrel.

Ordinary was known for keeping his guns well oiled. He was downright obsessive about it. When the killer from South Carolina wasn't screwing or looking for banks to rob or stages to hold up—the man did not drink or gamble—he could be found sitting back in a chair, drinking coffee and oiling his weapons.

A soft whistle rose from the direction of the whorehouse. Bob wheeled clumsily, knees wobbling, and almost tripped over his own feet.

Another Oldenberg rider—Ike Grayson—knelt in the whorehouse's front yard, in front of the porch. He held a brass-breeched Henry rifle negligently across his knee, a challenging grin spreading the clean-shaven cheeks of his moon-shaped face. He opened and closed his gloved hand around the rifle's stock, just behind the hammer, as if he were daring Bob or the other two men to fire on him.

The breeze plucked at the brim of his high, tan sombrero and lifted dust around his face.

"You're surrounded, Bob," Oldenberg called from the mercantile's loading dock. "Toss the iron into the street, a good ten feet away if you can make it that far, and tell Blackburn and Simms to stand down. I got me a real uneasy feelin' they ain't takin' orders from me anymore."

The gang leader's voice rose with shrill offense, and his teeth flashed whitely above the barrel of his leveled Winchester. "Looks to me like all three of you done double-crossed ole Karl. Tell me it ain't so, Bob. After all I done for you—got you back on track, got you makin' a good livin' again, with plenty of cooch and hooch and pistol poppin' to keep you interested. *Tell me ya ain't done me that way, goddamnit, Bob!*"

Bob dropped his bloody gun hand and, suppressing the hammering pain in his arm, stepped slowly back away from the barn.

"How you wanna play it, Bob?" Simms asked behind him.

Colorado Bob continued backing up past the still sobbing and groaning Alva, shuttling his gaze between Oldenberg on the loading dock about fifty yards away on his right, and Dewey Ordinary ahead and left. Both men stood statue-still. Bob didn't think Ordinary had even blinked.

Just softly for his own two men behind him to hear, Bob said, "Heed our asses, fellers. Oldenberg can't shoot a long gun fer shit. I'll worry about Dewey."

"What's that you're sayin' there, Bob?" Ordinary asked tightly, aiming down his Winchester's glistening barrel. "Thought I heard you mention my name."

"Yup," Bob said, wincing as the pain bit deep into his arm. He was all blood from shoulder to elbow. "I just said I was gonna shoot you first, you pig-diddling son of a bitch!"

He threw himself sideways, hitting the ground on his left shoulder. As Ordinary's rifle roared, blowing a gob of dirt and shit up from the street where Bob had been standing, Bob rolled off his shoulder and extended his Colt.

The gun roared. "God—!" Ordinary shouted as the bullet smashed into his left shoulder and threw him back against the livery's gray wall.

The report of Bob's .44 hadn't ceased echoing around the street before a veritable fusillade rose around him.

As Bob drilled Ordinary a second time, he could hear Simms and Blackburn shouting while others grunted and cursed and guns roared and bullets smacked flesh and bone and wood, and one slug spanged off a rock in the street between Bob and the now-screaming, butt-shot Alva.

On his belly, Bob turned toward Oldenberg.

The gang leader was shouting curses as he jogged forward in his heavy-booted, bull-legged gait, ramming a fresh shell into his Winchester's breech.

Bob squeezed off a shot.

The slug hammered through a mercantile window over Oldenberg's right shoulder, making the big man jerk his head down, throw an arm up, and curse loudly.

"Let's get inside, Bob!" Blackburn shouted above the staccato pistol pops and the resounding whip-cracks of rifles.

Several slugs plunked into the dirt around Colorado Bob. One burned his left calf while another blew his hat off his head and yet another traced a hot line across his cheek.

As he scrambled to his feet, his wounded arm forgotten, he whipped a glance around and saw smoke puffing from several places along the street—from behind stock tanks, rain barrels, brush clumps, and rooftops.

Yessir, Oldenberg had brought the entire gang—or what was left of it. Must be a good seven or eight cold-steel fellas, including big Karl himself, popping off shots at Bob and his two compadres. Just then he remembered Johnnie.

Where the hell was Li'l Sis? Must be in the house somewhere, covering him and the boys from a window.

Returning fire at the rooftop left of the livery barn, until his revolver hammer screeched down on an empty chamber, Bob beat a path toward the whorehouse.

Simms was on the porch, bleeding from several bullet burns and directing his fire toward the mercantile. Blackburn was on one knee in the yard, shooting up the street to his left while slugs peppered the ground around him and chewed into the freshly painted porch rails and the whorehouse's front wall.

Ike Grayson lay jerking near Blackburn, a bullet through his belt and another through the right center of his chest. Colorado Bob winced as another slug tore through his right side, just above his hip, while another sizzled so close to his right ear that he could feel the heat of its passing before it shattered a whorehouse window.

As Bob made for the porch steps, he caught a glimpse of Grayson's head jerking back as a stray bullet hammered into the dying man's temple. It blew Grayson's brains out the back of his head and put an instant end to his suffering.

Bob bounded across the porch and, as several slugs chewed slivers from the floor behind his hammering boots, thrust himself headlong through the open door. He hit the parlor floor on his wounded arm. Bellowing, a veil of yellow pain dropping down over his slanted eyes, he rolled onto his back to see Simms backing into the house behind him, flinging an empty, smoking Smith & Wesson aside while he triggered shots with another.

When that gun hammer clicked empty, he stepped back behind the door frame. His face looked as though someone had struck him with three ripe tomatoes. Screaming, Blackburn flew through the door, materializing from the wafting smoke cloud like an apparition, Ike Grayson's Henry rifle in his hand and several bullets chewing the outside door frame around him.

When the short, blond gunfighter was inside and had slammed the door closed, Colorado Bob shoved himself up against a heavy wooden cabinet and looked around. He pulled the hand of his useless arm onto his lap and jerked off his neckerchief.

Blackburn and Simms sat with their backs to the front wall, near the windows on either side of the door that jerked as bullets slammed against it, ripping splinters from the panels. Both men were filling their empty pistols from their cartridge belts.

"Where the hell's Fuego?" Blackburn barked above the hammering fusillade.

As if in response, a large shadow moved slowly down the stairs to Bob's left. It was Fuego, descending the steps slowly and buttoning the fly of his buckskin trousers. He had a bloody knife in his teeth.

Upstairs, a girl was screaming.

When Fuego reached the bottom of the stairs, he removed the blade from his mouth and crouched to peer out the nearest window. "You gringos sure know how to make some noise. Hard for a man to enjoy himself." He glanced at Bob. "You find the money?"

26

CUNO MASSEY CHECKED the brown-and-white pinto down in a six-foot gulley on the northern outskirts of Alfred. He leapt out of the saddle, slid the Winchester from the boot, and, moving up to the edge of the gully, racked a live round in the rifle's breech.

He'd been following Oldenberg's small group since just before dawn. Oldenberg had cut the trail of Colorado Bob and Johnnie Wade, and they'd led Cuno, trailing from about two hundred yards behind, here to the bailiwick popping like Mexican fireworks on Cinco de Mayo.

He peered over the gully's jagged, brush-tufted crest. Gunfire barked and cracked, with occasional whining ricochets. Cuno could see smoke puffing up above the frame, sun-weathered buildings, but he could see only one shooter, likely one of Oldenberg's men, crouched behind a rain barrel in a gap between two bulky, barrack-like business structures, shooting toward the south side of the street.

Cuno hoped they hadn't killed any of his prisoners. He'd started the job of hauling their sorry asses to Crow Feather, and he intended to finish it. Just as he intended to retrieve his horse and his guns.

He scrambled up out of the ravine, leaving the horse cropping grama grass behind him, and ran crouching through the scattered sage and rabbit brush. The town's crude, sparse buildings grew before him, as did a few scattered corrals, stables, and haggard-looking privies.

Smoke rose from a few chimney pipes.

Occasional shouts lifted beneath the staccato thunder of the lead swap on the town's main drag.

Cuno kept one of the large buildings—the fifth building down from the left end of the town—between himself and the street, out of sight from the gang members. Oldenberg's men were bearing down on Colorado Bob's group hunkered down in the little, pink house that Cuno had seen when he'd scrutinized the town from the main trail several minutes ago.

Cuno stole around a lean-to shed and corral in which three nervous horses snorted and knocked their stalls, then sprinted the last forty yards to the back of the building he'd been heading for. He pressed his back against the wall, tried to get a fix on the Oldenberg shooters, then jogged out from behind that building to the next.

He crept up to the gap on the far side of the building, pressed his left shoulder against the wall, and edged a look around the corner, glancing up the trash-strewn gap toward the main drag. He pulled his head back quickly, but he'd taken a good enough look to see the man firing a rifle over the rain barrel at the head of the alley.

The cracks of the man's rifle echoed off the buildings to either side of him. Cuno could hear his cartridge casings clinking into the dust behind him.

Somewhere along the street, someone suddenly started cursing sharply—either wounded or enraged or both.

Cuno edged another look around the corner of his covering building. The man at the head of the gap squeezed off another shot across the street and jerked his cocking lever down. He was a big, hatless gent with a cap of dark curly hair sitting close against his broad skull and long, broad sideburns. He wore a doeskin vest and brown chaps over black Levis.

His tan slouch hat lay crown down against the side wall of the building to his right, as though it had been blown there by the wind or a bullet. Cuno stole toward him, holding his Winchester up high across his chest and staying close to the wall on his left.

He wanted the man dead, but he couldn't shoot him in the back. Cuno had to give him a chance, even if it was only half a chance.

As the man ducked down behind the rain barrel to begin thumbing fresh shells from his cartridge belt, he gave Cuno his profile. Cuno took two more steps, adjusting his grip on the Winchester.

Suddenly, the man, having apparently spied Cuno in the periphery of his vision, snapped a look down the gap. He dropped his gaze back down to the Winchester resting with its loading gate up across his knee.

Frowning, he turned toward Cuno once more. His eyes widened and his broad nostrils flared.

"Hey, who . . . ?"

He didn't finish the question. He didn't know who Cuno was, but his instinct told him he wasn't on his side.

The man flung the Winchester aside and, keeping his startled gaze on Cuno, reached for one of the two Smith & Wessons jutting up from his tied-down holsters. Cuno snapped his own Winchester straight out before him and fired.

He winced as the man yelled loudly and, straightening, fell back over the top of the rain barrel. He hung over the top of the barrel, kicking as the hole in his chest drained the life out of him, his chaps flapping like giant batwings, and his big head swinging from side to side.

Cuno racked a fresh round and, crouching and staring cautiously into the street over the dead man on the barrel, moved forward, running his left shoulder along the building's unpainted, plank-sided wall. He didn't like that the gunfire had died off considerably, with only a couple of pistols popping from the direction of the pink-and-white house angled left across the street.

Oldenberg's boys had likely become savvy to the wolf in their fold—Cuno. The tentative shooting from the house told him the Colorado Bob group was puzzled, as well.

Cuno stopped at the building's front corner. He dropped to a knee, the rain barrel shielding him from the other side of the street, and glanced around the front of the building.

A man was crouched behind the rear wheel of a farm wagon parked at the edge of the street, just beyond the boardwalk. He had two Colt pistols aimed toward Cuno, holding them high so that they framed his gray, cunning eyes beneath the brim of a coal-black derby hat. He was grinning wolfishly, poking his pink tongue out between his ragged teeth, the silver cross thonged around his unshaven throat glowing in the sunlight angling under the porch roof.

Cuno's eyes snapped wide as both pistols exploded simultaneously, belching smoke and flames.

He drew his head back behind the wall as one slug chewed into the wood before him, peppering his cheek with stinging splinters, and another barked into the wall of the building on the other side of the gap.

Cuno dropped the Winchester, clawed the borrowed .45 from the borrowed holster, and snaked his arm around the corner.

Two quick shots—*k-pow! k-pow!*—and the derby-hatted gunman threw both his half-cocked pistols up over his head with a startled yelp and flew back against the wagon wheel. There was one hole in his cheek, and another beneath the silver cross at his throat. He was still staring, stunned, at Cuno, as a rifle popped on the other side of the street.

The slug hammered into the rain barrel.

Cuno dropped down behind the rain barrel, holstered his Colt, and picked up his Winchester. He racked a fresh cartridge as the gunman across the street, hunkered down behind a pile of crates in front of a drugstore, snapped off two more rounds into the water barrel, the heavy-caliber rounds echoing loudly, like thunder.

At the moment, he was the only one shooting, the other guns—even those inside the pink house—having fallen silent while the shooters tried to figure out who was who and what was what.

The man sent several more fifty-caliber rounds into the water barrel or skimming off the walls to either side of Cuno. The burly blond freighter sat tight, cheek pressed against the barrel's cool, smooth oak, squeezing the Winchester in his hands. A cricket of apprehension was scuttling along his spine.

The man across the street was trying to keep him pinned down while others flanked him just as he'd flanked them. Cuno had to keep moving.

Thwack! Another heavy slug rocked the rain barrel.

Cuno rose to his knees and slid the Winchester over the top of the barrel. A pale, creased hat crown protruded from above the crate pile on the other side of the street and left. Drawing a bead on it, Cuno fired three quick rounds.

The hat crown disappeared behind the wafting smoke veil. Cuno fired three more quick rounds, but before the sixth slug had hammered the crate pile, the man rose from behind the crates, screaming and staggering back against the wall behind him.

"Shit!" he cried, dropping his stout Spencer repeater. "I'm *hiiiiit!*"

Then he slithered around the corner of the building and dropped to his knees and out of sight.

Cuno bolted off his heels and, squeezing his empty Winchester in one hand—he'd have to find a secure hole to reload, for he sensed men trying to gain position on him—he ran onto the boardwalk before the building on his right. A second later, he was in the gap on the building's far side, sprinting down the gap toward the building's rear, lifting his knees high, hearing his heels thumping in the hard-packed dirt and gravel, his own breath rasping from exertion and nerves.

Those were the only sounds. The shooting had stopped. An eerie, brain-pulling silence had descended over the town.

Cuno had only accounted for three of Oldenberg's men. There were two, maybe three more. He had to buy some time to reload his guns. Getting pinned down between buildings, with an empty Winchester and a .45 holding only four rounds, was a sure way to end his journey.

As he bolted straight out the back of the gap between the buildings, he glanced to his right. His senses hadn't tricked him.

Smoke puffed from behind the livery barn, and the rifle's crashing report reached his ears at the same time the .44 slug threw up a sage clump in front of him, tossing it a good foot higher than Cuno's head.

"There!" the man who'd fired on him yelled.

Cuno gritted his teeth and angled slightly left, toward a two-hole privy sitting at the end of a well-packed trail and abutted on both sides by spindly cedars. His blood quickened as another gun popped behind him to the left, the slug slicing across his left cheek and spanking a boulder ahead and right of the privy.

Both men fired once more as Cuno bounded around the privy's right wall and dropped to a knee behind it.

There was a rustling thump to his right. He jerked his head with a start, sucking a tense breath. A coyote wrinkled his black-tipped nose at him and withdrew into a shadbush thicket. In front of the thicket lay a still-trembling cottontail splashed with blood.

The thumps of pounding boots and chinging spurs rose on the other side of the privy, as did the rasps of strained breaths.

"Is he behind the damn outhouse?" one of the men yelled hoarsely. "Did he stop there? Did you see him, Earl?"

"Didn't see him run beyond it!" The man's voice quivered as both sets of foot thuds grew louder. "Careful, Karl. The dry-gulching son of a *bitch!*"

Cuno was quickly thumbing cartridges from his belt into his Winchester's loading gate. The men were within thirty yards and closing when a gun barked a hole through the privy's back wall and whistled over Cuno's Winchester barrel, two feet in front of him.

He pivoted, pressing his back to the wall and stretching his lips back from his teeth as two more bullets shredded the wood of the privy's back wall, one blowing slivers three feet above his head and one within an inch or two of his shoulder.

Two more shots hammered in from the east flank, both over Cuno's head.

"Hey, bushwhacker!" one of the men shouted. "You back there?"

Cuno bolted up and turned to the privy. He loudly racked a shell, leveled the Winchester's barrel at the worn vertical boards, angling it slightly right, and fired four quick rounds. Amidst the cacophony of the Winchester's blasts and the bullet-riddled wood and flying splinters, a man screamed.

Cuno did not quit shooting until he'd emptied the Winchester and there were nine of his own holes in the privy's back wall—four on the right, five on the left.

Lowering the rifle and squinting against his own powder smoke wafting back from the wall to rise up around the corrugated tin roof, Cuno palmed his Colt. Rocking back the hammer, he moved quickly around the privy's west side.

One man lay on his back about ten feet beyond, one boot propped on a rock. His head was turned to one side, his rifle resting beside him. His boots trembled as though from an electrical charge, and blood bubbled on his thick lips pooching out from a heavy, salt-and-pepper beard with a white, lightning-like slash across one cheek.

Kicking the man's Winchester away, Cuno looked left.

The other rider was stumbling slowly back toward the line of widely spaced frame structures paralleling Alfred's main street. His black duster buffeted around his thick legs and high-topped, mule-eared boots into which his checked pants were stuffed. His rifle—a Winchester Yellow Boy with a scrolled receiver and initialed rear stock—lay in his trail behind him, near a shabby black derby hat with a brown band.

The rifle was splattered with bright red blood drops.

The man's boot toes began to drag along the ground. He stopped and dropped to his knees but kept his head up, facing the rear of the building before him.

He knelt there, unmoving, as Cuno walked up and swung wide around him, thumbing fresh shells into his Winchester's breech.

The man, balling his big, sunburned cheeks, rolled his befuddled gaze to Cuno and studied him in moody silence for a time.

"Who're you?" he said softly, knotting his thick sandy brows, as though trying to recall the name of a long-lost family member. He had muttonchop whiskers and an untrimmed goatee. In his right ear he wore a thin, gold ring.

"Cuno Massey. Who're you?"

The man winced slightly and his pensive gaze strayed over Cuno's right shoulder. "Karl Oldenberg." With a heavy sigh, he sagged forward onto his hands and rolled onto his back. The entire front of his white shirt behind his deerskin vest was bloody.

"Crazy damn world," he groaned. "Can't trust nobody in it. Not never."

The light left his eyes. He farted loudly, jerked, and lay still.

"No, you can't never," Cuno said.

Holding the Winchester out in front of him, he brushed a hand across his bullet-burned cheek and began tramping back toward the main street and the little pink house.

27

CUNO SWUNG WIDE of the little pink house and approached it from the backyard.

He stole slowly amongst the silk sheets and brightly colored women's underclothes flapping and dancing on the wind from two clotheslines, closing on the back door. He ducked inside, his boots crunching wood slivers on the puncheon floor, and moved through the empty kitchen and down the hall toward the front of the house.

The place was as quiet as a sarcophagus, with only the sound of the wind buffeting curtains and rustling under the eaves. The air was thick with the rotten-egg smell of gun smoke.

When he'd passed a couple of open doors on both sides of the house, Cuno stopped at the doorway to the front parlor and raised the Winchester stock to his cheek.

Three figures sat before him, on the other side of the room, facing him, their backs to the wall. They made no offensive moves but merely sat looking at him dully through the powder smoke hanging in webs.

Behind Cuno, the floor squeaked. A bulky shadow moved on the wall to his right.

Cuno wheeled just as Fuego, starting from five feet behind him, lunged toward him. Cold steel flashed in his right
fist, just above his waist—a long butcher knife with a
pointed, razor-edged tip. The blade point was only four
inches from Cuno's belly before the blond freighter
smashed the barrel of his Winchester against the half-
breed's hand.

Fuego screamed and whipped sideways, smashed the
knife against the freshly papered wall but retained his grip
on the wooden handle. Blue-green eyes on fire, wearing
only his bandanna around the top of his bald head, the half-
breed started bringing the knife back toward Cuno.

Spittle sprayed from his thick, chapped lips.

Cuno whipped his Winchester stock straight up in front
of him. It slammed against the underside of Fuego's chin
with a solid smack and a crunch of breaking teeth. Fuego
flew back against the wall. The knife clattered to the floor
at his feet. The half-breed groaned. Cuno silenced it with a
savage slash of the rifle barrel across the big man's forehead.

Fuego hit the floor so hard that several jars fell from a
kitchen shelf and shattered loudly.

Upstairs, a girl squealed.

Cuno wheeled back toward the parlor and snugged the
Winchester to his shoulder, sliding it across the three men
still sitting where they'd been sitting before, in the same
positions. None had reached for a weapon.

Cuno was wondering if they were all dead—they were
certainly bloody enough to be dead—when Colorado Bob
growled, "Stand down, Widow Maker. We're all outta cartridges."

He appeared to be wounded in the arm, low on his side,
and in his upper left thigh. About ten feet away from him,
and also facing Cuno, one leg stretched out before him, the
other bent and lying flat, Blackburn had taken a nasty burn
across his forehead and a slug about six inches below his
left shoulder.

Simms sat on the other side of the door. He had his

knees drawn up to his chest. He, too, was a bloody mess. Glowering across the room at Cuno, he fairly sobbed, "Goddamnit, boy, don't you have nothin' else to do with your time?"

He dropped his head to his knees and sobbed with abandon—an overgrown child who hadn't gotten what he'd been promised for his birthday.

Cuno shifted his eyes to Colorado Bob sitting with his head against the wall, left of the largest window in the room. "Where's Li'l Sis?"

"Done cut out on her big brother, I reckon." Bob chuckled without mirth, then winced as pain racked him. "She doesn't have the killin' fire to make it in this line. Needs to get her a job in a saloon somewheres. Anywheres but Texas . . ."

Cuno glanced around cautiously, then, seeing nothing of Johnnie Wade, he lowered the rifle and stepped into the smoky room. He saw his own Winchester leaning against the wall, near a pile of spent brass. Blackburn was wearing Cuno's wide brown cartridge belt and his Frontier model, ivory-gripped Colt. He nudged the man's boot with his own.

"I'll take my rig back now."

"Well, you'll just have to pull it off yourself, because I took a bullet through my hand."

When Cuno had his own gun belt around his waist, with the satisfying weight of the Colt .45 hanging off his hip, and his own loaded Winchester in his hands, he stepped out the half-open, bullet-riddled front door.

From the porch he saw a man hunkered down over a woman lying facedown in the street, as red as a side of beef. The man wore an apron, and he had a pencil behind his ear.

He looked at Cuno, and his eyes acquired a fearful light. He straightened and backed away slightly, holding his hands up feebly. "Look, mister, I don't know what the trouble is here, but—"

"There any law in this burg?" Cuno moved off the porch and across the yard, heading for the street.

The man wrinkled his nose and sniffed. "I . . . I reckon I am . . . when needed."

Cuno looked up and down the sun-blasted street. A few other men were angling toward him from a saloon at the far end of town, and a big woman in a shapeless gray dress stood outside a haberdashery, shading her eyes with a hand as she stared toward the brothel.

"You got some cuffs and leg irons?"

The man in the apron hiked a shoulder. "I reckon I can scavenge some from the jail."

"How 'bout a sawbones?"

"I last seen him playin' poker over to the Territorial Saloon."

"Round it up. The cuffs and the sawbones. A freight wagon, too. I got four wounded prisoners who need patching for the trail to Crow Feather."

When the man in the apron had limped off toward the west end of town, Cuno started back to the brothel. Slow hoof thuds drew his head around, and he saw a girl on a fresh buckskin riding toward him from the west, angling out of a gap between the buildings.

She came on slowly, her features set with a bored, tired air. Or was it a sad, defeated air? In her gloved hand she held a carbine across the pommel of her saddle, but she didn't seem inclined to raise it.

Cuno let his own rifle hang down beside his right leg as he scrutinized her critically, a feeble, remembered anger stirring in him but without the heat it had before.

"What's the matter, Li'l Sis," he said, putting some false steel into his voice. "Get a craw full?"

"I'll be pullin' my picket pin."

"What about your brother?"

"He ain't my brother. Leastways, he ain't the brother I thought he was."

Johnnie Wade filled her lungs wearily and looked at Cuno directly. "I'm sorry for what I did back there at the cabin. I figured to play this hand out different . . . for both me an' Bob. But he's just a killer like the others." The skin above the bridge of her nose winkled, and she lowered her eyes. "I'm sorry, Cuno, but you ain't takin' me in."

Cuno let a silence stretch. Her defeated air was infectious, and he suddenly just wanted to be in the driver's box of a freight wagon, hoorawing a team of mules through empty, quiet country, far away from people and all their troubles. "I'm not a lawman. I'm just finishing a job for a couple who can't."

"Maybe see you again sometime." Johnnie touched her spurs to the buckskin's flanks.

"Where you heading?"

She threw a glance over her shoulder and kept riding. "I don't know."

The buckskin stretched its stride into a trot, the hooves kicking up dust as the horse and its slender, tawny-haired rider trailed on out of town.

Cuno watched her for a time. Then, seeing a man in a shabby suit and carrying a black medical bag heading toward him, he tramped back into the brothel.

"Sit tight, fellas," he said. "The doc's comin' to patch you up for the hangman."

Blackburn cursed.

Fuego groaned.

Brush Simms continued to sob into his arms.

Colorado Bob laughed madly.

EPILOGUE

"IT'S . . . IT'S *Colorado Bob*!" a boy shouted, pointing. "And that's . . . why, it's . . . *Frank Blackburn*!" His face became all sparkling eyes in the late afternoon sunshine as he jumped around, pointing and yelling. "It's the *prisoners*, fellas! We can have the hangin', after all!"

As the coverless freight wagon and its four sullen, heavily bandaged, and shackled prisoners traced a long, last bend in the trail from Alfred, Cuno saw the boy fairly dancing a jig by the plank bridge at the far western edge of Crow Feather. He was a towheaded lad in coveralls and holding a cane pole. A line drooped from the pole into the creek that was swollen from the summer storms that had been assaulting the Mexican Mountains looming in the north.

Two other boys about the same age—ten or so—and one a couple of years younger leapt to their feet then, too, and, leaving their poles along the rocky, sage-stippled creek bank, wheeled and went running along the trail into the town, yelling almost in unison, "It's the prisoners! It's the prisoners! Colorado Bob and them! We can have the hangin' *after all*!"

"Kids," scoffed Colorado Bob behind Cuno. "Never cared for 'em."

"Me, neither," said Frank Blackburn. "Fact, that boy there needs to have his tongue cut out, dried, and hung around my neck for a fob to show off to my favorite two whores in Wichita Falls."

"Better make it fast," said Brush Simms, wincing and touching his bandaged forehead as the wagon bounced violently across a chuckhole.

Cuno glanced over his shoulder to see the redheaded outlaw straining to peer with a sour expression over the tops of the horses and into the fast-approaching town. Simms said, "I do believe that's a gallows I see yonder. Like as not, built just for us." He sank back down against the slats with a sigh. "Can't believe it. I just can't believe I'm really gonna die. *Me* . . . of all people!"

"You earned it," Cuno said, staring straight ahead as the Main Street business establishments of Crow Feather—sunbaked mud and whipsawed structures, and a few tents and log cabins—pushed up on both sides of the trail.

"I wasn't talkin' to you, you son of a bitch!" Simms barked, his voice cracking shrilly. "I'm all *through* talkin' to you!"

"Pardon me," Cuno said, feeling a smile lift his mouth corners for the first time in what felt like months. What a relief to have made it to his destination at long last.

"Easy, Brush," Colorado Bob counseled. "We each must die."

"But not me! Not today!" Blackburn chimed into the conversation. "And not account o' some wet-behind-the-ears gunslick like *him*!"

The wagon clattered along Crow Feather's wide, dusty main drag, the four boys running out ahead of it and yelling, waving their hands in the air as though to announce the circus was heading into town.

Dogs ran out from beneath boardwalks and from trash piles between the sun-seared buildings. One had been loitering under the gallows sitting before the county courthouse on the left side of the street, four hang ropes forlornly jostling over the raised platform in the vagrant summer breeze.

Now the spotted pup, as though with all the others intuiting what the commotion was about, came out to chase the wagon, yipping and howling like a crazed coyote.

Crow Feather was only about half again larger than Alfred, but Cuno could see the sprawling stone walls and guard towers of the federal pen at the far end, flanked by sage flats, low brown hills, and more mountains shouldering in the east. But it was the sheriff's office Cuno was heading for, the yelling boys leading the way. He remembered that the sheriff shared quarters with federal deputy marshals down a side street not far from the prison.

As he slouched in the driver's box, holding the horses steady despite the dogs bolting out to nip at their hocks and at the wagon's wheels and to jump up and snarl at the prisoners, he saw people stopping along the boardwalks to stare. More kids appeared as if from nowhere, and loafers rose from benches to shout and wave.

Several others—women as well as men—came out of the shops and saloons. A beefy, red-bearded blacksmith stopped hammering on his anvil between the open doors of his shop to regard Cuno and the wagon and then to yell something to another gent across the street.

Cuno couldn't hear much because of the rising din, but he'd thought the blacksmith had said something along the lines of, "I'll be damned—lookee there, Haskell!"

"It's them!" a man in armbands shouted from in front of a barber poll. "It's Bob and Blackburn and, shit"—he planted his fists on his hips and laughed—"they threw in a half-breed for good measure!"

Behind Cuno, Brush Simms gritted out, "Don't I count?"

Cuno slowed the wagon to let a farm rig pull out from a mercantile loading dock. As he did, he looked around for his old partner, Serenity Parker. His pulse hammered as he wondered—as he'd been wondering over the twenty long, hot, dusty miles from Alfred—if he and Serenity still had a contract waiting for them out at Fort Dixon.

He'd no sooner got the horses pulling again when his searching gaze held on a balcony over the Trail Driver Saloon and Dance Hall on the street's right side, just beyond the mercantile.

There were several girls up there, looking like exotic birds in their colorful dresses, hair feathers, and breeze-buffeted boas. They stood around laughing and smooching with half-dressed drovers and a couple of mustached younkers wearing the striped pants of cavalry soldiers. A potbellied corporal was feeling up a pretty little brunette from behind while the brunette laughed and sucked a cornhusk cigarette.

But the soldiers and the others were all in the periphery of Cuno's vision. What had caught the young freighter's incredulous stare was a plump whore dressed all in pink, and the scrawny little bird of a gray-bearded gent sitting crossways in her lap.

The little gent wore only threadbare longhandles and black wool socks through which most of his gnarled toes protruded. Tufts of cottony hair poked out from around the sides of his head, the freckled, age-spotted top of which was as bald as a turkey buzzard.

Indeed, Serenity Parker resembled nothing so much as a buzzard perched bizarrely in the lap of the chubby, pink-gowned whore whose swollen bosom he nuzzled and smooched, kicking his scrawny legs and swigging from a half-empty whiskey bottle.

Cuno hauled back on the horses' reins, glaring up at the balcony and his carelessly frolicking partner. "Serenity!" he called above the calls of the gathering crowd and the barking dogs. "Is that you up there, you old son of a bitch?"

Serenity was taking a deep sniff of the whore's cleavage. He jerked his head up suddenly and turned toward the street. "Huh?" he said, glancing at the whore. "Someone use my handle?"

"I believe it was the gent down there," the whore said, frowning down at Cuno and his makeshift prison wagon.

"Down where?"

Serenity wheezed and chuffed himself up off the whore's broad lap and, holding his bottle by the neck, moved up to the railing and squinted down toward Cuno. He had about three days' growth of salt-and-pepper stubble on his hollow cheeks and jutting chin, and judging by his hair as well as his attire, he'd been frolicking in the mattress sack for just as long.

"I'm glad to see you're all worried about me," Cuno chided, ignoring the cacophony around him. One of his horses pricked its ears and kicked a dog, making the wagon jerk. "Hope you didn't go to any extra trouble, saddling a horse and riding out looking for me."

"*Cuno?* I'll be goddamned!" Serenity exclaimed, widening his deep-set, frosty-blue eyes. "Where the hell you been, son? I been worried *sick*!"

Cuno glanced at the whore who'd come up to stand beside Serenity. She had a pretty, round face with a beauty mark on her chin, but she dwarfed the old gent.

"I see that," Cuno growled.

Serenity glanced at the whore and flushed.

"Ah, well, hell—what'd you want me to do? Lay around pinin'? I figured I might as well have a little fun while I waited for ya. Didn't see no point in ridin' out after ya, this country bein' as big as it is."

The oldster's eyes shifted to the back of the wagon. The bushy gray brows came down, and Serenity blinked as though to clear his vision. He ran a grimy sleeve across his eyes, then looked again and pointed with the bottle.

"Say, what the hell you got there, Cuno? I hope you realize you picked ya up some trash along the trail. Why, that there . . . hell . . . ain't that Colorado Bob King his ownself?"

Behind Cuno, Bob chuckled. Blackburn cursed. Simms asked one of the women gathered around the wagon to sit on his lap for "one last real good time." The target of Simms desires and several other women gasped.

Cuno frowned at the din and yelled up to Serenity, "What about the contract with Fort Dixon?"

Serenity rolled his shocked gaze from the prisoners to Cuno, bunched his lips, and shook his head. "It went to an outfit from Medicine Bow yesterday. You're a day too late."

The bottom dropped out of Cuno's stomach. He cursed and was about to lay into Serenity once more for cavorting and drinking while their business went down the privy pit, when the old man waved a hand in dismissal. "Not to worry, though, young'un. Serenity fixed us all up. A rancher named Trent from the Rawhide Range sent a man to town to secure a contract for hauling in winter supplies next month, and guess who landed it?"

As suddenly as Cuno had lost his stomach, it was back. He stared up at Serenity grinning proudly down at him. "Trent?"

"A damn lucrative deal, too," the oldster said. "But we're gonna need at least one more wagon and driver. It ain't easy country, either—them Rawhides."

A smile started to take shape on Cuno's mouth when a shutter opened behind Serenity, and a gent with thick silver hair and round, steel-framed spectacles poked his head out the window. He wore a silk undershirt and string tie. His hair was badly mussed, and his eyes were rheumy from drink. He wore as much beard stubble as Serenity.

Behind the man a girl laughed as he said, his resonant voice pitched with anger, "What the hell's all the commotion out here? Did I lose several hours, or has night fallen over Crow Feather once again?"

Long, slender, female arms wrapped around his neck from behind. A redheaded girl's pale face appeared over his right shoulder, smiling drunkenly as she nuzzled his ear.

Serenity turned toward the man, then gestured over the railing with his bottle. "Look, Judge—it's them prisoners you been waitin' on! Colorado Bob, Blackburn, some red-head, and the half-breed. The partner *I* been waitin' on brung 'em! Can you believe *that*?"

The judge blinked and frowned skeptically.

"Better hurry, try 'em, and hang 'em, Judge. All four of 'em look like they could give up their ghost at any second!"

Muttering and shaking his head, the judge pulled his head back inside the window. At the same time, two men approached the wagon from the right boardwalk, both wearing badges—one a sheriff's badge, the other the cop-per moon and star of a deputy United States marshal. The sheriff was sandy-haired, the marshal gray and sporting a hooked scar on his leathery left cheek, starting just above the tip of his salt-and-pepper mustache.

Both men were shuttling awestruck gazes between the prisoners in the back of the wagon and Cuno still seated in the driver's box.

"What the hell is this?" the marshal asked, moving with the sheriff up to Cuno's right front wheel. "What . . . what . . . what . . . ?"

"Where'd you find these men, son?" the sheriff asked, tipping his funnel-brimmed Stetson back on his thinning widow's peak. He had a half-smoked stogie firmly wedged in the right side of his mouth.

"Long story, Sheriff," Cuno said.

Relief washed over the young freighter. He set the wagon's brake. His job was done. His weariness was re-lieved by the optimism of Serenity's news of a freighting contract.

"Landers and Svenson are dead," he called down to the two lawmen as people of every stripe stood around the wagon, as frenzied as coyotes around a fresh gut pile. "Killed by Oldenberg. Wasn't no one else to get these owl-hoots to town for their appointment with the gallows, so I took over."

Cuno wrapped the horses' reins around the brake handle and started climbing down off the wagon while the two lawmen sized him up with awe.

"Killed by Oldenberg?" the deputy marshal muttered, half to himself.

"Yeah, but don't worry, Oldenberg's doin' the two-step with Old Scratch himself," Cuno said, leaping into the dusty street between two mock-fighting dogs. He slapped thick dust from his pants and his shirtsleeves. "I'll tell you everything you wanna know later. In the meantime, I'm officially turning these killers over to you for proper handling. All their friends are dead and, as you can see, they've been brought to heel. But I wouldn't put nothin' past 'em."

He gave the lawmen a cordial nod, then tipped his head back to stare straight up at Serenity grinning down at him from the saloon's second story, the oldster's arm angled around the pink-clad whore's broad waist.

"Come on down here and buy me a drink, you old coyote," Cuno shouted. "I wanna hear about the contract!"

An hour later, Cuno and Serenity sat around the Trail Driver Saloon that, except for them and one lone mouse, had emptied out when the four killers had been hastily tried in the Crow Feather county courthouse and led out to the gallows for proper disposal.

The crowd was jeering and laughing. Kids were running around playing lawman and outlaw. Dogs were barking and humping each other. Prim old ladies including the town schoolmarm were looking properly disgusted as they peered out from between splayed fingers at the gallows and the four doomed killers standing there while the judge, who doubled as the executioner, tightened the nooses around their necks.

The widows of the men killed by Oldenberg's gang stood nearest the gallows, each dressed in black and holding a rose. One held a small blond child in her arms.

Inside the Trail Driver, Serenity finished reporting to Cuno the details of their new freighting contract, sipped whiskey from his shot glass, and said, "Don't you wanna go out and join the festivities? Sounds like the town's having one hell of a hoof-stomping good time!"

It was so quiet inside the saloon that Cuno could hear the mouse on the bar nibbling a dry bread crust from a free lunch plate.

"Nah." Cuno kicked back in his chair with a sigh. "I like the quiet in here. Besides, those four were as good as dead back in Alfred."

"Well, then," Serenity said, holding up his whiskey glass. "Here's to four dead coyotes and a new freighting contract."

Just then the crowd quieted.

Cuno and Serenity turned to peer out the saloon's dusty front window. There was a shrill, horrified scream—it sounded like Simms—and then the raspy bark of four trap doors opening. The four men on the gallows shot straight down through the doors and out of sight behind the crowd.

The snapping of their necks sounded like distant pistol shots.

The crowd erupted, throwing their arms in the air and yelling.

Cuno clinked his glass against Serenity's.

"Cheers."

Peter Brandvold was born and raised in North Dakota. He currently resides in Colorado. His website is www.peterbrandvold.com. You can drop him an e-mail at peterbrandvold@gmail.com.